K2,

Quest of the Gods

K2,

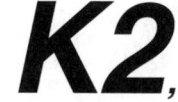

Quest of the Gods

The location of the legendary 'Hall of Records'

Ralph Ellis

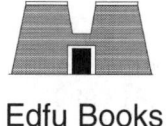

Edfu Books

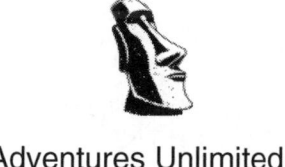

Adventures Unlimited

K2,
Quest of the Gods
First published in 2000 by Edfu Books

Published in the U.K. by:
Edfu Books
PO Box 165
Cheshire
CW8 4WF
info@edfu-books.com
U.K.

Published in the U.S.A. by:
Adventures Unlimited
PO Box 74
Kempton, Illinois
60946
auphq@frontier.net
U.S.A.

Prototype Edition Mar 2001
revised & updated
First Edition Aug 2001

U.K. paperback edition
ISBN 0 9531913 62

U.S.A. paperback edition
ISBN 0 932813 992

Printed in the United Kingdom by T. J. International, Padstow

Muse

Men called him Gobhan Saer, and many a tale
Yet lingers in the byways of the land
Of how he cleft the rock, or down the vale
Led the bright river, childlike, in his hand:
Of how on giant ships he spread great sail,
And many marvels else by him first planned.

Goibhniu the Great Architect
D'Arcy M'Gee

Dedication

To anyone who has sacrificed weekends or holidays, in order to
contemplate the design of the pyramids.

Acknowledgements

It has been a long, hard and rocky road to reach this stage in the search for the historical truth. Apart from the publishing mishaps, I must have sat and studied the Great Pyramid layout for years before coming to the conclusions that follow. All credit, however, must go the Rudolf Gantenbrink for not only exploring the shafts in the Great Pyramid, but also publishing that data on the internet. Without this precise information on the dimensions of the shafts, a full and final analysis of the Great Pyramid would not have been possible.

My thanks go to Himalayan Kingdoms for arranging the K2 trek and to all the staff in Pakistan who made it possible. Special thanks go to Altef, my *sirdar* guide, who had to help me in some of the more difficult sections of the trek.

Greg Taylor of the *Daily Grail* web-site needs a mention at this point. He started his site with a few hits a day and desperate pleas for more news, I can well understand these problems. Less than a year later, however, he was being besieged with correspondence, apologising for taking days off, and getting 1,000 hits a day. Many thanks Greg, for your interest and support in these books and I wish you every success in your enterprise.

Thanks also go to Jane Tatam, who has to interest the media and sort out the UK distribution. Daria Renshaw, my editor, deserves a commendation for sorting out the convoluted text. Finally, many thanks to David Hatcher Childress at Adventures Unlimited, who has done some sterling work in controlling the USA distribution

Ralph Ellis
March '01
Cheshire.

Gantenbrink http://www.cheops.org
Daily Grail   http://dailygrail.com
Edfu Books http://edfu-books.com

Contents

Chapter I

Roof of the World

I awoke from a fitful sleep in a panic, breathless, gasping for air. My brain was dulled by the lack of oxygen and I really thought I might expire there and then in this dark little nylon 'tomb'. I needed fresh air urgently. With a sense of rising panic, I fumbled with the flap on my tent and ripped the zip open. The air outside was indeed fresher and it filled my lungs and satisfied my senses like a blustery ocean breeze. The night air was frosty and still, my exhaled breath billowing in great balloons of ice-crystals in front of me.

I was disorientated for a while; just where was I? After a while the hyperventilation slowed and I was able to concentrate. In the crisp moonlight, the rugged outline of mountain tops loomed through the sparkle of ice-crystals and here, right in front of me, was the second highest peak in the world – K2. It rose up at a 45° angle just in front of my tent, a black and white chequer-board of jagged shapes that continued to rise for another 3,000 meters above the level of my tent. High as I already was in the Himalayas, these peaks were still awe-inspiringly massive.

Then a curious noise wafted up the glacier from far below, it was almost mechanical in nature, a rhythmic wurr-wurr-wurr. My brain was befuddled again, we were in the most remote region in the world, so what on earth could be making such a noise? A military helicopter? Certainly the Pakistan military had a great presence on the glacier, but this did not sound like the standard issue Mil helicopter that was used in this region. Then, much to my amazement, two geese flew past the

1. Roof of the World

entrance to my tent! Our camp was at an altitude of over 5,000 m, while the direction that the birds were flying in, led to the Terrace Pass, which tops out at 6,000 m. Many a light aircraft runs out of both lift for its wings and air for its engines at anything greater than 5,000 m; whereas these geese were admirably coping with both deficiencies. The mechanical waft of their wings slowly faded into the distance, and the valley returned to its usual silence.

Some degree of normality having returned, I pondered my situation. The purpose of this trek to the roof of the world was not simply for the pleasure or the challenge of the journey. No; just around the corner of this peak, so I believed, lay the fabled 'Hall of Records' – the fabled lost repository of the gods. This morning, I would at last find out how right or wrong that prediction would be; whether there was any justification in this arduous expedition. At last I might be able to see direct evidence to support this crazy notion of an ancient 'Quest of the Gods'. My mind was beginning to wander – just what was I doing here? Here was a sane and rational professional person, sitting on the roof of the world looking for evidence of a fable! Just how had I arrived in this peculiar position?

The answer was long and complex, and it involved a great deal of research into the form of the ancient megalithic monuments that are dotted around the globe, especially those in Britain and Egypt. Just what was their true purpose? Many people have claimed that the pyramids, for instance, contained some kind of mathematical riddle and many have claimed to have solved that puzzle. But invariably the answers involved complicated maths, seemingly for the sake of it; there was no end result, nothing positive or verifiable. I, too, had become hooked on the maths inside the pyramids, but I knew that if this maths was a real artifact and not the result of fevered imaginations, it had to have a very simple meaning and a verifiable answer.

There were many fruitless days in this search for the historical truth. I had sat there looking at the Great Pyramid diagrams for hours on end, idling with many strange concepts. In the book *Thoth, Architect of the Universe* (see advertisement on forepages), I had attributed the design of this pyramid to the Egyptian god, Thoth, for he was the god not only of writing, but also of much of science and technology. I had done this, in part, because I wanted to free my mind from the established dogma surrounding the site. If one thinks in terms of a Neolithic/Bronze-Age construction, the baggage that goes along with that association

1. Roof of the World

severely limits the options available. By attributing the design to a god, I had at one simple stroke lifted that veil and allowed myself the more visionary concept that just about anything and everything was possible.

The sky was the limit, any technical possibility could be explored in these chambers and shafts; some, perhaps, well in advance of our own abilities. But, tempering this bold vision with some sober reasoning, it occurred to me that if there truly was a quest tied into the design and construction of the pyramids (and the henges of Britain), then the solution to this quest would have to be relatively easy – it would have to be well within our technical understanding of the wider world, otherwise the quest would be self-defeating.

With the mind free to roam, and with a little lateral thinking, I suddenly saw that the outline of these monuments looked suspiciously like the features that can be found on our own Earth. In short, the design of these monuments was based on maps – maps made to be indelible by their other-worldly construction in massive Cyclopean stone blocks.

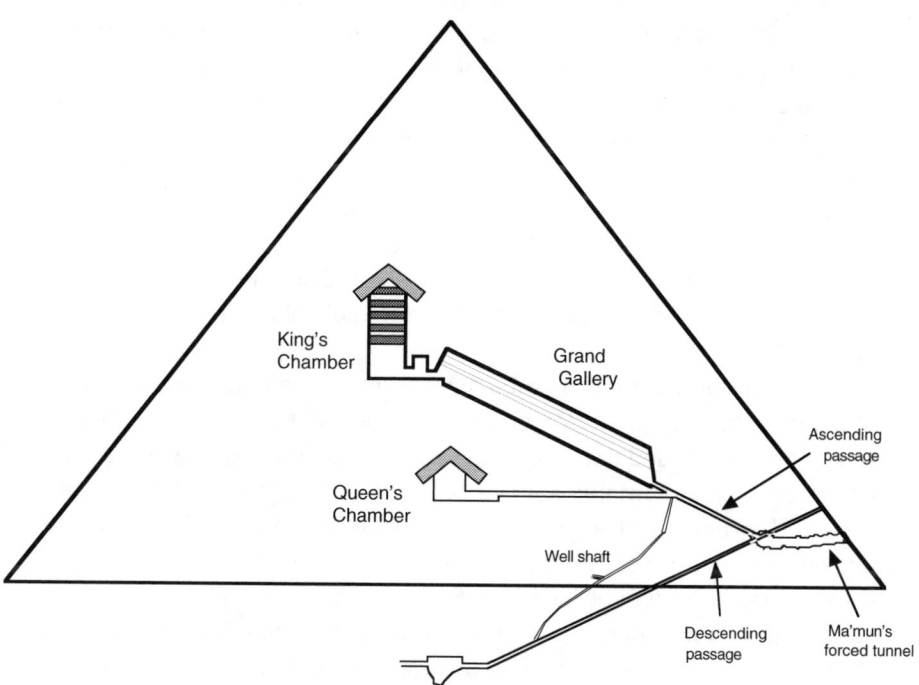

Fig 1. The Great Pyramid of Giza.

1. Roof of the World

The final piece of the jigsaw puzzle, that made everything fit, was the supposed 'hidden maths' in the fabric of the pyramids. This too, it turned out, was based on maps – it was nothing more complicated than cartographical coordinates. The concept was complete: all of these monuments not only appeared to resemble the outlines of maps, but these maps had coordinates too.

This concept was very radical, of course, but here at last was a very simple, consistent hypothesis that explained each and every last feature of Stonehenge, the Avebury henge in Britain, and the complex internal structure of the Great Pyramid on the Giza plateau – how many other hypotheses could do that? The principle of Occam's Razor dictates that the simplest theory is often the truest and it was on that basis that this whole mad caper into the Himalayas began.

An alternative viewpoint may be, as many opponents have pointed out, that the simplest answer to these problems is that the Great Pyramid was a tomb for a fourth dynasty pharaoh and nothing more. Indeed, that is a simplistic answer, but in reality it does not explain very much about the site – it is more a statement of ignorance than evidence.

It does not, for instance, explain the exact number, size, location, layout and complexity of the internal chambers in the pyramid; whereas the 'map' hypothesis explains all this, and more besides. It does not explain why the chambers were apparently sealed during the building phase, not after completion; nor does it explain the complexity of those small 'air' shafts and the absurdity of the design of the 'attic chambers' above the King's Chamber – these items are so complex they may have doubled the construction time for the pyramid. One must also ask why a simple tomb has to contain so many mathematical functions: what was the point of all this?

There is something substantially more complex about these structures than a simple tomb – they have function. Some historians have even concluded that sites like Newgrange, in Ireland, were tombs; yet to see the midwinter sunrise inside this henge would mean the annual desecration of a grave – an unlikely hypothesis. Some of the smaller sites around the world are undoubtedly tombs, but equally clearly, there are deeper functions to some of the major monuments; a cathedral is not simply a tomb because people are buried there! In Egypt, when one looks at a sixth dynasty pyramid, or the chambers in the Valley of the Kings, the function of these constructions seems pretty obvious. One can definitely detect the atmosphere of a tomb.

1. Roof of the World

There is no such atmosphere to be found within the pyramids on the Giza plateau.

Mountains

Although I was relatively confident about this 'map' hypothesis, there were still some loose threads to tie up. I had a deep conviction that the small shafts in the Great Pyramid pointed to the location of this legendary 'Hall of Records', but their precise meaning eluded me. They were definitely not the Egyptologists' original concept of 'air' shafts, and I was equally suspicious of the idea that they pointed to stars. There seemed no rhyme or reason in the star theory, promoted by Robert Bauval.

Giorgio Santillana and Hertha von Dechend had formulated a method by which the era for the construction of the Giza plateau could be calculated by the precession – the gyroscopic wobble – of the Earth and the position of the plateau of the Sphinx. The era obtained by this method, which was publicised more widely by the author Graham Hancock, indicated a construction date for Giza of some 10,000 years BC. There seemed much merit in this concept, but the star-pointing theory for the small shafts, promoted by Robert Bauval, clashed head-on with this and indicated a construction date in the third millennium BC.

Thus, the compromise argument was that the design and layout of the Giza plateau was constructed in 10,500 BC, but the pyramids themselves were not built for another 8,000 years. Somehow, however, the designs and goals of the original architect were preserved though this enormous span of time and the people of an entirely different epoch suddenly decided to build the Giza pyramids. As a complete explanation for what we find on the plateau, it is a complete nonsense. A later modification of these ideas was then floated – the design was all made in the third millennium BC, but it reflected, and was dedicated to, a much earlier epoch. Hence the design in part comprised the 10,500 BC precessional date. Frankly, this argument is not much better.

I had an intuitive feeling that the method for the precessional dating of the pyramids, indicating an earlier date for their construction, was substantially correct. But if this were so, then the idea that there were specific alignments between the small shafts and particular stars had to be either greatly modified or dropped. This freed up the small shafts for other uses and I toyed for many months with their being markers, indicating latitudes and longitudes. The search was not terribly fruitful, even with the new data supplied by Rudolf Gantenbrink, in his 1993 exploration of the small shafts. But then I noticed a small error in Rudolf's data – a small gremlin had worked its way into his technical drawing; a numerical spoonerism that gave an impossible result.

Spurred on by this 'discovery', I quickly saw what the designer had been up to. Rudolf himself saw the mystery, in part, when he mentioned that the King's northern shaft was designed around the ratios of 7 and 11, the very Pi-based ratios I had been trying to explain in the book *Thoth.* Suddenly, the meaning of the shafts was obvious and, in turn, the meaning of the shape, and even surface-covering of the pyramids was equally obvious. Everything in the pyramids means something. It is actually a mind-bogglingly simple (but very lateral) conundrum and an allegorical tale of momentous importance.

A quick illustration of the subtle, yet obvious, nature of the pyramid's design will suffice at this point. Yes, the pyramids were representations of stars – the belt of Orion – but they were also representations of something else: mountains. This is the reason for their shape and the strange choice of covering material, as will be shown later. It was obvious to me that the pyramids represented mountain peaks and thus began my epic trip to the Himalayas.

Hindu Kush

The Boeing 747 made a firm landing during a rainstorm at Islamabad airport, my first taste of Pakistan. It was hot and muggy and the arrivals hall was a scene of chaos and confusion; in many other places around the world, tempers might have begun to fray, but obviously the service here met the expectations and everyone was happy.

The hotel made a refreshing change from the disorganisation all around it, with chirpy and attentive staff and perhaps more importantly, a functioning air-conditioning unit. I had a chance to relax before the arduous journey ahead. But as soon as I had made myself comfortable at the hotel it was time to leave, and a car was detailed to take me up into the Hindu Kush – the foothills of the Himalayas. We sped off on a journey that took us out of the metropolis of Rawalpindi, with all its political and military architectural splendours, and into the real Pakistan

1. Roof of the World

that the elite most probably either never see or, more likely, ignore.

Now we were battling against the tide of donkeys and cattle, as well as the usual melee of motorbikes and mopeds. The road wound its way ever upwards, through terrain that began to look distinctly Alpine. Indeed, the midday cafe was modelled on that very theme and almost made the illusion complete; the daydream was only shattered by the punka walla, whose task was to keep the marauding flies at bay. I sat back on the small verandah, savouring the last of the surprisingly tasty chicken korma and viewing the distant mountainous terrain. There, in the distance, were the green peaks that line the foothills of the Hindu Kush.

Green Man

The cafe obviously marked the crest of this particular mountain pass, so as soon as we set off after lunch, the road began to drop down again towards our first objective, the Indus river. This was the mighty waterway that had been here long before the collision between India and Asia, which had uplifted and caused the Himalayas in the first place. We know this because, despite the massive physical barrier of the Himalayas and the Karakoram, the Indus river simply cuts straight through them, creating some of the deepest river gorges anywhere on the planet. The perfectly reasonable geological deduction is that the river was there first and has resolutely maintained its course, while the terrain all around it has inched remorselessly upwards.

The modern road joins the Indus river at Thakot and thence becomes the Karakoram Highway, the route of the original Silk Road. This junction is actually an historically convenient location in this quest, for the mountain on the opposite bank of the Indus is Pir Sar – the Green Man.

Here, there is a large and verdant mountain rising up steeply from the banks of the Indus, which was foaming and tumbling wildly over the rocks far below us. The significant point about this mountain is that there is a flatter top to it, that is both cultivatable and defensible. It is reputed to be the mountain that the god, Hercules, was unable to capture during his mythical war with the Indians; it is also the location of a slightly more recent battle – one which may be of interest to this ancient quest – the battle in which Alexander the Great bettered the demigod, Hercules, and routed the defenders of Pir Sar.

The link between Alexander and the Great Pyramid of Giza may seem obscure at this stage, but consider for a minute just what Alexander was doing in the Hindu Kush, and what drove him to force-march an army through such inhospitable terrain? The reasons will become apparent, but only once we have confirmed the assumption that the Great Pyramid is a representation of a Himalayan mountain.

Chapter II

Vega and Draco

An intense debate has been raging over the last few years, regarding the mathematical capability of the ancient Egyptians. Were they, or were they not, incredibly numerate? Were the dimensions and slope angles of the pyramids derived by accident, or were they cognitively designed by a competent architect?

I will try to prove the latter, which unfortunately means that we must look at a little maths. This is unfortunate, for what is supposed to be a mass-market book. However, the designer put the maths there, not myself, and if the fundamentals of the pyramids are to be explained, then these little mathematical tricks need to be explained as well.

Luckily, none of the maths is very complicated. Indeed, one does not need to understand the maths at all. All that is required is to be able to compare two diagrams and to see that there are similarities between the various lengths and angles; that's it.

Pythagoras and Pi

The two main pieces of maths that have been used throughout the Giza and Dahshur pyramids are the Pi formula for a circle, and the Pythagorean formulae for deriving triangles. They are very simple pieces of maths and the following will serve as a little reminder of how they are used.

a.   To derive the length of the perimeter of a circle, the radius is simply multiplied by 2 and then by Pi. The Pi value used throughout the pyramids is the fractional approximation of Pi, or 22 : 7. (Perimeter = $2\prod r$)

b.   If the length of two sides of a right-angled triangle are known, the length of the remaining side can also be found. ($A^2 = B^2 + C^2$)

c.   If one side-length of a right-angled triangle is known and also the size of an angle, the remaining angles and side-lengths can also be found. (Tan a = Opp / Adj, etc)

Normally, when calculating values for these triangles, the vast majority of them end up with fractional side-lengths. However, there are a few triangles that are different; they can be resolved with whole numbers on all three sides. These special triangles are relatively rare, considering the almost infinite number of angles that could be used, and so they stand out as mathematical beacons shining in the gloom.

These special triangles are known as Pythagorean triangles, after the famous Greek astronomer and mathematician who is reputed to have discovered them. To come across a Pythagorean triangle is a sure sign of cognitive mathematical intervention. These special triangles do not occur in buildings by chance; they have to be designed in by someone who is familiar with the formulae by which they are derived. To find Pythagorean triangles in the pyramids is to firstly understand that the pyramids were designed by a competent architect and, secondly, to understand that Greece was not the originator of these formulae. The ancient Egyptians must have known of them many thousands of years before the Greeks got to hear of them.

This may seem a small point to make, but it effectively overturns all the established history of Greece. While the Greeks were knowledgeable and articulate, they most probably derived a lot of their knowledge from Egypt. Thus, it is to Egypt we must look to for evidence of how these formulae were derived.

Blueprints

So, were the pyramids thrown together, or were they designed on the drawing-boards of a competent architect? In the book *Thoth*, I tried to show that the pyramids were indeed designed using these special

2. Vega and Draco

Pythagorean triangles. They were seemingly used in the slope angles (and therefore the base lengths and vertical heights too) of the Great and Second Pyramids. The Great Pyramid uses the Pi formula for a circle as its fundamental design criterion, whereas the Second Pyramid uses instead the Pythagorean triangle with side-lengths of 3-4-5.

That was not all; it also appeared that the Dahshur pyramids followed these same principles – they, too, were based on these special Pythagorean triangles. Indeed, it also seemed like the two pyramids were actually copies of each other, with the sides of the Vega (Bent) Pyramid simply being trimmed down a little.

The classical explanation for the shape of the Vega Pyramid is that it suffered some cracking during the construction phase, and so the builders decided to reduce the slope angle of the upper parts of the pyramid to prevent it collapsing. Some cracks in the structure are cited as being conclusive evidence of this.

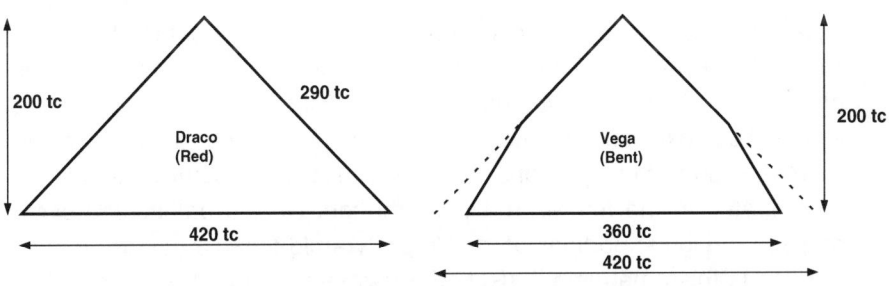

Fig 2. The Draco (Red) and Vega (Bent) Pyramids.

Looking at the diagrams above, it can be seen that the design of the Draco (Red) Pyramid clearly used the special Pythagorean triangle of 20 - 21 - 29. To prove that this was so, the designer arranged that the linear dimensions of the pyramid mimic these Pythagorean numbers, but they were simply multiplied by ten to make the pyramid larger. This was the beacon in the dark that I had been looking for, proving that the design

was deliberately made this way –
the very Pythagorean numbers were
a part of the design.

Thus, the upper levels of
the Vega Pyramid were actually
made using the very same angles
as the Draco pyramid. They were
following the shape of a cognitively
designed structure and forming a
pair of monuments that were almost
twins. This seemed to be conclusive
evidence that the change in slope
angle of the Vega Pyramid, at that
precise point above the ground, was
due to prior design and not imminent
collapse. That is where we left the
story in the book *Thoth*, as the data I

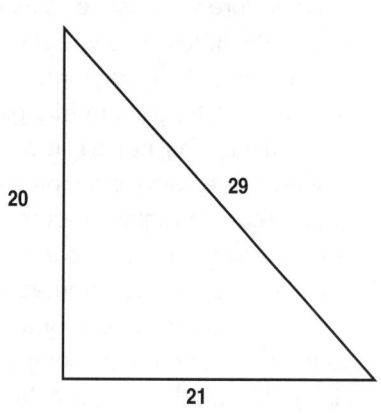

Fig 3.   The 20-21-29 triangle.

had did not seem to justify any further conclusions. However, as is often
the case with these structures, there was more to the story than this.

While the upper and slightly flatter section of the Vega (Bent)
Pyramid had the same slope angle as the Red Pyramid, it also had its
own very different set of dimensions. If the dimensions of the Draco
Pyramid were shouting 'Pythagoras' at us, in multiples of ten, then what
would these new dimensions from the top of the Vega Pyramid tell us
about the designer's intentions? A quick calculation using the
established texts quickly showed what this pyramid was supposed to
represent and even, perhaps, how other similar structures should be
investigated in the future. The trick, though, was to amend the slope
angle of the lower portions of the Vega Pyramid to make things 'fit'.

Is this amendment justified, or simply fiddling the figures? The
results will prove it to be totally justified. Besides, to derive this stunning
mathematical symmetry, the slope angle of the outer casing only has to
be tweaked by just four minutes of arc, which is a thoroughly trifling
amount. As will be explained later, the designer was only counting on an
accuracy of +/- half a degree with most of the angles in the pyramids,
and it is doubtful whether the artisans could complete a pyramid with a
angle of elevation to the nearest minute of arc. Also, having made this
little tweak to the Vega Pyramid's slope angle, the resulting structure
has *such* a degree of symmetry to it that it simply could _not_ have

happened that way by chance. By making this little amendment to the angle of elevation of the Vega Pyramid, the dimensions given in the diagram overleaf result. (All measurements are in Royal or Thoth cubits - tc.)

So, what does this new diagram prove, you might be thinking? The Vega Pyramid, as it lay on the boards of the cunning designer, now seems to have been composed entirely in odd and fractional units of length. What, then, was the marvellous mathematical 'grand plan' that was being projected into the future?

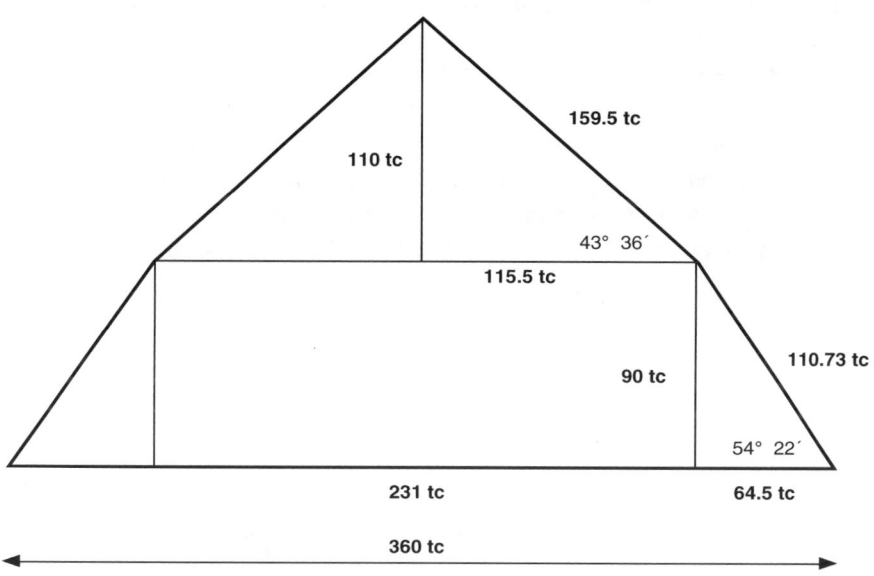

Fig 4. The Vega Pyramid, as the designer intended.

The answer lies in the real units that were being used on these sites: were they simply cubits, or was there a larger unit involved? In the book *Thoth*, I made the suggestion that the unit being used a lot at Giza was the rod length, which comprised $5\frac{1}{2}$ cubits. This may seem like a very peculiar unit of length to use, but it was also explained that this unit of length was the originator of the British rod unit, which also measures $5\frac{1}{2}$ units in length ($5\frac{1}{2}$ yards). The precise reason why this unit of measure should be taken as a valid unit known to the Giza designer will be discussed later. Indeed, it will be shown later that this unit was used a great deal in the dimensions of the Great Pyramid. For the moment, however, please accept that this unit of measure was known and used by the architect; in fact, the following 'coincidence' may be sufficient to persuade most people that this is so.

To see what the designer was really up to, all that has to be done is to divide all the dimensions of the flatter, upper portions of the Vega Pyramid by the rod length of $5^1/_2$. The results are shown in the diagram overleaf. (All dimensions in Royal or Thoth rods - tr.)

Now, the simplicity and elegance of the original design of these pyramids is laid bare for all to see. The top of the Vega Pyramid, when expressed in rods instead of cubits, is simply a copy of the 20 - 21 - 29 triangle once more, and therefore it is also a smaller copy of the dimensions of the Draco Pyramid. Even the dimensions of the stone blocks that were used in the upper portions of the Vega Pyramid have been scaled down by roughly the same amount, in order to confirm that this upper section really was meant to represent a scale copy of the Draco Pyramid that lies next door. Plainly and simply, the Vega Pyramid has a smaller copy of the Draco Pyramid siting on top of it.

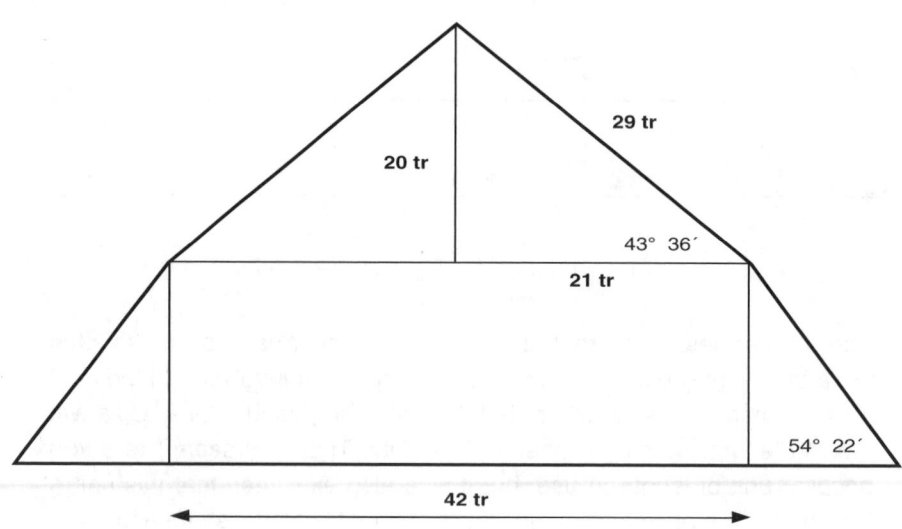

Fig 5. The Vega Pyramid in rods.

2. *Vega and Draco*

This whole quest is about simple similarities and symmetries; difficult maths does not need to be understood. The numbers 20, 21 and 29 can be seen to be repeated throughout these two pyramids, and the knowledge that these numbers are somehow special in formulating triangles is quite sufficient to prove that the Egyptians knew of, and applied, Pythagoras' geometrical theorems. It also demonstrated that there was supposed to be a link between the two pyramids at Dahshur; that they were a part of the same grand plan. The reason for this link was probably something to do with the 'precessional layout' of Giza and Dahshur, as was explained in the book *Thoth*.

There will be more of this simple maths later in the book, but it does not get much more complicated than this. This quest was never supposed to be about applied mathematics; it is a simple quest with simple answers so that anyone can follow it. Maths was only used because it is a useful tool that does not alter or get distorted down the millennia. The maths that was encoded in these pyramids will last for eternity, as far as we are aware, and so a researcher in any era, using any language and applying any numerical system, will see the same mathematical patterns emerge.

Hint?

But does this little numerical game at Dahshur have any other lessons for us? Does it mean something more than it seems on the surface? To be honest, apart from the explanation given in the book *Thoth,* I cannot think of anything fundamental that can be derived from this symmetry. In addition to this 'precessional layout' explanation, what I believe is going on here is a simple and graphic example to any potential investigator, which should be applied in any future research on these pyramids.

The Dahshur pyramids are not the most important pyramids in this quest. The prime site lies a little further to the north; on the Giza plateau. What the Dahshur pyramids may represent, however, are simple mathematical examples for a researcher to follow and apply later in the quest. Indeed, it was from this very mathematical hint at Dahshur that I later derived the full solution for the design of the Great Pyramid. What, then, have we learned from this diagram of the Vega Pyramid?

a.   That Pythagorean triangles are important.

b.   That whole-number lengths are significant.

c.   That if whole numbers are not derived immediately, try looking for rod lengths instead, using $5^1/_2$ as the unit divisor.

The last point is very important. The designer had simply placed another layer of obfuscation over the plans. A set of meaningless lengths and angles may put off a researcher who is just giving these structures a cursory glance. It takes a dedicated researcher to see through the second veil to the whole numbers that lie within.

At the same time, the rod length also gave the designer greater design flexibility. A design using only cubits has to be of a certain physical size, whereas a design using rods as well as cubits can be two different sizes for a given numerical length. Look at the two 20-21-29 triangles in the two pyramids at Dahshur (figures 2 & 3). They are saying the same thing and using the same numbers, but they are doing so using radically different physical dimensions for the structures.

Not only did this give the designer greater flexibility in the design; it also gives the researcher more confidence to say that this was a deliberate design. If the two pyramids at Dahshur were exactly the same size, then this may have been due to simple copying – it does not tell us that something technical or mathematical was going on behind the scenes. The actual design that we see today is much more convincing. There is the basic concept of the Pythagorean 20-21-29 triangle displayed at the Draco Pyramid, which was then repeated on the top of the Vega Pyramid; but this symmetry can only be understood after the side-lengths (in cubits) have been divided by 10 and multiplied by $5^1/_2$ – a sure sign of a cognitive design.

Even after this subtle manipulation of the physical size of these pyramids, the two structures are mathematically exactly the same – the only difference being that one is measured in cubits and the other is measured in rods. This is compelling evidence that this was the intended design, and it is also a strong hint that the same techniques should be tried on the Giza plateau. One thing is for certain, however. The Vega Pyramid was not redesigned at a late stage due to internal cracking of the structure. The Dahshur pyramids were deliberately designed in the fashion that we see to this day.

Chapter III

Blueprint

Looking at that great edifice known as the Great Pyramid of Giza, often called the Khufu Pyramid, is a moving experience no matter how often one visits the site. That great, unbelievable mountain of rock, hewn from the quarries along the Nile and piled high into the sky, higher than many of the world's modern skyscrapers. Yet, however peculiar the exterior of the pyramid may seem, the form of the internal galleries is even more puzzling. Here, we find not only the fine engineering and embodiment of mathematics – as can be found on the exterior – but also some strange ideas which don't fit at all well with the traditional image of the pyramid being a tomb.

There is the Grand Gallery, which appears to have no function whatsoever. There are the peculiar small 'air' shafts – some of which were wholly entombed in the structure and had no contact with the other chambers or the pyramid's exterior. Finally, there is the extremely odd roof structure over the King's Chamber, for which there is no structural explanation or precedent.

Much of this subject is covered in great detail in large sections of the book *Thoth*, and some intriguing concepts were aired in those chapters that clash strongly, both with the established understanding of these monuments and also the more radical 'new age' interpretations. The ideas I put forward in that book were extremely simple and yet they managed to explain all of the internal elements of the Great Pyramid. The proposal was that the internal galleries and chambers, when viewed from a certain angle, formed themselves into the outline of the continents of the Earth – the Great Pyramid was simply a 'map' of the continents of

3. Blueprint

the Earth, formed from megalithic masonry. It was a pretty wild and provocative idea; one that managed to generate a lot of criticism even from those with more liberated viewpoints. Yet, here was such a simple and elegant method of explaining every single component inside the pyramid, that I instinctively felt it had to be true. Proving it to be true to any degree of satisfaction, however, was to be a long and tedious business; hours of staring at diagrams, just hoping that inspiration would generate that 'eureka' moment.

The reality of research is never quite so dramatic. If anything, it was nothing more than a series of small breakthroughs that slowly amalgamated over time into an all-embracing explanation for the layout of the pyramid. My simple theory had, at last, come of age. But having constructed this thesis, it still demanded a rationale; for if an architect had indeed drawn such a massively complex 'map' many thousands of years ago, it needed a purpose. The working-theory I chose for this aspect was to be equally logical and simple. There is only one reason for producing a map, and that is to mark something upon it. Unbelievably, this seemed to be a good old-fashioned treasure-map with an 'X marks the spot' scribbled on it somewhere.

The small breakthroughs, teased from the drawings with much patience and tedium, were enlightening in themselves, because all these discoveries continually pointed towards the same incredible explanation. I had an idea, in the back of my mind, that the location the pyramids were pointing to would be the same as the location I had already found when looking at the Avebury henge in Britain. It was a good enough guess at what may be marked on an ancient map, but it was a fruitless task that failed miserably. Despite this failure, it was actually one of the main factors that drove me ever onwards; for despite my every effort to make the pyramid 'map' point towards the Atlantic, as my research at Avebury and Stonehenge indicated it should, the evidence always pointed in another direction. The data was not only obstinate; it was consistently obstinate.

Design

Many books have been written on the unbelievable precision that was achieved in the construction of the Great Pyramid, and it is frequently claimed that the design and construction of this vast edifice was made to within so many seconds of arc and to the nearest millimeter. The texts ramble on and on in this refrain and perhaps with some justification, because this pyramid especially is truly awe-inspiring in its accuracy, for what is described classically as a Bronze Age edifice. But the working-theory that I was using dictated that the entire structure was, and is, nothing more than a giant drawing-board carved from monumental blocks of stone. The myriad of chambers and galleries are simply the outlines of a technical drawing; a blueprint from a master craftsman with an idea at the back of his mind and a gleam in his eye.

If this was the case, the question of the pyramid's construction accuracy must be turned around completely. The question is not how precise *is* the pyramid, but what sort of precision was the master architect looking for in the first place? In other words, to understand the function of the pyramid, to what degree of accuracy must we measure? If we find a particular measurement to be 30 seconds of arc or five millimeters adrift from our expectations, should this be considered a significant finding or the slip of a mason's mallet?

Previous works appear to have led us to expect the former; they have sought solace in every last millimeter of measurement. The author, Peter Le Mesurer (an apt name!), took all his measurements to five decimal places of an inch; that is, to the nearest two microns! Clearly expecting such precision in any building is a complete nonsense, but the question remains – to what precision must we measure to develop a serious theory and discover an explanation?

Rudolf Gantenbrink, the German engineer who explored the shafts in the Great Pyramid, had probably found the best evidence for the true accuracy of the pyramid. As his little robot crawled up the shafts, Rudolf measured and described every detail of these complex and enigmatic structures that branched off from the main chambers.

The shafts were each constructed from an upper and lower block, and each of these blocks seems to record an entire history of the construction of the pyramid. The manufacture of the blocks was far from consistent and there were many periods of poor workmanship, which probably indicate that the master designer was often away from the construction project for some considerable time and left the project unsupervised. Errors in the main chambers and the pyramid exterior could always be altered at a later date, but the errors in the shafts were buried deep inside the superstructure of the pyramid and were thus

3. Blueprint

impossible to correct. Rudolf says of these limestone blocks that form the sides of these small shafts:

> Blocks No. 8 and 9 were evidently built into the structure in unfinished form. In 1992 we also found three unfinished blocks in the upper shafts ...
>
> The far end of Block No. 5 is unfinished. As a result, the height of the shaft drops to only 9 to 10 centimeters ... This is an obvious example of inferior workmanship, what we refer to as a 'Monday morning block'.
>
> Block No. 5 was almost certainly inserted without authorization from the architect or master builder. The discovery of a number of such unfinished blocks in both upper shafts and in the lower southern shaft as well would seem to indicate that the 'shaft builders' made up a separate working group. This group apparently lagged behind at times, pressured by the rapid rate of growth of the pyramid layers and the construction of the chambers. [1]

Quite clearly, there were many areas of the pyramid that did not live up to the high standards the architect required. But a sensible project manager will understand the limitations of his or her workforce and set tasks that they *can* accomplish; goad them on to higher achievements perhaps, but not stretch them to a point at which they consistently fail. Put it this way, if understanding the design of the pyramid required measurements to the nearest millimeter and second of arc, we have failed at the first fence because the pyramid cannot, and does not, live up to that expectation.

The answer to all this, however, is actually perfectly simple; a sensible architect would have protected their design with liberal margins of error, to ensure that the finished product always lay within the achievable limitations of the workforce. Plans that were drawn up to the nearest cubit and the nearest degree were most probably quite good enough and that is what we are about to find. Again and again, these extremely simple answers to the problems posed, reinforce and confirm that the explanations to be shortly given are true explanations and not ideas found by forcing the data.

The great importance of these enigmatic 'air' shafts is about to be laid bare, piece by piece. The first thing they can do is to convincingly

3. Blueprint

decide for us the level of accuracy that the designer was expecting from his construction teams. That this is possible at all is solely due to the courage and tenacity of Rudolf Gantenbrink, for his dogged determination to explore, measure and map the precise details of these shafts with his small robotic vehicle, known as Upaut II. The precise measurements he made are the sole means of exploring the mathematics in the shafts and the fact that these figures are now freely available on the internet is a major benefit to everyone interested in the subject of ancient Egypt, and a great credit to the man himself. [2]

Shafts

For all the following discussions on the dimensions of the shafts I shall be using the Egyptian Royal cubit, or the Thoth cubit (tc) as I christened it in the book *Thoth*. This has been done for a specific reason – the true meaning of the design cannot be seen until the original units are used, as I have explained in the previous chapter. The explanations that follow rely on being able to understand that a particular measurement is significant or not. It is not immediately apparent whether a figure like 26.17 meters, for instance, is significant. Only through a conversion to Thoth cubits and the discovery that this length is in fact 50 Thoth cubits, can the truth emerge.

For the time being, only measurements that result in whole numbers will be considered significant. This rule is changed in later, more complicated sections of the Second Pyramid in particular, but it is still a good general guide. The Thoth cubit (tc) measures 52.35 cms and it was the prime unit of measure used in all the pyramids of Egypt.

What is required now is a small demonstration that some shaft lengths in the Great Pyramid resolve into whole-number units of cubits, and can therefore be considered to be significant measurements.

The first measurement to be studied is the King's southern shaft itself. It starts its journey high up within the structure of the pyramid, inside the King's Chamber. The shaft is tiny, just a quarter of one Thoth cubit (tc) high, and it heads off perfectly level for a distance of 3.25 tc. At this point it begins its upward journey; not at the normally quoted angle of 45° but at a much shallower 39.2°. After a little while it bends upwards again at a much steeper angle, before finally settling into a steady 45° all the way to the exterior of the pyramid.

3. Blueprint

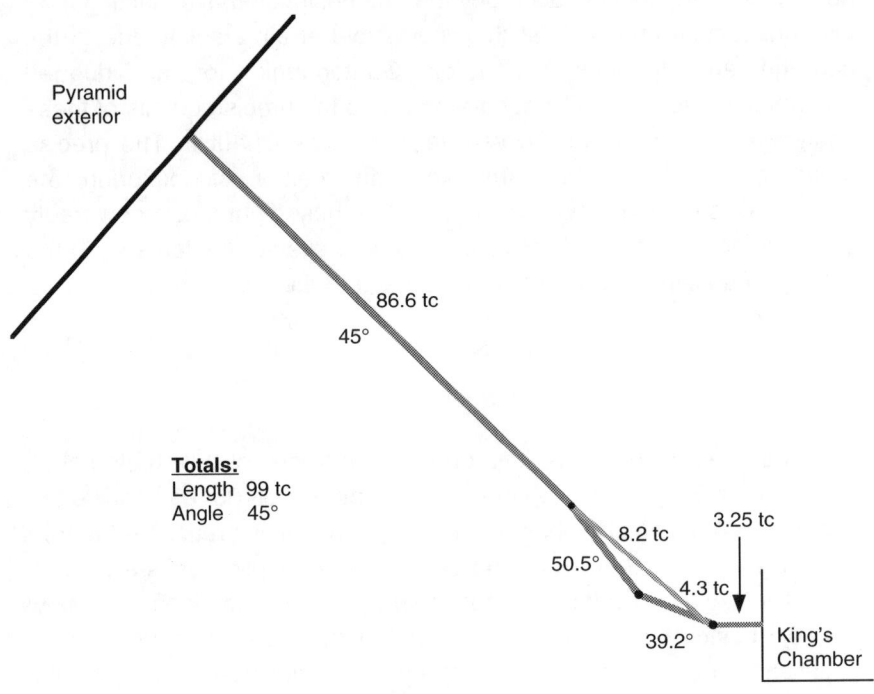

Fig 6. *The King's south shaft.*

There are a couple things to note about this shaft. Firstly, the initial wild swings in the angle of this shaft nearly cancel each other out, so that the general line of the shaft is 46.5° in the 'bendy section', then 45° from there on, making an average of 45.2° for the entire shaft length. Taking the direct line, instead of measuring through the bends, the length of the shaft from the initial first bend to the exterior of the pyramid is 99 tc. So was the length of 99 tc the true designed length of this shaft – just as it appeared on the drawing-boards of the architect? Are we taking liberties in measuring the direct length instead of the true length through the bends (although the latter only adds 0.1 tc to the length)? Did Rudolf Gantenbrink really measure the shaft accurately enough to deduce this length?

A little simple maths will prove that the result is a valid one. If the rise in the shaft is calculated over that distance of 99 tc, using the desired angle of 45°, the result is precisely a 70 tc rise, as is shown on the next diagram. In fact, if horizontal and vertical lines are drawn from the extremities of the shaft, again as shown on the following page, the resulting triangle formed by the these lines and the shaft is almost

3. Blueprint

Pythagorean; the result gives whole numbers to three decimal places on all three sides. But does the simple presence of whole numbers in the shaft and the imaginary triangle indicate that this was the designer's intention? Perhaps that is not the immediate conclusion, but there are some other clues to be found that indicate this was so.

In the previous chapter it was argued, with a large amount of supporting evidence, that the British Imperial Measurement system was based on the same principles as the Great Pyramid's measurements, and that the 5 $\frac{1}{2}$ unit rod-length was perhaps a significant unit of measurement within all of these pyramids. Indeed, the rod length works especially well in the dimensions of the Vega Pyramid at Dahshur, as we have just seen, and now it will be shown to work well in the Great Pyramid too. Thus, it can be seen that, like the 1,760 tc base length of this pyramid, the shaft length measurement of 99 tc that has just been found can also be divided up into rod lengths – Thoth rods (tr) each measuring 5 $\frac{1}{2}$ cubits in length.

1,760 tc divided by 5.5 equals 320 tr.
99 tc divided by 5.5 equals 18 tr.

When based on this symmetry with the Imperial measures, it would now appear that 99 cubits is a significant number, as it is now a whole number in both normal units (cubits) *and* the new rod unit. But more evidence was to follow that would reinforce the view that 99 tc *is* a significant measurement.

In figure 6 it was shown that the shaft itself forms a triangle of specific dimensions, as has just been demonstrated. But the end of the shaft – where it meets the exterior of the pyramid – forms another triangle, and this also appears to have 'significant' dimensions, as can be seen in figure 7. The most important thing about this triangle is not the measurements as such, but the fact that this small triangle measures exactly $\frac{1}{4}$ of the dimensions of the Great Pyramid itself. The height of the pyramid is 280 tc and the 70 tc rise of the shaft is, of course, exactly $\frac{1}{4}$ of this. Since this triangle is also bounded by the exterior of the pyramid, the other dimensions of this imaginary triangle are all $\frac{1}{4}$ of the dimensions of the pyramid itself. Now, that just has to be significant by any standard. By judicious use of shaft angles and lengths, the designer seems to have drawn a small diagram of the pyramid itself on his blueprint – and with good reason.

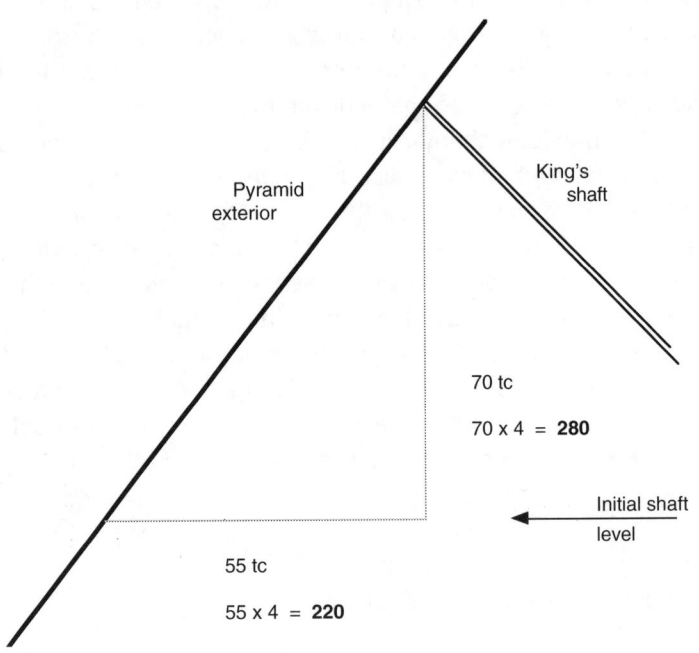

Fig 7. End of King's south shaft.

This seems to mimic, in some respects, the explanations for the Avebury site in Britain, where I attempted to explain that one of the features inside this massive henge was actually a small copy of Stonehenge. There may be an oblique reason for this similarity. It is difficult, perhaps, to find a significant artifact that can be marked on a monument that is itself supposed to last for thousands of years, because the environment and topography can change so much over that amount of time. If a particular outcrop of rock were to be copied, for instance, perhaps that outcrop would be quarried and destroyed in a few thousand years. But the monument itself (or a sister-monument) is an obvious choice for marking a reference point on a monumental 'map', as that is one of the few artifacts that is designed to last for so long. Indeed, one can only 'read' the map in the first place if the monument has survived the millennia.

Because the King's south shaft appears to draw a picture of the pyramid itself – and further justification for this theory will be explained

3. *Blueprint*

later – the lengths and angles involved in this shaft can be taken as being the original dimensions intended by the designer. All of these dimensions were apparently drawn using whole-number lengths and whole numbers of degrees, although later shaft angles will use half degrees as well. Note that the bends in the lower section of the shaft are being ignored at the present; the reason for this will be explained in a later chapter.

Northern

The second shaft to look at is the King's north shaft. Now this shaft was a lot trickier to decipher than the southern shaft, because it not only bends in the vertical plane, it also bends in the horizontal plane to wind its way around the Grand Gallery. As Rudolf Gantenbrink has pointed out, the bends in this shaft must have been very important in some respect, as the designer has gone to a great deal of time and trouble to produce them:

> (It is presumed that) the shafts simply constitute an afterthought, or an insignificant architectural change. This hypothesis defies all logic and basic engineering knowledge. The shafts, despite their small dimensions, greatly complicated the construction and required massive static changes, endless additional work, time and energy. Any builder forced to penetrate vast horizontal layers with diagonal structures, faces enormous challenges and headaches. Not to mention the fact that both northern shafts had to be bent several times at different angles – a masterpiece of engineering – to get around the vast obstruction of the Great Gallery. [3]

One obvious riposte to this would be that the designer was a little 'sloppy' and the bends were in fact a last-minute correction to get out a sticky situation; namely the Grand Gallery being in the way. Basically, this argument goes, the designer had made a big mistake in the starting point for these shafts and the resulting bends were a clumsy solution. This may sound reasonable, but Rudolf deals neatly with this one too:

> Until 1993, when we discovered that the lower northern shaft also

bends to avoid the Great Gallery (sic), it was generally assumed that the bends in the upper northern shaft were simply the result of a planning mistake made by the pyramid builders. In other words, not until actual construction was underway did the builders supposedly realize that extension of the upper northern shaft conflicted with the Great Gallery. Based on our present knowledge, this assumption no longer makes sense.

The northern shafts' structural conflict with the Great Gallery (sic) was obvious to the builders much farther below, during construction of the shafts emanating from the Queen's Chamber. Based on the experience gained there, the builders could have shifted the King's Chamber shaft inlets farther to the west, in order to correct their 'planning mistake' without great effort. Instead, the builders repeated the conflict situation, a fact which again cost them immense time and energy. [4]

It is most unlikely that the same mistake would have been made twice on the same building project, so an alternative explanation is required. The precise reason for the horizontal bends will be dealt with in a later chapter; but, for now, the 'blueprint' concept for the pyramid only requires that we take a vertical section through the pyramid – like projecting an image of the shafts onto a screen out to the east or west of the pyramid. In such a scenario, all the bends in this shaft to the east and west, that snake around the Grand Gallery, will be erased from the picture. All that is left on the screen is an image of the shaft slowly increasing and decreasing its angle of climb, and then becoming constant at 32.6°. As in the King's south shaft, we are only left with vertical changes in angle to explain at this stage of the investigation.

However, the precise layout of these vertical undulations was further confused by a small error in the diagram given by Gantenbrink on his web-site. Each of the shaft lengths and angles can be resolved into a triangle, which can then be solved using the standard Pythagorean rules. The last triangle proved to be impossible to resolve – there was an error somewhere. Many alternative lengths and angles were tried and each failed. The calculation would not give consistent answers when approached from different starting points. It was only when I thought logically about the possible errors that could have been made in drawing the diagram, that an elegant solution became obvious. The lengths and angles were diligently measured by Rudolf, so the error was unlikely to be found here. In this case, the error must lie in some of the lengths that had been *calculated* from that initial data.

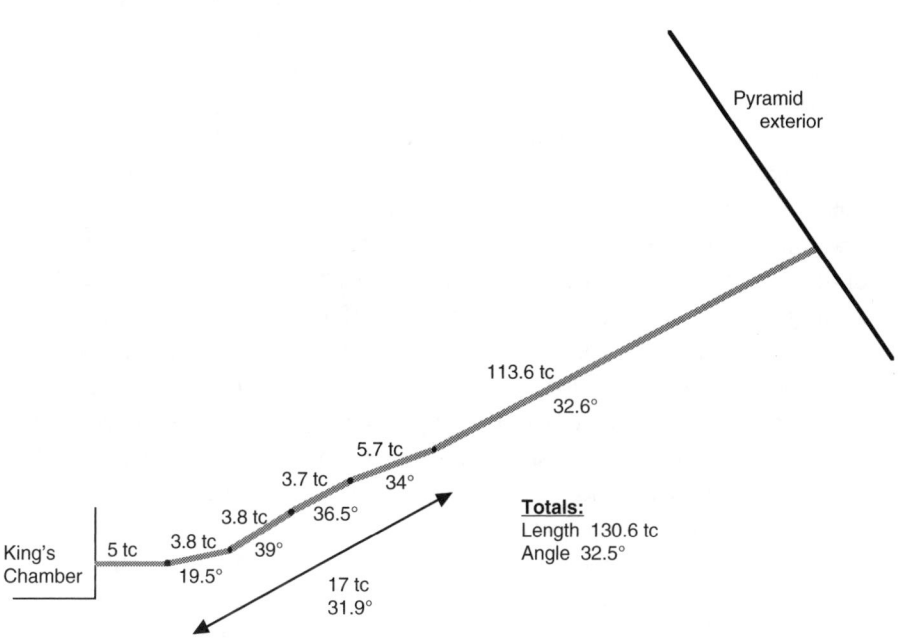

Fig 8.   King's north shaft.

Just as expected, the rise of the final section of the bends looks to be in error – the total rise from the initial level of the shaft was given as 4.48 meters, whereas the figure that resolves the whole problem is 4.74 meters. The adjusted figure not only gave a whole number for the total rise for this 'bendy section' of shaft (that of 9 tc), but the resulting rise in elevation was exactly the same as for the undulating sections in the southern shaft. This evidence was convincing enough to assume that this was the real figure to use in later calculations.[5] Armed with this revised data, the total length for the entire shaft can now be correctly calculated, as is shown in the previous diagram.

As in the case with the southern shaft, there are a whole series

3. Blueprint

of bends in the shaft; but the average trajectory is very much the same as the rest of the shaft, without the bends. The average track of the undulating section of shaft is at an angle of about 32.0°, whereas the rest of the shaft was measured as being 32.6°. Thus the total length of the shaft is about 130.6, tc at an angle of just under 32.6° – in fact, the average angle appears to be 32.5°. Again, the question must be asked as to whether these were the precise units that the designer intended in the original plans? The answer has to be yes, and for precisely the same reasons given previously for the southern shaft.

If the full dimensions of the triangle formed by the shaft are calculated, using an average angle of 32.5°, the rise in the shaft from its initial position can be found to be exactly 70 tc – exactly the same measurement as found previously for the southern shaft. The northern shaft seems to be mimicking the southern shaft, in rising exactly the same distance from the initial bend to the exterior of the pyramid. This would mean that the southern shaft (without averaging out the bends) exits the pyramid just 0.1m or 0.2 tc above the level of the northern shaft. In comparison, Sir Flinders Petrie, in his calculations, determined that the southern shaft exited the pyramid 1.4 tc above the northern,[6] whereas Rudolf Gantenbrink says that the northern shaft is 1.7 tc higher than the southern one.[7]

There is a slight discrepancy here which needs addressing in a later survey; but why should such errors exist in such a well-documented structure? There are a few possibilities as to why this should be so. Both surveys faced the difficult task of calculating exactly how much cladding material has been removed from the pyramid where the shafts make their exit, as this will greatly affect the results. Additionally, Rudolf was using the internal shaft dimensions recorded by his robot to derive the shaft length, and it is a fact that his calculation of the lower portions of the northern shaft is incorrect. The calculations of the lower part of the shaft, where the bends are located, make the shaft both 0.45 tc too low and 1.0 tc too long. This in itself will affect the results, but the nett effect of these errors should not actually make the results very different from my own. In fact, using Rudolf's own data, I make the south shaft just 0.5 tc higher than the north, a discrepancy which is a little puzzling.

With this uncertainty surrounding the precise measurements of the shafts, the question has to be asked – will this line of enquiry be able to proceed further with any degree of certainty? How can one speculate on data that appears to have up to one tc (0.5 m) of possible error?

3. Blueprint

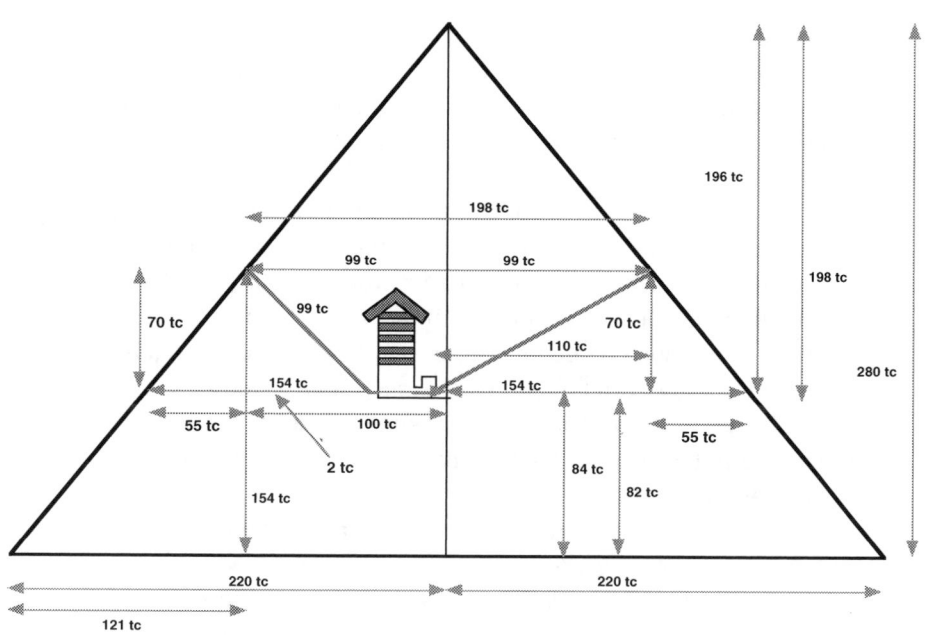

Fig 9. *Dimension symmetry – cubits.*

Personally, I think there is a sure way out of this cul-de-sac; a route that was preconceived and deliberately employed by the designer to overcome any such trivial obstacles. Once more, it would seem that the true dimensions of the internal shafts and chambers can be deduced mathematically, as there is some symmetry in the dimensions that makes the whole scenario about to be explained ring very true. Incidentally, the dimensions achieved by assuming the following symmetry agree very precisely with most of the other measurements given by Petrie in his 1883 survey; although Petrie does not, himself, draw the conclusions made on the previous diagram because he did not

3. Blueprint

have access to the correct angles and lengths of the small shafts. The previous diagram is measured in Thoth cubits of 0.5235 m length, and it begins to demonstrate what the true dimensions of this pyramid really were supposed to be.

It was ascertained by Petrie, in his survey, that the floor of the King's Chamber was built at the point in the structure where the area of the pyramid, at that level, is half the area of the base of the pyramid – an interesting observation that serves to confirm the technical abilities of the designer, and the mathematical nature of everything inside the pyramid. Accordingly, the floor of the King's Chamber is 82 tc above the base of the pyramid.

In figure 9, this concept can be taken a few steps further. It can now be seen that the height of both the small shaft's exit points above the ground, equals the horizontal distance from the center of the pyramid to the exterior casing – at the height of the shafts themselves. Similarly, the length of the angled section of the King's south shaft is equal to the horizontal distance from the center of the pyramid to the exterior casing – at the height of the exit point for the shafts. Indeed, the total width of the pyramid at this level is equal to the height of the pyramid above the King's Chamber floor-line.

Not all of these measurements are exact, of course, as not all of these triangles are precise Pythagorean triangles, with nice whole-number lengths to them. However, the results are as close to whole-number answers as it is mathematically possible to get, in these circumstances. There follow some examples of the accuracy achieved:

a. King's north shaft length, using 70 tc rise and 45° angle:
98.995 tc instead of 99 tc.
b. Height of the level where the floor area is equal to half the floor area at the base of the pyramid:
82.010 tc instead of 82 tc.
c. Width of the pyramid at 154 tc above the ground
198 tc exactly.

Clearly, there has been some mathematical symmetry designed into the structure here, and I would suggest that it is there for only one purpose: to overcome any misconceptions and to confirm the theory as outlined so far. There are so many things that could have confused a potential researcher; the masons on the site may not have built the pyramid to

30

3. *Blueprint*

quite the architect's specifications (examples of this will follow), or perhaps there may have been some subsidence over the years (as indeed Petrie noted on a few occasions). To overcome these problems, the architect simply built in a few mathematical tricks to confirm that these were the true dimensions required. It does not matter about the odd five centimeter slip here or there; the mathematical symmetry will always shine through.

But just in case this was not enough for the intrepid researcher, there is another confirmation built in that is so sweet, it is simply perfect. As already mentioned earlier in the chapter, the $5\frac{1}{2}$ cubit rod was often used as a measurement unit by the designer, to prove that certain measurements were really designed in the way that we appear to see them.

If this was indeed the case, then some measurements using the Thoth rod should also be apparent in the Great Pyramid. There were a few rod units found in the internal chambers, including the Queen's Chamber and the Grand Gallery, but in retrospect the rod unit seemed to be remarkably lacking in the measurements of the structure. This was a slight problem with the theory – until the internal lengths between the pyramid's more distant features were calculated. The diagram is therefore repeated in figure 10, but this time all the measurements have been divided by $5\frac{1}{2}$ to derive the Thoth rod (tr).

The rod length is a particularly odd measurement, consisting as it does of a non-whole number – $5\frac{1}{2}$ cubit length – and it might be expected that very few measurements would be divisible by it. However, the opposite is true; most of the lengths within the Great Pyramid are divisible by $5\frac{1}{2}$. The fact that so many of the internal dimensions of this pyramid are divisible by this odd unit not only indicates that the rod unit is a valid measurement, as I have already proposed; it also reinforces the conclusion that the measurements I have outlined previously are the correct units that were intended by the designer.

It is inconceivable that so many coincidences and rod lengths should be derived from the measurements – that were derived by both Petrie and Gantenbrink – by sheer coincidence. The fact that some of the lengths and angles have been adjusted by the odd couple of centimeters, or the odd minute of arc, does not in any way invalidate this claim. In this case I would propose that figure 10 was last seen in this format and with these units on it, when the architect unfolded it on his table many thousands of years ago.

3. *Blueprint*

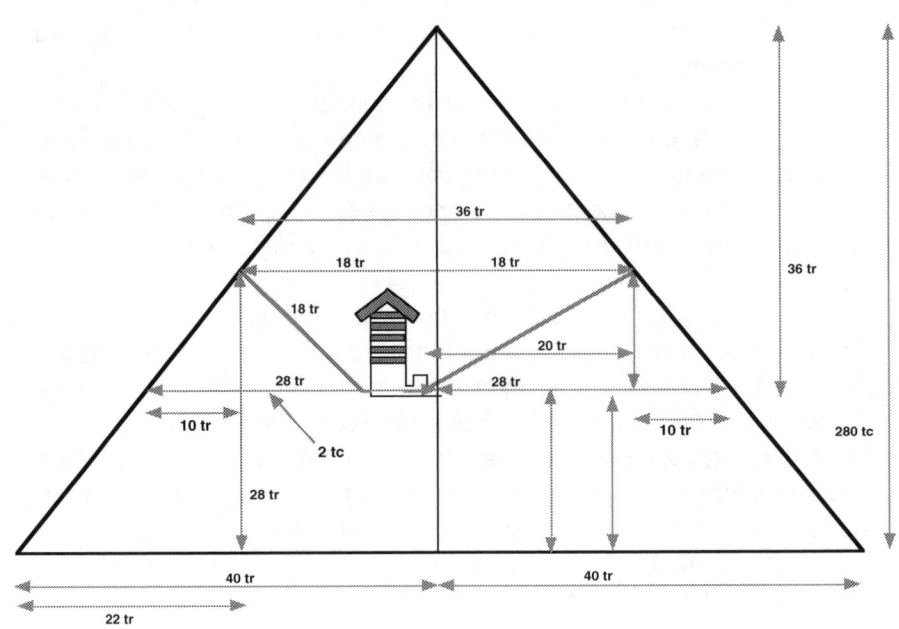

Fig 10.   Dimension symmetry – rods.

Doppelganger

Looking once more at the end of the northern shaft, where it exits the pyramid, the 70 tc rise in the shaft from its origins in the King's Chamber would mean that another $^{1}/_{4}$ copy of the pyramid itself would be drawn at the end of the shaft, where it meets the exterior of the pyramid, just as was proposed for the southern shaft. Thus, although the two upper shafts look to be very different from each other, they actually mimic each other very closely in their design; there is a cognitive symmetry here that is difficult to explain away as coincidence.

If further proof were needed that this is a true result and that the data is not being fiddled to suit the theory, it is to be found in the Queen's Chamber shafts. The Queen's shafts, of course, are an even deeper

3. Blueprint

mystery that the King's shafts – for these lower shafts were seemingly not 'completed'. The lower ends of these shafts were not cut through into the chamber itself; the last few centimeters were left intact, so the presence of these very complex and tedious-to-construct shafts was simply hidden from view.

In effect, the architect had left us a tantalizing mystery to be unearthed by a dedicated researcher. The full significance of the whole edifice cannot be deduced without the Queen's shafts and so hiding these shafts just makes the quest a little more challenging. Little snippets of evidence like this serve to confirm what I had suspected all along; this was indeed a quest, one manufactured to last several millennia. It is quite a sobering thought to understand that we are all following a test that was conceived and fabricated many thousands of years ago.

Luckily for us, the Queen's shafts were discovered by the ever-industrious Victorians and their form has, for the most part, been diligently mapped by Rudolf Gantenbrink. The southern shaft was fully investigated by the little robot, which provided the surprise of the little enigmatic 'door' at the end of the shaft. The northern shaft proved more difficult due to the tortuous bends, which the robot was unable to overcome. Not wanting to get the robot stuck, the attempt to chart this shaft was abandoned. For the purposes of this analysis of the pyramid, however, the layout of the northern shaft will be assumed to have generally the same form of bends as the Kings's north shaft, and the same length and angle as the Queen's south shaft. This may sound like a huge assumption, but the following evidence will show why this scenario is highly likely.

In their general format, the Queen's shafts are very similar to the King's Chamber shafts; they are just a little higher above the chamber floor and a little taller, at 0.35 tc against 0.25 tc. Firstly, we shall look at the Queen's south shaft. From the first bend in the shaft, up to the enigmatic door, the robot measured a slope of 39.6° and a length some 57.48 m, or 109.8 tc. Once again, the question has to be asked as to whether this is the correct construction length the designer intended? Once more, the answer just has to be yes, and I can say this with some confidence because of another, rather glaring, symmetry that a very small change in these measurements will make. If the length of the shaft is changed from 109.8 tc to the whole number of 110 tc, and if the angle is lowered very slightly from 39.6° to 39.5°, then the rise in this shaft from the first bend to the little 'door' will be 70 tc, just like in all the other shafts.

Here is the stunning symmetry that all the shafts reflect, despite their initially different appearances. Someone has gone to very great lengths to ensure that the rise in each shaft is 70 tc, and it is no coincidence that this figure is just $^1/_4$ of the 280 tc height of the pyramid itself. Each and every feature of the pyramid has a function in this quest, and the ultimate function of this part of the design will be fundamental to understanding what this megalithic message, encoded within the fabric of the pyramid, really means.

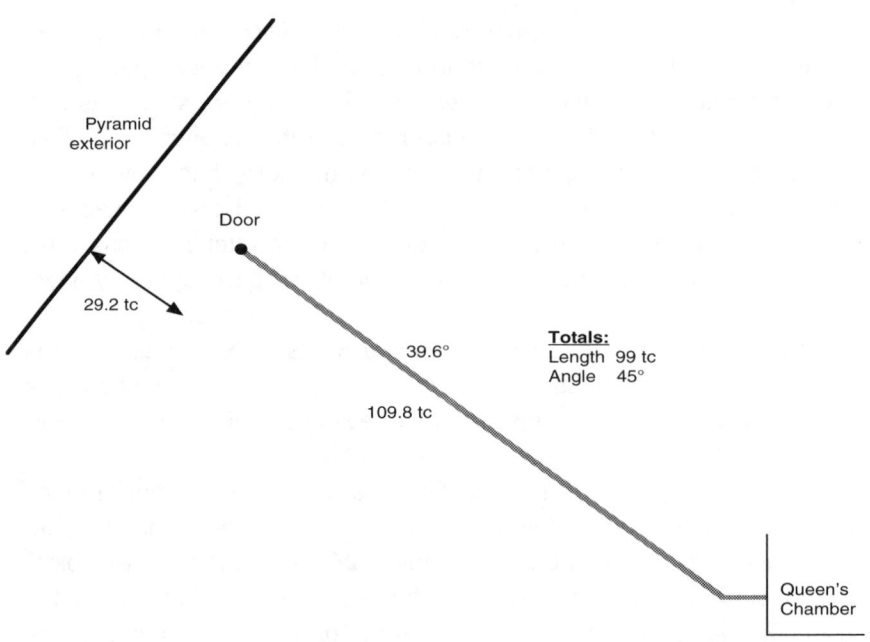

Fig 11.   Queen's south shaft.

The number of coincidences, which will pour forth from the few lengths and angles involved in the pyramid's construction, are phenomenal. I have looked into many alternate scenarios with alternate dimensions to see if the same coincidences will arise, but with little success. It will become apparent in later chapters that these figures are, in some way,

3. Blueprint

special numerically; they seem to cascade with whole-number answers to calculations and those answers are often linked to the mathematical constant, Pi. The numbers *are* special, and their deliberate choice by the designer will become proof-positive that this whole business is a real cognitive test and quest. As a taster of what is to come, the revision of the shaft angle to 39.5°, as just shown, gives another little quirk – the number 39.5 is related to the Pi formula in the following fashion:

$$39.5 = (2\Pi)^2$$

Hopefully, the previous few pages have not been too much like hard work, mathematically. But it may help to recap what has just been looked at diagrammatically, as this may quickly solve any misunderstandings. As can be seen in the following diagram, all of the small shafts now have a rise of 70 tc; a figure that is directly related to the pyramid height of 280 tc – it being exactly $^1/_4$ of the pyramid's height. (The Queen's north shaft is assumed to be symmetrical to its neighbour for the reasons given in a later chapter).

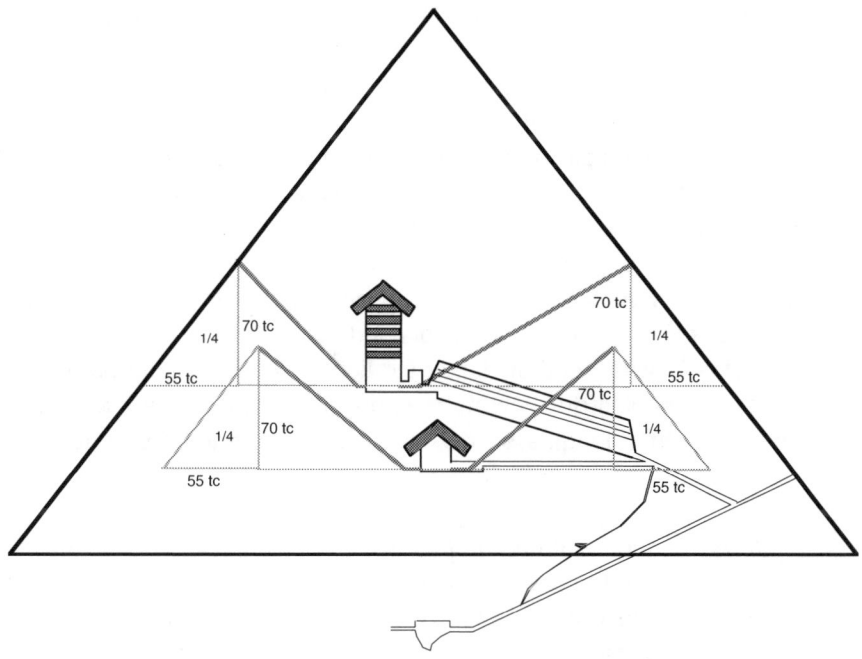

Fig 12.   The $^1/_4$ pyramid triangles.

3. Blueprint

But it is not just the rise of the shaft that is important here; so is the line of the outer casing of the pyramid, which intersects the shaft. The vertical height of 70 tc, when taken together with this angle of the outer casing of the pyramid, forms small triangles that are therefore exactly $\frac{1}{4}$ the size of the pyramid itself. Thus, the designer's original drawings for the pyramid probably looked something like the diagram below:

In order to draw this diagram, the numerical values measured by Rudolf Gantenbrink have simply been rounded to the nearest cubit length or the nearest half degree. Remember that 0.1 of a Thoth cubit is only 5 centimeters, and an angle of 0.1° on the entire length of the Queen's south shaft represents a difference of just 10 centimeters. These are very small errors that can easily be explained in terms of construction deficiencies, measurement error or mathematical constraints. As explained at the beginning of the chapter, there are sufficient examples of poor-quality workmanship in the shafts for us not to get too excited about a 5cm deficiency in a shaft length of 57 meters. After all, this only represents an error of 0.1% in the length of the shaft. Far harder to explain are the numerical symmetries that occur when the whole numbers are used, as shown in figure 12.

Besides, these are not any old whole-number angles and lengths; they are quite specific to this project. For this is not simply a tale of strange, unfathomable mathematical symmetries; there are some really interesting things that can be derived from these measurements.

When the small shaft's lengths are multiplied by four, to scale up the 70 tc rise to the size of the Great Pyramid itself, the angles that have been chosen for these shafts produce lengths that are related to the dimensions of the pyramid itself; as can be seen in the following diagram. This is yet another reason to believe that these shafts have been designed just as has been explained.

This is also another demonstration of the ingenious nature of these chosen angles; for how many other angles are there that would mimic the pyramid lengths so closely? The base lengths produced in figure 13 are:

280 tc – the height of the pyramid.
440 tc – the base length of the pyramid.
340 tc – the length of 340 tc is not very significant, but to balance this, the hypotenuse of this triangle conveniently resolves itself to 440 tc, which again is the base length of the pyramid.

3. Blueprint

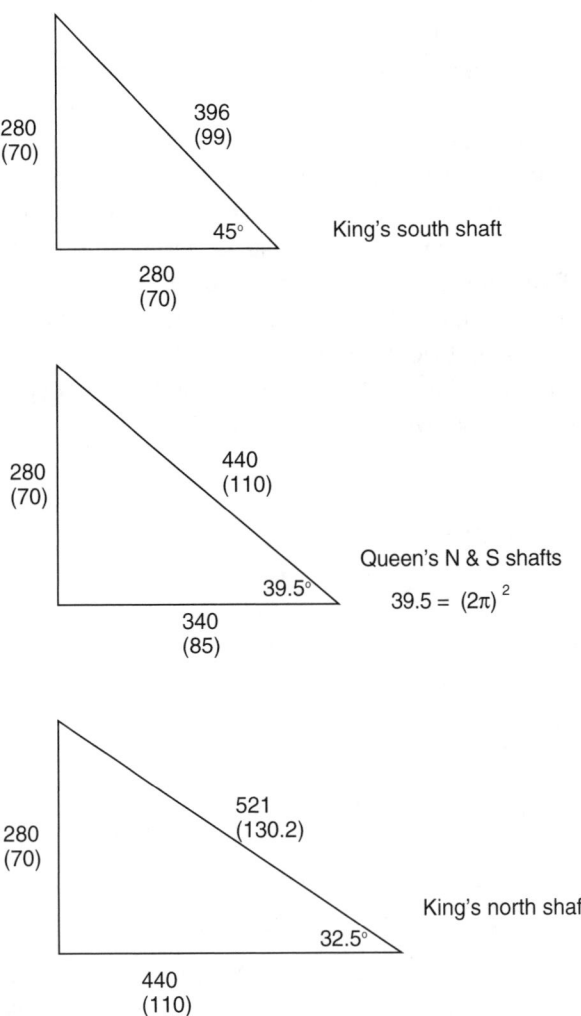

Fig 13.   *The shaft triangles.*

Once more, this is direct evidence that the best accuracy the designer was looking for in this blueprint was just to the nearest half cubit and the nearest half a degree. The pyramid itself may well be much more accurate than that in many places, but to understand the technical drawing that has been built for our benefit, the nearest half cubit and degree is quite sufficient. Understanding this is a great benefit in this quest, for there is no longer any need to get carried away with a multitude of confusing decimal places and, in addition, the length and angles that *do* resolve into fractional units can generally be discarded as irrelevant.

From the very start of this whole enterprise, the megalithic monuments have consistently indicated to me that this quest was not supposed to be hugely difficult. There is no great mathematical complexity in the drawings; just a little understanding of Pi and the theorems of Pythagoras is more than sufficient. The problems are not supposed to be *that* difficult, as this would probably defeat the whole rationale of the quest. It would seem that the whole conundrum is simply a test of lateral thinking and the validity of this concept is further reinforced by the simple whole-number lengths used.

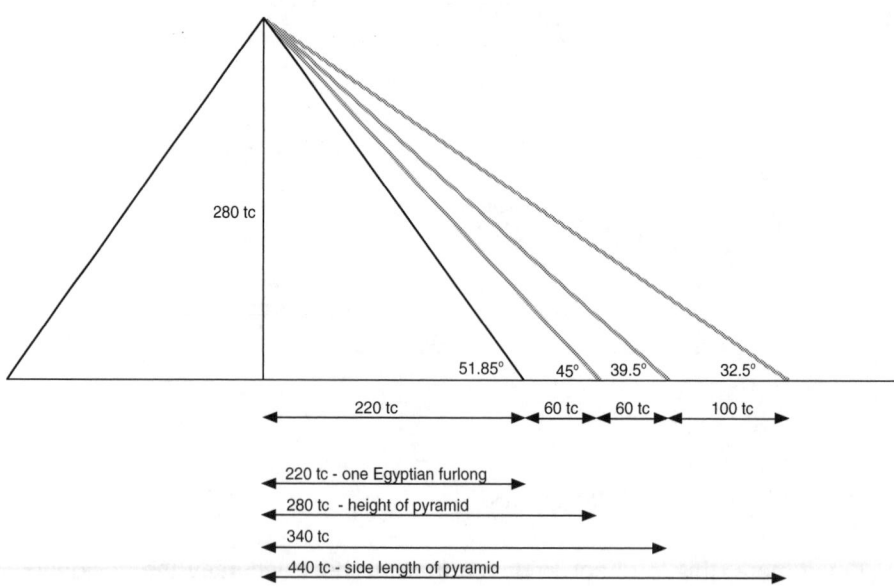

Fig 14.   Great Pyramid shadows.

3. Blueprint

In this case it can be stated, with some confidence, that these little triangles, which are formed by the chamber's shafts, are not simply there as a part of some unfathomable equation to be number-crunched by a team of mathematicians; neither are they there as a decoration, or a figment of my fevered imagination – they have a specific purpose. Like most things in this quest, the picture that has just been drawn of the shafts and their triangles is representational – a picture.

Perhaps it is becoming obvious now that the little $^1/_4$ scale pyramid triangles are intended to be scale images of the pyramid itself. Thus, the lines of the chamber's shafts on this drawing are seen to be originating at the top of this smaller, imaginary pyramid and descending at specific angles down to an imaginary ground. In effect, they are rather like representations of a shadow being formed from the top of the Great Pyramid and being cast onto the ground. Indeed, that is probably the correct answer. To see the equivalent dimensions that a real shadow would make when cast by the Great Pyramid, take a look at figure 14.

That the shadow projected from the top of the pyramid is important is implicit in the theology of Egypt itself. In the book *Tempest*, I cover in some detail the fact that the shadows of the pyramids were used in the original Giza rituals. At the very least, these shadows were used for determining the seasons of the year, but it is not beyond the realms of possibility that there may be other, deeper layers of this quest that lie below this simplistic level. In appendix 1 it will also be shown that the Second Pyramid was specifically designed around the concept of shadow angles, but this investigation did not discover a rationale for this design – hence the reason for this very interesting topic being relegated to the appendix. It is a topic that is not to be missed, however, just because it is in the appendix – at the very least, it clearly demonstrates the methods that the architect used when designing these monuments.

This whole shadow concept was definitely a theory that was well worth investigating. Was this, for example, the origin of the ancient imagery for an eye located at the top of a pyramid? Take a look at the pyramid on the back of the American one dollar bill. The imagery here is nearly the same as that in figures 14 and 15, except that the all-seeing eye on the dollar bill appears to take up a larger proportion of the pyramid. But that is most likely to be artistic licence, in order to make the eye large enough to be visible in the picture. What if the original eye was supposed to be only located on the pyramidion – just on the very top two cubits or so of the structure. In this case, the eye could be envisaged as projecting rays outwards, just as Plato thought that light travelled, from the very top of the pyramid down to the ground. These rays would then form the angles that we have just deduced.

Many pyramidions have the Sun-disk inscribed at the very apex, giving the impression that the Sun's rays shining over the pyramid are somehow important. This kind if imagery would seem to indicate that the pyramids could possibly be used like a large gnomon at the center of a huge sundial, with the shadow of the pyramid falling on a specific point. The pyramidion of Amenemhet III, however, has a more familiar imagery. In addition to the Sun-disk, there are the two eyes of the king himself looking down and across the Nile Valley, and the towards the rays of the rising Sun.

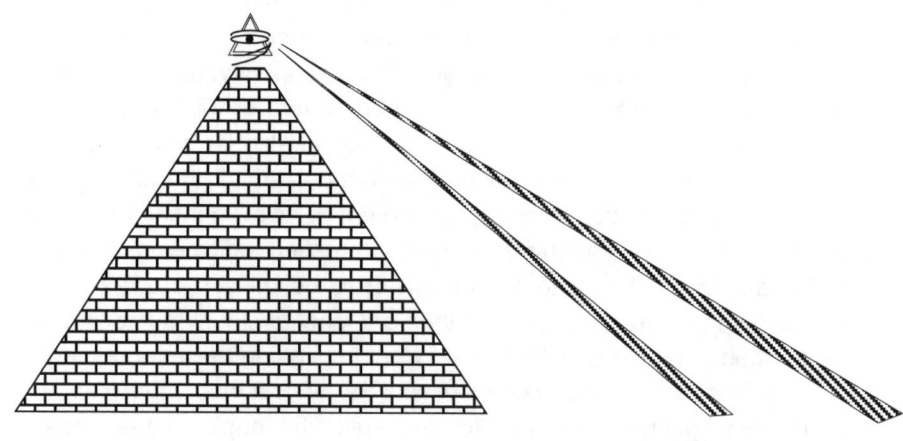

Fig 15.   The pyramidion all-seeing eye.

Ra was perhaps the oldest deity in the Egyptian pantheon of gods and it had many other forms. Ra, the Sun god of Heliopolis. Amun, the hidden one, an equivalent deity who was based at the southern temple of Karnak. Atum, the creator god, who merged into a manifestation of Ra.

3. Blueprint

Aten, either the Sun-disk itself or the power that lay behind the Sun, which was the monotheistic deity of Akhenaton.

The primary temple for Atum-Ra worship resided just a few kilometers down the road from Giza, at Heliopolis – literally the city of the Sun. In the ancient theology of this land, Ra was presented with the Sacred Eye, the symbol of the cosmic order, by Thoth. Old Kingdom pharaohs were regarded as manifestations of Ra, guardians of the cosmic order, and their royal titles invariably included a reference to Ra.

The Sun's rays were thus, somehow, bound up in the form of a pyramid. Tentative confirmation of this idea is to be found on the aprons of the pharaohs themselves. Just as in the modern Masonic world, the pharaohs of Egypt and their chief priests and advisors wore aprons, and the aprons in the Old and New Kingdom were distinctly pyramidal-shaped. From the aprons of the tomb guardians that were discovered in the tomb of Tutankhamen, it can also be seen that the pyramid shape has distinct rays of light, being shone from suns at either side of the pyramid. The suns depicted here may be shining upwards rather than downwards, but after several thousand years of maintaining a tradition, some differences are bound to creep in. What is clear, however, is that there is a distinct and ancient tradition that links the rays of the Sun and the apexes of the pyramids.

This argument is explored much further in the book *Tempest*, where it is convincingly shown that the shadows projected from the pyramids were very important in Egyptian rituals. At the simplistic level, the reasons for making these observations was that the pyramid's shadows crossed the pyramid causeways at certain seasons of the year. Even if the pyramids were not used for daily timekeeping, it is highly likely that they were used for calendrical purposes.

But what if there were a dual usage to the pyramid shadows. What if there were something more esoteric? As already mentioned, in appendix one there are details of a perfect piece of calendrical symmetry that has been embodied within the shadow-length of the Second Pyramid, and which may well indicate that there are some deeper meanings to these observations. For instance, if the Great Pyramid's shadow was directed downwards at a specific angle, the tip of the pyramid shadow could easily point to the location of a hidden chamber at a certain time of year. Is this another part of the imagery that is being indicated on the plateau? Due to parallax, the tip of the pyramid's shadow would never be more accurate than 5 cubits, but this is sufficiently accurate to find a chamber entrance. So if we were to measure out from the base of the pyramid for a certain number of cubits, would we stumble across a hidden shaft that takes us far below the pavement – down into the bowels of the plateau to discover a sacred chamber?

This is certainly a possibility, but as I have said on many previous occasions, I do not believe that a secret chamber would be on the plateau itself. In my estimation, the individuals who have been swarming around the plateau, digging for treasure, are deluding themselves; for what kind of simpleton would place a secret chamber on the Giza plateau, a location where every vaault robber that mankind has ever produced has been plying his or her trade in one era or another? It is my assertion that this quest has to be more secure than this; a sacred chamber should not be subject to the ignominious possibility of being discovered by someone installing a new set of latrines for the tourists. Once more, logic and lateral thinking suggests that a remote location would be more suitable; somewhere that was not only remote during the era of the pyramid's construction, but was likely to remain remote for a very long time indeed.

While toying with this 'shadow' theory, though, it might be interesting to see on which dates the shadow will actually produce the angles given in the diagram above. With the help of a computerised planisphere, the dates specific to the angles are easily obtained. For the following it will be assumed, for simplicity, that the angle is taken at midday, with the shadow lying due north of the pyramid. [9]

Angle	Autumn date	Spring date
45°	5th November	7th February
39.5°	24th November	19th January
32.5°	n/a	

The Sun at Giza never drops below 36.6° above the horizon, due to the latitude at which it is located; so the Sun will never reach the 32.5° position.

Cartography

Having shown that the location of the Sun's shadow might quite possibly mark the site for the entrance to a secret chamber – a potential Hall of Records – I have subsequently casually dismissed that idea. But if the Sun's shadow is not marking a location on the plateau, what are these explanations all about? The answer is perfectly logical: the *true* location of the Hall of Records has not yet been deciphered. There are several layers to this conundrum, and having found just one of them does little to further the cause. One could spend a lifetime grubbing around the pyramids and find nothing, for the true location is rather more inaccessible than this. The location will be found by simple deduction later on in the book, but it is interesting that the location – or more likely the general area in which to look – was known long before the upper chambers in the Great Pyramid were opened and explored.

Many of the pyramids, including the Great Pyramid, were open to the priesthood in early dynastic Egyptian eras. Flinders Petrie also noted anecdotal evidence that the Romans still knew of the entrance to the Great Pyramid around the turn of the first millennium. It was not until the coming of the Arab invasion that the location of the entrance appears to have been lost, and a forced entry had to be made into this pyramid by the Caliph al Ma'mun. In making this forced entry, the ascending passage was discovered, so it is only in the last thousand years or so that the layout of the upper chambers in the Great Pyramid has been known.

Tunnel vision

The classical story of the discovery of the upper chambers inside the Great Pyramid at Giza is well known. In the ninth century, an Arab governor of Cairo, known as the Caliph al Ma'mun, decided to see for himself what lay inside the Great Pyramid and began to excavate a tunnel bodily, through the casing and core blocks, with hammers and chisels. Fortuitously for the caliph, the tunnelling shook the structure so much that the capstone fell off the end of the ascending passage.

The resonating crash was heard by the workers, who dug in that direction and found not only the descending passage, but also the ascending passage and all the upper chambers in the pyramid. After thousands of years lying undisturbed, deep inside the Great Pyramid, the King's and Queen's Chambers were opened at last and their treasure would soon belong to the caliph.

3. Blueprint

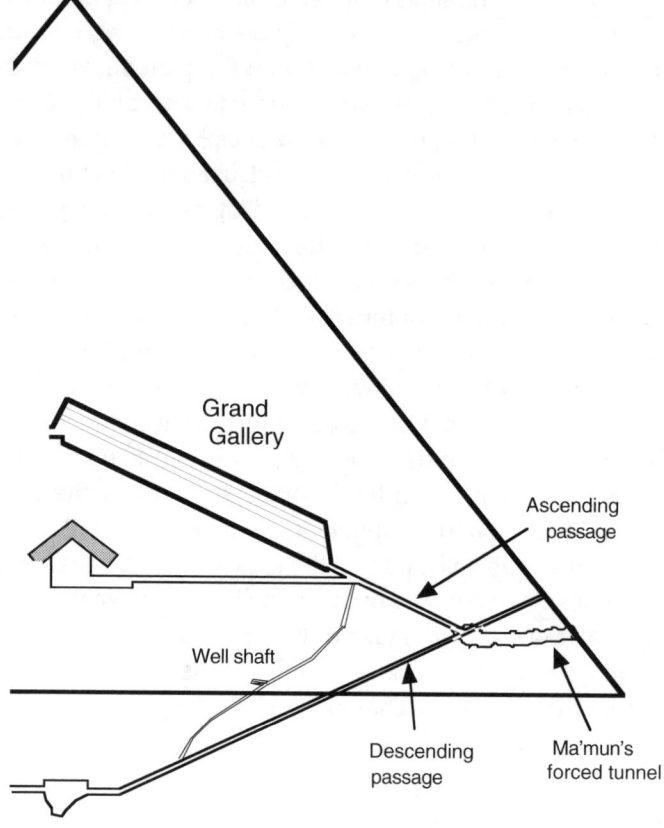

Grand
Gallery

Ascending
passage

Well shaft

Descending
passage

Ma'mun's
forced tunnel

Fig 16.   Section of the Great Pyramid.

But, as the story goes, there was no booty; apparently this most ancient and precious of cupboards was absolutely bare. There were not only no burial artifacts, but no burial and no inscriptions either! The first thought to cross the mind of the caliph must have been that the 'tomb' had been robbed; but how? Even if the secret 'well shaft', deep inside the pyramid, had been found at this stage, it is hardly a suitable tunnel through which to strip a wealthy burial chamber totally bare. So where was all the loot? The caliph and his excavators must have not only been very exasperated, after all their work, but mystified too.

Are we so sure that this is what really happened, just over a millennium ago? Are we simply complacent because this is what we have been taught by respected authorities for centuries? Perhaps it is merely easier to agree with the established consensus of opinion, rather than thinking positively and laterally about the problem.

Fortunately, there are a few individuals out there who are more than happy to challenge a whole raft of classical myths; and so it was, one day, that a short e-mail arrived in my in-box from a like-minded colleague, Mark Foster. [10] Mark had an idea that had been bothering him for some time and he wanted to throw it around a bit. A quick read convinced me that it was a highly original idea and definitely worth some further thought. After a few debates here and there, we together devised the following alternative scenario to the classical story, which is quite attractive in many respects. The new explanation not only answers some irritating puzzles, but it also poses some interesting and fundamental questions in return.

The basic problem with the classical explanation was that Ma'mun's tunnel is rather too accurate for comfort. It tracks into the pyramid in a direct line for the all-important junction between the descending and ascending passageways. It is often cited that Ma'mun had to turn the tunnel sharp left to discover the original passageways; a fact that Mark and I had in the back of our minds when we first visited the Great Pyramid. But as Mark and I ambled down the forced tunnel, we were both equally rather mystified because the left turn could not be found! Having backtracked the tunnel and tried again, that 'left turn' seemed to be no more than a slight widening of the tunnel at this point. In actual fact, the diggings were almost right on their target. So how did this happen? Was Ma'mun just lucky and happened to pick the right spot? Did he have an idea of where to go to?

There is also the problem of why Ma'mun was tunnelling inside the pyramid in the first place. Not only was the presence of the true entrance to the pyramid well known in classical times, but people were also aware of the descending passage and the subterranean cavern at the very bottom of the pyramid. Strabo says of the original entrance to the Great pyramid:

> The Great pyramid, a little way up on one side, has a stone that may be taken out, which being raised up there is a sloping passage to the foundations. [11]

Strabo seems to be describing a door, made of stone, that is movable in some way; it can be moved upwards and outwards at the same time.

3. Blueprint

This sounds like a hinged flap arrangement, with the hinge at the top of the stone. Strabo was clearly familiar with the internal layout of the lower portions of the pyramid; he calls the rough-hewn hole there the 'foundations' rather than the more obvious term of 'chamber', and he is also familiar with the form that the entrance stone took.

We shall look more closely at the exact design of this entrance stone later in the book, but to gain entry to the pyramid so high up its northern face was obviously not easy. A series of ladders would have to have been erected against the pyramid to reach the entrance. Wobbling at the top of this construction, the new initiate then scrambled into the thin hole and down the descending passage. A knotted rope would also have to be fed slowly down the length of the passage, to allow for an easy exit from the dark and foreboding depths of the sacred pyramid.

Undoubtedly, all of this frenetic activity would have scratched and pitted the entrance to the pyramid over the millennia in a very obvious fashion. Yet, it is generally accepted that the casing blocks must have been intact during the rule of Ma'mun, as the casing blocks appear to have been used by Sultan Hasan for the construction of his mosque in 1356.

The question is, therefore, why could Ma'mun not see these telltale marks, and the original entrance to the pyramid that lay only a few meters above him? Why could he not see the handle on the door, or the scuff-marks on the smooth exterior? The knowledge of the true entrance must still have been known, so why could none of the locals be 'persuaded' to point it out? This apparent invisibility of the original entrance could not have been because it was covered by sand, for instance, because Ma'mun's tunnel lies below the level of the real entrance. So what was the problem? Why was so much effort expended in digging a new tunnel, when an easy entrance lay just above?

Two very important questions have just been posed – why could Ma'mun not see the real entrance, when it was so well known? And why was his alternative tunnel so accurate, if he did not know where the real entrance was? Bit of a catch-22, really.

Guide passage

Mark Foster [12] had an idea that Ma'mun already knew of the original

3. Blueprint

entrance and the descending passage, and had used the new forced-entry tunnel for another reason – perhaps to get around the granite plug-blocks in the ascending passage, or perhaps to get the necessary equipment into the right position to dig around those blocks. But if Ma'mun did not discover the ascending passage while he was creating his new forced tunnel, how did he know it was there? The ascending passage was, after all, completely secret and unexplored at this time, so how was it discovered?

Mark and I both came to the same conclusions on this topic. The key to discovering the ascending passage lies outside the pyramid; just to the east of the base and to the north of the causeway. Here, there lies what Petrie called the 'trial passage', which is simply a foreshortened replica of the Great Pyramid's descending passage and the junction with the ascending passage.

As everything on the plateau has a purpose, why is it there? Petrie thought it was a test-bed on which the architect could test out the procedures for laying out the internal passageways to the pyramid. This is a possibility. However, we both think that the real answer is that it is not a 'trial passage' but a 'guide passage'. Any interested party looking into this short passage system will clearly see the symmetry with the real descending passage inside the pyramid, but a little further down they will come across a junction with another ascending passage. The idea might dawn on someone that the real pyramid passageways just might have exactly the same configuration.

Thus, the ascending passage was quite possibly found by Ma'mun's men entering the original entrance to the pyramid and tapping down the ceiling of the descending passage, searching for that elusive passageway that was hinted at by the 'guide passageways' outside. Success at last: the men found a concealed entrance! But as they were not able to penetrate the granite plugs that blocked this ascending shaft, a small tunnel was dug through the softer limestone core-blocks, around the granite plugs, and up into the ascending passage. Ma'mun was at last able to enter the Queen's and King's Chambers and to plunder his expected booty.

If all this is so, however, it may also be an indication of another passageway inside the Great Pyramid. The only difference between the 'guide passageways' and the real passageways, is that the guide system has a vertical shaft attached to the junction of the descending and ascending passages. Mark believes this to be a sure sign that a similar vertical shaft lies undiscovered within the Great Pyramid – it is a distinct possibility.

This is all very well as scenarios go, you might say, but if this is the case then why on Earth is that great forced tunnel of Ma'mun's there? Surely the classical explanation is correct; Ma'mun came in via this crude excavation! Perhaps, but here is where some of my traditional lateral thinking came into play. Tunnels are not only for getting in, but also for getting out...

It is highly probable that the real reason for the forced tunnel was not to get *into* the pyramid, but rather to get something *out*. Whatever it was, though, it must have been small enough to go down the first part of the ascending passage, but too long to go around the bend between the descending and ascending passageways. The only alternative for the intrepid explorers was to dig a tunnel directly outwards from the junction of the two passageways, bypassing the internal passageway constriction.

This explains both of the questions posed earlier. The original entrance had been known about and used, and the reason for the accuracy of the forced tunnel is now obvious; because it was started from *inside* and dug *outwards*. This may also explain why so much rubble was later found in the bottom of the descending passage – it came from the forced tunnel's excavations.

So what was the long, thin booty that Ma'mun had found and 'liberated' from the King's Chamber? Had the chamber been filled with sacred and valuable artifacts, and the mummy of a great and ancient king? Had Ma'mun discovered a king's ransom in bullion? Perhaps, but personally, I think that the real answer is probably more prosaic and poignant than this.

The Caliph's tale

Ma'mun laboriously climbed his way up the 41.2 cubits of swaying ladders to the original entrance of the Great Pyramid; a difficult task for an obese caliph and a worrying moment for his advisors. After a short slide down the descending passage, he entered the small rough shaft that his men had dug around the granite plug-blocks and scrambled into the ascending passage. From there he struggled up the Grand Gallery, his men cautiously pushing his bulk from behind. Sweating and cursing, he finally

3. Blueprint

crawled on hands and knees into the King's Chamber, a degrading and exhausting experience that no caliph had endured either before or since.

Ma'mun was flustered, even angry, but also elated. Although he had been briefed that the King's Chamber was basically empty, what it did possess was an untouched, enigmatic and completely sealed sarcophagus! This was the prize that justified these privations. Ma'mun was going to be at the opening of this sarcophagus, at whatever cost – he was not about to let his chief vizier run off with the treasure of the ancient kings, or perhaps even the secrets of the gods themselves!

A disorganised rabble of workmen arrived and prised at the coffer lid with crowbars; they cursed, swore and shouted, but the lid just would not budge. Finally, in a state of ecstatic anticipation, Ma'mun pushed the rabble aside and ordered the coffer to be smashed with sledgehammers. The chief gaffir aimed a few heavy blows and with a great crash, one corner of the sarcophagus flew off – the result of this still being visible today.

Ma'mun ordered the workers away, yelled for silence, grabbed a flickering lamp from a soldier and approached the hole in trepidation. Then, the significance of the moment struck him. He was standing inside the greatest of all the world's ancient monuments, a structure rumoured to have been constructed by the gods themselves. Here, at the heart of this sacred monument, lay a simple, unadorned, solitary black-granite coffer, that had been sealed for thousands of years; and he, Caliph al. Ma'mun, was going to be the first to see inside. His hand began to tremble at the thought and he quickly steadied it with his other, lest the workers see him as apprehensive.

The light flickered and it was difficult to see, but at last it steadied and he saw for himself that the sarcophagus was .... empty!

This is exactly what happened to the archeologist Zakaria Goneim a millennium later. He was excavating the pyramid of Sekhemkhet at Saqqara, when a sealed sarcophagus was found complete with its 'funereal wreaths' still on the top. With great difficulty, the sliding end of the coffer was raised and it was ... empty!

Whilst Zakaria Goneim was greatly disappointed, the Caliph al. Ma'mun was absolutely livid. Suspecting, perhaps, that one of his workers had manufactured this little ruse, he flew into a violent rage and vented his anger on a few unfortunate victims of summary justice.

3. Blueprint

Ma'mun, however, was not about to go back to his palace empty-handed, after all he had been through. But the chamber only contained the sarcophagus, and it was quite obvious that it was bigger than the entrance to the chamber. As a consolation prize, they found that the lid of the sarcophagus could be turned diagonally and just about squeeze through the King's Chamber's tough granite entrance blocks. Ma'mun was going to have it as a memento at all costs.

Unfortunately for the workers, however, after sliding the great block of stone down the Grand Gallery, they found that the lid was not going to squeeze around the plug-blocks and into the descending passage. Besides, the lid must have weighed a tonne, and if it ever got into the descending passage, nobody could think of a way of preventing it from plunging all the way down to the bottom of the pyramid. In addition, the original entrance stone-flap was far too small to get the lid through. It was all becoming a bit of a nightmare.

Spurred on by an enraged caliph, however, the chief of engineering came up with an answer. The only practical solution was to force a new tunnel from the junction of the descending and ascending passageways, horizontally through the core blocks of the pyramid and into the open air. *This* is Ma'mun's forced tunnel.

Ruse

Although the forced tunnel is therefore a much later addition to the Great Pyramid, it would appear that the subterranean chamber, and perhaps the chambers of some of the lesser pyramids, were known of and explored over many millennia. The entrance to the Third Pyramid is, for example, too obvious not to have been noticed and opened at some point in the dynastic era. Again, in the book *Tempest*, I argue that the biblical Esau was the guardian of the Giza plateau, and that this tribe of Israel was responsible for the upkeep of the pyramids and their chambers. However, none of the chambers in these other pyramids are as complex as the Great Pyramid's upper chambers, and the location for any potential Hall of Records could not have been derived without knowing the layout of these upper chambers.

The Great Pyramid's lower chamber is not a part of this quest, and so it was deliberately left unfinished by the designer to avoid confusion with the rest of the finely worked chambers. In addition, it was

3. Blueprint

most probably left open to the priesthood (and later tourists) as a deterrent to potential tomb-robbers; for if the pyramid was already open and empty, what was the point of anyone trying to force an entry or to search for treasure? Thus, with this little ruse, the designer had deliberately placed another crafty layer of confusion in the way of any potential researcher or robber – the all-important upper chambers in this pyramid were not only secret, but also cleverly sealed and concealed.

So, throughout the vast bulk of its existence, the only parts of the Great Pyramid which were open to the priests were the descending passage and the subterranean chamber; the block covering the ascending passage to the upper chambers being sufficiently well-disguised to prevent any inadvertent discovery. Frustrated at only finding this incongruously rugged 'cave' at the bottom of such a magnificent construction, various individuals resorted to digging further down and sideways from this chamber in order to find something – anything – of interest. But there was nothing to be found; the quest was not understood.

Although the upper chambers were not discovered at this time, it is quite probable that they were known to have existed, in some form or other, in the ancient past. The evidence for this comes from the story of the pharaoh looking for the lost chambers of an unspecified pyramid, and the flint chest in which their plans resided. This story tends to support the idea that the reality of hidden chambers in one or other of the pyramids was known to the priesthood. Equally, the presence of a 'large pebble' of flint, discovered by Sir Flinders Petrie under the sarcophagus in the King's Chamber, tentatively points towards the Great Pyramid being the location of those rumoured secret chambers. [13]

Thus, it is quite possible that little hints had been dropped by the designer, or perhaps even the workers on the site, who had passed down their own traditions of secret chambers, to be discovered within the Great Pyramid. On balance, the former is perhaps the more likely as the next rumour to spread across the land involved something that only the architect was likely to have known – the general location of the Hall of Records itself. Knowing about some secret chambers you had just built in a pyramid would be one thing, but knowing the mind of the architect is quite another matter.

As I suspected previously, the location of any potential Hall of Records was likely to be quite remote, perhaps quite removed from Giza, and even Egypt itself. To mark such a remote location on the

3. Blueprint

Earth's surface, a map is required, and a map is exactly what we have in the design of the Great Pyramid. As explained in the book *Thoth*, the form of the upper chambers of the Great Pyramid gives us a real map of the world to work with, a fact that shall be looked at in more detail in later chapters. This may appear to be speculation at the moment, but if the Great Pyramid map is a reality, then we now have the means at our disposal to point at any location on the surface of the Earth.

Initially, the evidence in the book *Thoth,* pointed towards some Atlantic islands, but even if that were so, there was another problem to solve. Such a large-scale map would be quite unsuited to marking the location of something as small as a hidden chamber. Each tiny dot on the Great Pyramid 'map' would encompass hundreds of square kilometers of land. The problems that the quest was posing appeared to be insurmountable, and yet, it was interesting that the ancient traditions of Egypt were constantly pointing in another direction − not to the west and the Atlantic, but eastwards.

Perhaps hints had been dropped by the architect to the priesthood long ago, and passed down through the ages. Each chief priest, and possibly a pharaoh or two, if he or she could be trusted, was told of these ancient rumours. There was treasure to the east of Egypt, perhaps even the lost scrolls of Thoth/Hermes himself; the repository of the gods. Each pharaoh and priest must have nodded sagely and thought privately that this was an impossible quest into uncharted territory. Such distances to cover, such hardships to endure and so many tribes to vanquish enroute, to get to the end of the world. The quest was impossible, and besides, only the general location was known; without a detailed map, discovering the exact boulder that covered these ancient secrets would be utterly impossible.

One pharaoh, however, was different. At the tender age of 24, he had already lost count of the number of times he had dared the impossible and succeeded. His reign had only just begun and yet he had already achieved the impossible. Surely the gods were smiling on his exploits? Surely he could push through to the ends of the Earth and beyond? In the next few years, he would indeed achieve the impossible and as a result of his sacred quest, he was to push the boundaries of 'Egypt' far beyond anything that had been seen before. His throne name was Meryamun Setepenre Aleksanders. He was born a Macedonian but, nevertheless, he was now a pharaoh of Egypt and he is more popularly known in the historical record as Alexander the Great.

Chapter IV

Repairs

The story of Alexander will have to wait until the next chapter, but in the meantime, one other thread of the story needs further analysis – the true age of the Giza and Dahshur pyramids. Were these pyramids simply tombs for the pharaohs Khufu, Khafre and Menkaure, or had they been standing on the Giza plateau for millennia before the fourth dynasty even come to power?

There has been much debate on this topic. Perhaps we have all heard about the discussions and arguments that have erupted in books and on the internet regarding the era in which the Sphinx at Giza was constructed. John Anthony West and Robert Schoch have made a veritable industry out of speculation regarding the amount of weathering that is present on the Sphinx itself and its enclosure, and in turn how the era of its construction can be gauged by these observations. It is an interesting discussion and one that apparently has much life left in it, and I am sure it will run and run.

But, erosion of the Sphinx is only one small aspect of the evidence available when assessing the age of the pyramids. There are plenty of other examples of erosion that also point towards an earlier date for the pyramids' construction. Personally, I think that many of the early dynastic monuments in Egypt have a tale to tell in the weathering patterns that scour their fabric, and in the book *Thoth,* I try to explore many of these telltale features. So, let us indulge ourselves in a quick tour of Lower Egypt and see what other evidence there is to support the concept of a very early construction date for the pyramids.

In the book *Thoth,* I made two observations that pointed towards some of the pyramids being older than classical Egyptologists will admit. The first involved the fate of the pyramid of Meidum, which has plainly not collapsed but has instead been slowly eroded away. This can clearly be seen at the base of this pyramid, where the cladding stones show clear evidence of a gradual erosion. The cladding stones vary, from perfectly preserved at the base of the pyramid, to heavily and completely eroded at the top. Obviously, the lower cladding stones were protected by the material falling down from above. The question posed by this, of course, is how long does it take to completely erode the cladding stones of a pyramid?

The second example was the pavement of the Great and Vega Pyramids, which showed a clear differential erosion line where the lowest course of cladding stones had been removed. Knowing the date at which these cladding stones were removed allows us to calculate, with some confidence, the true age of the pyramids and this appears to be much older than traditional estimates imply.

But there is more evidence for an earlier date to some of the pyramids' construction. For this, we must travel south of Giza once more, to Dahshur. Passing through the small military area and on to the Dahshur plateau, the vast bulk of the Draco (Red) Pyramid lies before you. The casing blocks have, of course, been removed and what are visible are the rough-hewn sandstone core-blocks. The sandstone is relatively friable, but its high ironstone content seems to form a tough, oxidised, ruddy layer on the surface of the blocks; hence the usual appellation for this pyramid.

That most of the pyramids are in this ruinous state is a great shame. We would know so much more of the era and methods for their construction if they were still in pristine condition. But there *is* a pyramid that can give us some clues here; take a look around the corner of the Draco Pyramid, and the curious form of the Vega (Bent) pyramid looms into view once more.

More important than the strange shape to this pyramid, is the fact that the Vega Pyramid retains much of its outer casing, which forms an impressively smooth, straight surface all the way to top. Approaching the base of the pyramid, the fine workmanship of the massive casing blocks is easy to see. Other items are not so obvious – the core of this pyramid, despite being right next to the Draco Pyramid, is made from a different material; rough limestone blocks instead of sandstone blocks, with a mud mortar in-between, form the basic shape. For the casing blocks,

4. Repairs

however, the rough mortar is replaced by a fine pink mastic, apparently so strong that many of the casing blocks have split into two before the mortar itself gave way.

But this is not all. The basis of this new evidence for the age of the pyramids is another curious feature – the surface of the cladding stones. At some time in the long history of these pyramids, a long-forgotten pharaoh looked at the Vega Pyramid and said to his chief of public works; 'We must do something about the condition of this pyramid!' The chief acted immediately on these orders and started erecting scaffolding all over the four faces of the pyramid. This was no mean feat, for wood is not a readily available commodity in Egypt, and convoy after convoy of Lebanese cedar had to be brought in to provide the working materials. Slowly but surely a great latticework of poles covered the entire face of the pyramid – right to its very apex.

A team of several thousand artisans – some skilled, some not quite so – started chipping away at the casing blocks. Stone is not a uniform material, of course, and small fault-lines, cracks, and shoals (sand inclusions) within the limestone blocks each weather at a different rate. Over the years, the Vega Pyramid had become pockmarked with thousands of small patches of erosion in the casing blocks. Some were minuscule, only a few centimeters across; some required the removal of the face of an entire stone (not the entire stone, as the casing blocks are some 2m thick, so only the outer face was taken away and replaced). Each and every defect was chipped smooth and a new piece of limestone was neatly placed in the hole and smoothed down to a perfect surface. The pyramid then began to look like it had acne, with the fresh white of the repair blocks contrasting strongly with the older surface.

So, the entire face of the pyramid was then scrubbed clean of the sandy-coloured patina that had developed over the years, to display the brilliant white Tura limestone casing, just as it was in its new condition. Pharaoh looked at his achievement with pride; the pyramids were as new again, sparkling in the ruby glow of a bloated setting sun. He truly must be one of the greatest pharaohs in the history of Egypt to have achieved such a feat and the gods *must* have been pleased. As a record of his great achievement, the pharaoh dared the almost sacrilegious; he carved his cartouche in the lower casing blocks to the pyramid, and within the mortuary temple.

The description above is of my own invention, but the fact that

4. Repairs

something very like this has occurred in the distant past is self-evident by the thousands and thousands of little repairs that have been made all over the Vega Pyramid, from the bottom to the very top. The question is, though, who made them? The records not only fail to mention the actual construction of these pyramids, they also fail to mention the repairs that were made to them.

Era

So in what era were these repairs made? Some people have contended that the repairs may have been done at the time of construction, to rectify faulty workmanship, or that the repairs were required very soon after construction because of weak pieces of stone. Frankly, I do not agree whatsoever with such arguments. It is clear to me that these repairs are later additions to the pyramid, and for the following reasons:

a.   If the repairs were needed at the time of the Vega Pyramid's construction, then the stonemasons who built it were truly incompetent. The pyramid is absolutely covered in repairs from top to bottom; at a rough estimate, there are half as many repairs as casing blocks (some blocks have more than one repair). Also, some of the blocks have had their entire face replaced. If these defects had been noticed in the building stages of the pyramid, the entire casing block could have been replaced rather than just the face. That the masons could only repair the face of the block, indicates that the pyramid had been completed well beyond that particular course of casing stones.

Also, it has to be pointed out that the surface of the Draco Pyramid that was protected by the adjacent mortuary temple has no repairs on its surface. Clearly, the original workmanship was competent and the repairs we see were made to a surface that had been eroded over many millennia.

b.   The vast majority of the repair blocks are to the face of one casing stone only, and the repair finishes directly it meets another casing block. Had the repair been due to damage of the face during the pyramid's construction, it would be more than likely that the damage would also have been done to the face of adjoining blocks – therefore

4. Repairs

the repair would also have crossed the block boundaries. That the repairs terminate on a particular block edge is better explained as being due to one particular block being softer than its neighbours, and weathering more than them. Thus, the repair was made to one block and one block alone.

c. One can see repair blocks that have been added to the surface of the pyramid, and yet the surrounding casing block has continued to erode around the inserted piece. If this insert had been added at the time of construction, due to someone damaging that block, there would be no reason for rock surrounding the repair to erode more than usual. The more probable explanation is that this patch of casing stone was weaker than usual and had begun to erode, leaving an eroded hole. At a much later date, a mason cut out that hole into a nice rectangular shape and inserted a repair block. But, over the subsequent millennia, the casing stone continued to erode around the repair block because it was of inferior material in comparison to the repair, and so it presents us with the picture we see today – a repair block surrounded by a patch of eroded casing block. It all points towards later repair work, when the pyramid was already finished and quite old.

Personally, I think that if such a feat of repairs were achieved in the relatively well-documented New Kingdom era onwards (c 1500 BC), we would have heard all about it. There are records that document the repairs made to the Sphinx by Tuthmoses IV during the New Kingdom era, yet the surface repairs to the Dahshur pyramids were a far greater undertaking than this. This tends to indicate that the repair work was actually completed in the ancient past – much earlier than the New Kingdom era.

Remember that the present condition of the pyramids is due to their deliberate destruction in relatively recent history. Had this not taken place, the major pyramids at Giza and Dahshur would have been in relatively good condition to this day. So, if these pyramids have lasted so well in the 3,500 years since the New Kingdom and not needed much in the way of repairs (as the evidence from the cladding stones of the Vega and Second Pyramids indicate), then why did these pyramids need repairing so quickly after their supposed construction by Snorferu in the

4. Repairs

fourth dynasty (c 2,600 BC, or 4,600 years ago).

There is a deep conundrum here that is presented by something as mundane as an inserted repair block. Just when was this major feat of repair work carried out? Can such a date be found in the records?

Egyptology has attributed the Dahshur pyramids of Vega and Draco to the pharaoh Snorferu, and they indicate that he built both of these, plus the pyramid at Meidum, in the space of just 24 years. But a convincing argument as to why a pharaoh would want to go to the bother of constructing three pyramids is not forthcoming. Not only does this seem illogical, and physically impossible in terms of manpower requirements, the pyramids themselves have no inscriptions within them to confirm this proposal – just a few cartouches on the outer casing and on a stele in the mortuary temple. A much simpler solution, which will help considerably with the dating process above, is that Snorferu is intimately associated with these three pyramids, not because he built them all but because he *repaired* them all.

Having completed this great feat, the pharaoh Snorferu then performed the almost sacrilegious act of carving his name within the sacred precincts of the pyramid, so that his name would evermore be associated with these three pyramids. This is the true reason for Snorferu being associated with three of the largest pyramids in Egypt. If one is prepared to accept this, then these pyramids have apparently lasted for some 4,600 years without any further repairs being made to their fabric. Therefore, the true construction era for these particular pyramids must have been many thousands of years *before* the reign of Snorferu.

If the pharaoh Snorferu were indeed responsible for these repairs, then the surface that we can see today appears to have lasted for some 4,600 years or so, without further attention. Thus, it would be sensible to assume that 4,600 years would be the minimum time required, after the Vega Pyramid's first construction, before the pyramid began to look shabby and the first repairs were contemplated. If this is so, then the minimum age for this pyramid is some 9,200 years ago. The extent of the repairs, however, indicate that much more time passed before the first repairs were made than is required at the present time. If the time period that elapsed up until the first repairs were made by Snorferu were double this 4,600 years time-span, then the original construction of this pyramid would have been some 13,800 years ago.

4. Repairs

Myths

Such a scenario may be based on an amount of guesswork but it does make a great deal of sense, and the underlying evidence is irrefutable. Taken together with the data from Meidum, Giza and at the Sphinx, does this not all tend to reinforce the emerging evidence that these pyramids are indeed much older than we have traditionally been taught? The weight of evidence appears to be mounting relentlessly; the pyramids would seem to be as much as double or treble the orthodox age – a notion which conflicts strongly with all the established chronology of Egypt. It is no wonder that historians would resist such an interpretation of the erosion evidence; it would be too radical to even be contemplated.

Had the pyramids really been constructed that long ago, however, it should be of no surprise to us that knowledge of the presence of upper chambers within the Great Pyramid had been reduced to just vague myths. But were there other myths that had been passed down through the millennia as well; myths that spoke not just of hidden chambers, but of the location of the Hall of Records itself? Maybe it was only when these myths were whispered into the ears of the pharaoh Alexander that any credence was given to these strange stories. Alexander is known as 'the Great' for his unstoppable campaigns across the mighty kingdom of Persia, but there was possibly another unknown element to his greatness; his was the first, the most expensive, and perhaps the most extensive, expedition ever mounted to search for the Hall of Records.

Chapter V

Alexander

A great deal has been written about the life and times of Alexander the Great. A mighty king and warrior, he took his small army down through Asia Minor during the years of 334 to 331 BC, and into Egypt, putting to flight the mighty army of Darius III, King of Persia. Alexander entered Egypt in the winter of 332 BC and his first act there was to commune with the gods. Why was this? [1]

Alexander was born a prince and he was educated by none other than Aristotle of Stagira, who has been called the spiritual father of the Hellenistic age. Here was a prince who was born, bred and influenced, not only by the wisdom of Aristotle, but also most probably the legends and myths of Egypt – the land that most influenced Hellenistic literature and theology. What would Aristotle have told the young Alexander of the myths and legends of the Egyptian gods Thoth, Osiris, Seth and Horus? Each and every one of these was identified with a god in the Greek pantheon, so it is likely that Alexander saw Egypt as the foundation stone upon which all classical wisdom had been laid.

This is more than speculation, for it does appear that the initial thrust of Alexander's campaigns was directed straight at Egypt. Alexander did not have a great navy, and the superior navy of Darius III would have decimated any ships that Alexander could have mustered. But his army was a competent military machine, so if Alexander's primary goal had been the conquest of Egypt, the only option available to him would have been a land assault through Asia Minor and Phoenicia (modern Syria, Lebanon and Israel). The fact that the world's largest empire and army stood in the way, it seems, was of little consequence to

5. *Alexander*

Alexander and he merely brushed them aside in his frantic march on to Egypt.

If, however, one takes the classical view of his campaigns, and presumes that the destruction of the Persian empire was Alexander's primary goal, then he made some very curious decisions. Alexander had some skirmishes with the Persian vanguard in Asia Minor, but his first real battle with Darius III and the Persian army was at Issus, in south eastern Turkey, in November 333 BC.[2] Alexander was heavily outnumbered by the mighty Persian army, so the task of motivating his commanders into battle against this overwhelming force just across the river must have required almost superhuman confidence. But attack they did, and the surprising result was a resounding defeat for Darius and the mighty Persian army.

As is usual in these battles, the result was not total carnage. It is understood that a sizeable proportion of the Persian army escaped the battlefield and limped back into Persian territory, perhaps even without their armour to hasten their retreat. Darius and his army were on the run, and vulnerable to a sustained pursuit and another daring attack. If Alexander had wanted to defeat the entire Persian empire and gain access to their vast treasury at Persopolis (in modern Iran), then the obvious strategy would have been to chase after the ragged rabble and enter Persia triumphant.

Alexander's reaction was more enigmatic; he left the Persians alone to lick their wounds and regroup, while his army rode south instead. Leaving his flank open to possible attack by a re-equipped Persian army, he then engaged in a battle with the Phoenicians and there followed a bitter struggle to take the strategic Phoenician city of Tyre, on the Lebanese coast. Alexander's historian, Arrian, sees this diversion in purely military terms. It was explained as an attempt to deprive the Persian navy of a stronghold in this Phoenician port and thus secure Alexander's western flank; and also to stop the Persian garrison in Egypt from sailing to mainland Greece and attacking the motherland.

But the reasoning is muddled. The Persian navy could not attack Alexander's land-bound army and the Egyptian garrison was too puny to mount a sustained assault on Greece. In strict military terms, the taking of Tyre must have had more to do with a conquest of the Levant; either because it was important in itself or perhaps because Alexander wanted to secure the overland trade route to Egypt.

Whatever the case, with the fall of Tyre and Gaza, the road was open all the way to Egypt. There was no further opposition. Egypt had been controlled by the Persians for many years and was not able to muster an army equipped to challenge Alexander's battle-hardened troops. Likewise, the small Persian garrison in Egypt was ill-equipped to take on the mighty Macedonians. But why was Alexander here? Why had he let Darius temporarily off the hook? Why the rush into Egypt?

Oasis of the Oracle

Egypt possessed two major export commodities – grain and wisdom. The grain would have been useful; the wisdom invaluable. Egypt had been the land of the gods and their secrets for millennia; the pharaohs were not simply kings, but gods incarnate. The gods, of course, knew everything, and it is inconceivable that Alexander, tutored as he was by Aristotle, did not know of, and crave, that knowledge and divinity.

In *Jesus, Last of the Pharaohs,* I observed that many centuries before Alexander, the Egyptian veneration of the Apis bull was probably based on the constellation of Taurus. As Taurus moved away from its prime location in the heavens, due to the precession of the equinox, it was replaced by the constellation of Aries – a difficult transition period had begun in Egypt. The new followers of Aries had their own pharaohs, the Hyksos or Shepherd Kings (Kings of Aries), and the resulting civil war had seen the Hyksos followers ejected from Egypt.

This is a logical extension of what the historical record tells us. However, the really radical notion that I overlaid on this hypothesis was that the Hyksos pharaohs were, in fact, the biblical patriarchs. The biblical patriarchs were not only known as simple shepherds, but the Bible and the texts of the first-century historian, Josephus, also strongly indicate that they were kings. The conclusions are inescapable, and it was no surprise to me when many of the names of the biblical patriarchs could be found among the Hyksos pharaohs of Egypt.

What does this have to do with Alexander? There are two things to bear in mind when one considers the true rationale behind Alexander's strange tactic. The first of these involves a strange report by the first century Jewish historian, Josephus.

Josephus maintains that Alexander entered Jerusalem and paid homage to the high priest there. His courtiers were amazed; Alexander was rapidly becoming the most powerful individual in Europe and needed to pay homage to no-one. The courtiers were on the verge of questioning Alexander's sanity, when he is reputed to have said to his confidante, Parmenio:

> I did not adore the high priest, but that god who has honoured him with high office. [3]

We are being led to believe that Alexander was showing deference and respect to the Jewish deity. But if the courtiers had thought this utterance by their great leader to be rather strange, then their worst fears must have been confirmed when Alexander is supposed to have continued and said that the whole purpose of his campaigns thus far had simply been to visit Jerusalem. Apparently, according to Josephus, the Israelite god, Yahweh, had once appeared to Alexander in a dream and had promised to lead the Macedonians into battle and give them military success over the Persians.

Modern historians, however, must have read this account of Josephus and chuckled to themselves; was Josephus really so naive that he thought anyone would believe his absurd Jewish propaganda? The Israelites must have been grateful, of course, that Alexander had relieved them from the Persian yoke; but did Josephus really think that we would believe that a 'pagan' Macedonian king would enter Jerusalem on the hand of the Israelite high priest, to believe in, respect, honour and make sacrifices to the Israelite god?

The account of Josephus is odd to say the least, but I am prepared to take his account at face value; that Alexander visited Jerusalem and made sacrifice – not because of Josephus' unblemished integrity as an honest historian, but because in the book *Jesus,* I make a good case for the Israelites being the descendants of the Hyksos peoples, who were exiled from Egypt circa 1550 BC. According to this scenario, Alexander was in Jerusalem, not because he believed in the emerging Jewish beliefs, but because he knew and understood that their ancestors had been Egyptian pharaohs and had held the secrets and traditions of that society – with all the similarities between Egyptian theology and the Greek pantheon of gods. Alexander was on a sacred quest, like the twelfth-century Crusader Knights in pursuit of the Holy Grail, and just possibly, Jerusalem held some of those ancient and sacred secrets.

5. Alexander

But perhaps that particular avenue in this quest of Alexander's failed, because his next diversion, yet further away from the Persian army (which was busily re-equipping itself over in the east) was into the very fringes of these sacred lands – the inhospitable western desert. In the book *Jesus,* I also narrate this new twist to the itinerary: the story of Alexander's trip to the Egyptian oracle at the oasis city of Siwa – the ancient temple of Amun. Just as I had guessed, Alexander's primary goal was not Egyptian grain, but to commune with the gods. Accordingly, his first act on reaching the Nile was to set off on the long and hazardous journey to Siwa.

At Siwa, Alexander not only communicated with the gods and was anointed as a pharaoh of Egypt, but he also became a god incarnate himself. In recognition of this, Alexander became the 'two-horned one' and he was pictured with the two horns of a ram. He had become the latest in a long line of Hyksos (and biblical) followers of Aries, a Shepherd King. This much I have covered before, but what else did the oracle at Siwa impart to Alexander? Were there also tales of a long-lost treasure, a repository of the gods, a Hall of Records?

The subsequent campaigns of Alexander speak volumes. As a god incarnate, Alexander appeared to have presumed himself to be invincible and so he set off on his most hazardous campaign so far, straight into the lion's den – the regrouped and re-equipped army of Darius III.

Alexander smashed through the Persian-held lands of Assyria and Mesopotamia; he faced a force estimated at between 5 and 20 times the size of his own at Gaugamela; and yet still he won through and continued his campaign to take Babylon. Pushing yet further into the heart of Darius' empire, he again defeated Darius' army at the Persian gates, just outside Persopolis. Persopolis, the capital city of the Persian empire, was now within reach and Alexander not only took it, but captured the royal treasury as well. Here was the untold wealth of the whole Persian empire; a treasury so massive that contemporary reports say it took 7000 pack animals to carry it back to Greece. [4]

Thus far, one might suspect that Alexander was primarily on the trail of Persian gold and the blood of his opponent, Darius III. It is true that he chased Darius and the remnants of the Persian army up to the Black Sea, where the once mighty king of Persia met his final demise. But for some crazy reason, this is only the beginning for Alexander's campaign, and he urged his men on to yet mightier feats – a campaign into the Hindu Kush and the foothills of the Himalayas. The Greek historian, Arrian, says of this part of Alexander's campaign:

> Nothing put him off. Starvation, the freezing cold, nothing – he just kept coming on and on. And in the end his enemies were struck with fear and amazement. [5]

What was Alexander looking for in the Hindu Kush; the high foothills of the Himalayas? Michael Wood, the BBC historian, indicated that he could have been mopping up the last little pockets of Persian resistance. But was this the real reason? Was it just for this that Alexander goaded his faithful followers through such extremes and privations? They experienced the chill of freezing mountain-tops; the thirst and hunger of arid deserts; and the desolation and the precipitous mountain passes of the Hindu Kush. Alexander was taking a vast army, and all its baggage, through passes that were designed for a shepherd and his donkey, so what was the real purpose behind all this?

Arrian, the historian of Alexander's campaigns, obliquely hints at another reason. At Nysa, a small town on the borders of Afghanistan and Pakistan, the inhabitants declared that they were descendants of the followers of the Greek god, Dionysus, who had passed this way back in ancient times. Dionysus was the Greek god of ecstasy and wine, and the Greek counterpart of the Roman god Bacchus. The Roman, Bacchus, was the god that I closely linked to the biblical Jesus the book *Jesus, Last of the Pharaohs;* Jesus' best friend (and father?) being Zacchaeus Bacchus, the publican.

In that book, I also declared Jesus to be a Hyksos (Shepherd) pharaoh in exile, a 'Lamb of God' as he became known. Jesus was a Lamb of God and Alexander, like Moses before him, wore the two horns of a ram; thus, both Jesus and Alexander were linked to Egypt and the history of the Hyksos pharaohs. Now, both are linked once more to Bacchus, for Alexander, too, was a follower of Dionysus (Bacchus). It is not beyond the realms of possibility that this expedition by Alexander into the Himalayas was driven by these ancient legends.

> There were legends that Dionysus (Bacchus) and Hercules had come this way, and the Greeks were quite prepared to believe that these wild valleys had seen the footsteps of the gods in ancient times. [6]

5. *Alexander*

This, I believe, was Alexander's true mission. He was in the footsteps of the ancient gods and, no doubt, this was a part of the wisdom that he had gleaned from his travels in Egypt, as the king of those lands. The Greek gods were based on Egyptian counterparts and the gods themselves had been very interested in the Himalayas for some reason.

Wisdom

So, who were these gods and what was so special about the knowledge that they had imparted to mankind? Unfortunately, due to the tragic burning of the libraries at Alexandria, we are unable to say exactly what the Egyptians did or did not know of our Universe. But we do know that the ancient Egyptians' corpus of knowledge was quite extensive, and the evidence for that comes from the Greeks who studied in Alexandria.

Archimedes was one of these individuals who had deep insights into Egyptian scholarship. Whilst not wishing to detract too much from his own achievements, it is highly likely that he developed some of his insights having read Egyptian texts. Archimedes is primarily known in our era for his water-screw. The Archimedes screw comprises a helix inside a tube, and when rotated it becomes a highly efficient, if quite technically complicated, method of pumping water. Yet, recent scholarship has cast some doubt on Archimedes being the first in history to invent this procedure.

The Hanging Gardens of Babylon is counted as one of the seven wonders of the ancient world, yet a question still remains as to how it was watered. The explanation, given in the contemporary cuneiform texts, declares that it was achieved by 'bronze tree-trunks and palm trees', but what this actually means has remained a mystery. Recent scholarship, however, has indicated an intriguing possibility. The term 'tree-trunk' was often used in the cuneiform texts to indicate a tube of some kind; in this case, it sounds like a rather large bronze tube. The palm tree reference was more cryptic, but then it was noticed that the trunks of palm trees were always depicted, in Sumer, as being helical. Thus, the ancient texts seem to be indicating a bronze tube and helix – a giant Archimedes screw. This interpretation is still regarded as being speculative, but it does have a rather compelling ring of truth to it, and if correct, it would place the development of the water-screw back into the ancient past, well before the era of Archimedes.

5. Alexander

Other ancient Greek authors can give us cryptic windows into the ancient knowledge of the Egyptians. Plato's *Timaeus* was not simply dedicated to the story of Atlantis; it also comprises a long treatise on the form and function of the Universe. Plato is much criticised for some of his strange scientific concepts, but there are perhaps a few mitigating circumstances for this. Plato was not a 'scientist' as such: he was primarily a philosopher and, perhaps, the understanding of scientific principles was not a natural subject for him. Also, Plato did not receive his understanding of the Cosmos from the Egyptians themselves; it was third-hand through Solon and Socrates, and we have no way of telling how meticulous these people were in comprehending these concepts and keeping them true to the originals.

Thus, Plato only understands the geocentric solution to the mysteries of the Solar System, whereas there is good evidence to suggest that the heliocentric concept was widely known and understood, even in this era. [7] There again, Plato also seems to have a peculiar explanation for the theory of light and how our eyes detect it, so is Plato misinformed about science? Not entirely, and it is probably worth looking at the areas where his knowledge does indeed concur with modern concepts of the natural world. These can be summarised as follows:

a. The Universe is spherical and therefore has no up or down. Whilst Plato's understanding is strictly three-dimensional, it is more analogous to modern concepts that the later 'flat-Earthers'. [8]

b. The Universe is not eternal, it came into being. A concept which is not dissimilar to the modern big-bang theory. [9]

c. Time was created with the Universe, and will end when the Universe does. Quite a concept for the era, one might say.

> For before the heavens came into being there were no days or nights or months or years ... for they are all parts of time, just as past and future are also forms of it ... So time came into being with the heavens in order that having come together, they should also be dissolved together if ever they are dissolved; and it was made as like to eternity; for that was its model. [10]

5. *Alexander*

d. Stars are on fire, whereas planets simply reflect light. This is a very intuitive insight for in the night sky, stars and planets look much the same.

> ... god lit a light, which we now call the Sun, to provide a clear measure of the relative speeds of the eight revolutions (orbits of the eight planets) ... The divine form (stars) he mostly made of fire so that it should be as bright and beautiful to look at as possible. [11]

e. The planets not only have motion, but relative motion. Quite Einsteinian in an empirical kind of way. [12]

f. We are made from small cells and matter is made of atoms. This is not necessarily the first idea that springs to mind when one looks at materials.

> ... the bonding they used was not indissoluble, like that by which (the gods) themselves were held together, but consisted of a multitude of rivets too small to be seen ... We must, of course, think of the individual units of all four (types of matter) as being far too small to be visible, and only becoming visible when massed together in large numbers. [13]

g. That light has the finest particles, and cooling is due to a loss of light. Indeed, infrared cooling by the loss of photons is often the primary way in which materials cool.

> And the loss of fire (Plato calls light a manifestation of fire) is called cooling. [14]

These and other insights indicate that Plato had quite a reasonable grasp of the nature of science. What this does not tell us, however, is the true level of understanding of the ancient Egyptians. The Greeks may have studied in Egypt, but were they given all of the valuable state secrets? Were they allowed to copy this all down verbatim from the Egyptians' vast ledgers, or did it all have to be remembered from a simple and brief instruction? We have no way of telling. Even if we knew the sum of all this knowledge, it would still not answer other fundamental questions. How did the Egyptians know so much? Was it guesswork?

5. *Alexander*

Was it due to a long process of deduction and experimentation? Or was it divine instructions from the gods?

The ancients themselves would have had no hesitation in their answer to this. Most definitely the sum of all human knowledge came from the gods; they were responsible for everything in this world and their knowledge was infinite.

Alexander's India

Why was Alexander heading eastwards into the unknown with such tenacity, and why was he so interested in sacred mountain peaks? It is quite apparent that Alexander was in the footsteps of the gods, so does this mean that his goal was more theological than the simple temporal search for fame, glory and plunder? On the surface, this campaign may seem like the latter – a quest for riches – but in so many respects this does also seem to have been a sacred quest. But if that was the case, why was a sacred quest directed towards the barren and empty wastes of the Himalayas? Surely a sacred quest would lead to the magnificent temples of Upper Egypt, central Persia or even lowland India. Why, then, travel into the highest reaches to be found on Earth?

That I am following in the footsteps of Alexander, into the Hindu Kush, is rather intriguing. This book and the trek to the Himalayas is being inspired and directed by the mathematics to be found inside the Great Pyramid; an avenue of research that was denied to Alexander. The fact that both quests still resolutely point in the same direction seems to indicate that the ancient myths were correct in many respects. It would appear that either the secrets of the architect's plan have leaked out at some time in the ancient past, or perhaps an ancient peoples saw some strange goings-on in this part of the world and fuelled the legends with their stories.

Whatever the case, the tenacity with which Alexander drove his men on is perhaps without parallel in the history of mankind. Having defeated what was probably the most powerful army in the world at the time at Issus, Alexander then casually turns his back on the fleeing Persian hoards and proceeds into Phoenicia. Here was Alexander's chance to finally wipe the Persian empire off the map, while his foe was in total disarray, yet he looks south instead – to Egypt and the power of the gods.

5. Alexander

Imagine the pyramids at Giza in the time of Alexander, when his army first passed through the region in the autumn of 332 BC. What would those young soldiers have seen as they marched down the Nile? The first thing to remember is that, in such an era, even the largest of the civic and private buildings were comparatively small by modern standards. In comparison, the pyramids must have seemed like mountains built by the gods themselves. The great Parthenon back in Athens was just celebrating its centenary that very year, yet this little Lego set was child's play in comparison with the mighty Great Pyramid at Giza. Not only were the stone blocks used in the pyramid's construction far larger than anything in Greece, but the pyramid was nearly 15 times as high and 15 times as broad as the Parthenon. In addition, it was composed of solid rock, from top to bottom.

As the nervous soldiers approached the base of the pyramid, the flat expanse of cladding stones must have seemed to thrust up towards infinity, with barely a ripple or blemish on the entire surface. Running a trembling hand over the stones, there was hardly a joint to be found between any of them It was as if the pyramid had been cut from a single block. In an age when the power of the gods loomed large in the daily lives of every individual, this must have seemed, to the uneducated soldiers, to be the closest they would ever get to a real creation of the gods. Of all the countries they had visited and conquered, this was the place to be if one wished to be in communion with the deity. It shows the strength and character of Alexander that despite this, he could drive his men on into defeating a people who were so obviously blessed by the gods.

Walking around the Giza site, however, it would have been immediately apparent that not all the pyramids were constructed in quite the same fashion. There were distinct variations on the grand theme and the next pyramid down the plateau, the Second Pyramid, was graced by a rather fetching low line of granite; forming a double-layered ring around the base in a deep pinky-red. [15] The fine Tura limestone in the upper cladding had taken on a buff, sandy hue, but in its prime, that Tura limestone cladding must have been as white as snow, gleaming in the strong Egyptian sunshine. The contrast between the snow-white and the dusky-red must have been dramatic in the extreme and even the awe-inspired soldiers of Alexander must have wondered, in the back of their minds, why this had been done.

Certainly it was not for structural reasons, for it is only the cladding stones that are made of granite, not the core stones. The larger Great Pyramid just next door does not need a stronger layer of granite at the base, so therefore this design cannot be a structural requirement. Yet it must have been important to the architect to include these granite layers in the design, for the granite was not only much tougher and more difficult to work than the limestone, but it also had to be brought all the way from Aswan, nearly 1,000 kilometers to the south!

This was a prodigious undertaking for a Bronze Age society, so what was it all for? Why go to this enormous trouble? In addition, it would appear that the similar, lower granite layers on the Third Pyramid were left in the rough. Was this design intended or was it simply easier that way? The fact that the Egyptians could have smoothed all the granite down to match the contours of the upper limestone portions of the pyramid is self-evident, as all the other faces on each block *had* to be smoothed down quite precisely in order to fit alongside the neighbouring stones. Was it so much extra trouble to smooth down the last remaining outer face? This was, after all, the face that defined the whole character of the pyramid and displayed, for all to see, the capabilities of the designer and his artisans. Was it really too much trouble to smooth down that extra face and finish the job properly?

The artisans on the site obviously had the capability to smooth down the granite blocks quickly and efficiently, as they had to smooth down at least four sides on each block. This strongly suggests that a contrast was intended between the perfectly smooth, brilliant white Tura limestone and the dull, red and roughened surface of the granite layer at the base of the pyramid. It strongly suggests that this was somehow part of the designer's plan. But if that is the case, what does this imagery mean? What concepts are being suggested to us here? Why is it so difficult for us to understand what the designer really intended? Another clue to this conundrum is that the Third Pyramid has a quarter of its base covered with this rough granite casing. So why was the change made from granite to limestone at this point? Was the construction of this pyramid running behind schedule, as Egyptologists have suggested, therefore necessitating a switch to an easier-to-cut limestone surface?

The evidence from the Second Pyramid, next door, would suggest not. They had, under the classical dating system, just been through the same process with the fabrication of the previous pyramid. The length of time taken to work the granite layer should have been a known science to them by this time.

5. Alexander

But if fabrication expedience was not the reason for the resulting appearance of these pyramids, what was the true goal? To answer this question, I would propose that the resulting visual imagery is one of the most important properties that the pyramids displayed in their prime. Like so many other aspects of this quest, the pyramids are representational in some manner. It has already been proposed in a famous work that the pyramids are representational of stars – the belt stars of Orion to be precise. I believe this is actually quite likely, but is that all there is to it? Do stars need a granite base? Perhaps in our haste to assume we know everything about this site, we are missing something here.

What we are looking for here is an image of something that is very tall and pyramidal in its general form; something that is snow-white on the top and a dull, rocky-red at the bottom. Not only this, but that something must also lose more and more of the white surface material when the structure becomes smaller. When this happens, the smooth white material is replaced by more and more of a rough and red-looking material at the base. So what artifact achieves all of this in a few words? Simple – a snow-covered mountain range!

A simpler, more elegant, explanation would be hard to find. The Great Pyramid is the largest peak in this dynastic mountain range, and it is completely covered in fresh snow. The Second Pyramid is a little smaller (lower down the range) and so it has a snow-line, with a small but distinct dark and rocky layer that is visible at its base. The Third Pyramid in line is much lower still, and so it only has a snowy peak with the rest of the mountain showing its rocky underskirts. This *is* the reason for these three pyramids' construction details; they are simply representations of mountains.

Alexander was right; the place to look for a sacred depository was on the mountain-tops of the world. Was this the inspiration for the greatest building programme in the ancient world? Had the priests been to the high peaks far to the northeast of Egypt, and been awed by their lofty majesty and rugged beauty? Had someone from faraway lands told the priesthood of these natural monuments and dictated the form that the pyramids should take? We shall see very shortly that the architect knew exactly where the largest mountain range lay on the surface of the Earth, and from where the inspiration for the Great Pyramid was derived. The 'natural' model for the design of the Great Pyramid could not be more compelling.

5. *Alexander*

The pity for Alexander, and his weary army, was that he did not know exactly which mountain to look at; so he scoured the Hindu Kush looking for sacred places. Any peak with a monastery or a town on the top, he was interested in; anything that smacked of an ancient tradition of a sacred mountain.

Pothos

While high in the Hindu Kush, Alexander learned from the locals that Dionysus had indeed been down these very valleys. Incredible as such stories may seem to us, Alexander broke off from his military expeditions and went, with a party of troops, to a mountain that they thought may have been Mt Meros; the mountain where Dionysus was reared by his nurse, Nysa. It is recorded that on the mountain, the troops engaged in a Bacchic frenzy, no doubt lubricated with liberal quantities of Bacchic wine, dancing and singing and shouting the toast of Dionysus – *Euoi, Euoi.*

The Bacchic cry of Euoi is not too dissimilar to Jesus' penultimate cry, while on the cross, of *Eloi, Eloi.* This is a fitting similarity considering the link between Jesus and Zacchaeus Bacchus, the publican. Indeed, this most ancient and pagan of chants was apparently adopted, and continued well into the Christian era by the monastic orders. It would appear that the ending to the Gregorian chant, *Gloria Patri,* was "Et in saecula saeculorum Amen", from which the underlined vowels were bizarrely taken to form a shorthand version. The more obvious method would involve taking the first letter of each word, but by this curious method the monks derived the acronym, "Euouae", and thus appear to have continued the Bacchic traditions in their morning prayers.

The derivation of the Bacchic cry is uncertain, but Robert Graves claims it derives from the sacred alphabet. In his prodigious work, *The White Goddess*, Graves indicates that knowledge of the alphabet was secret, sacred and allegorical. Among the claims imbued within many ancient myths, the general thrust of his explanation was that the letters of the alphabet were linked to the seasonal cycle; the names of the calendrical months; and thence the names of the flora that grew within those months. Through this obscure method of letter substitution, many a secret message could be hidden within a simple poem about a forest, for instance. Graves works mostly within Celtic mythology, but closely links this with the Greek beliefs, and thence to Dionysus.

Central to the secrecy that surrounded the sacred alphabet were the vowel characters, which were traditionally absent from many Middle Eastern languages, including ancient Egyptian and Hebrew. This practice of vowel deletion meant that, even if one could read the consonant letters, the meaning of the text could not always be understood without a knowledge of the vowels that should be inserted into those words. In practice, this probably made the exclusive club of literate individuals that bit more difficult to join. The sacred vowels were, of course, A, E, I, O and U, and when read in the fashion that Graves carefully explains, they originally produced the name "Euoi", which he claims was a sacred name for Dionysus. [16]

The Bacchic frenzy over, Alexander moved his men on to investigate other mountain peaks and, among others, the hilltop towns of Ora and Bazira were investigated and taken. Finally, when approaching the mountain of Pir Sar – thought to be the impregnable fortress of Aornos – Alexander experienced another pothos, or violent longing. Pir Sar was reputed to have been the fortress that Hercules himself had failed to capture, during the Indian wars of the gods. Alexander was going to capture it at all costs – and he did.

But each and every mountain that Alexander battled for proved to be barren. It was a futile quest which must have drained the spirit of the most dedicated of individuals, for there are literally thousands of peaks in the Western Himalayas to choose from. It was the proverbial needle in a haystack.

There was another problem for Alexander. The truth is that any location for a sacred chamber has to be remote to prevent an unplanned discovery, and thus a location under a working monastery or town does not really fit that bill. Alexander simply did not have the full explanation, so he was a few miles wide of the mark in his quest. It was a shame for Alexander, he was trying so tenaciously and valiantly to succeed; but the upper chambers in the Great Pyramid that marked the location were not going to be opened for another 1,000 years or so, so the truth still remained hidden under thousands of tonnes of rock.

Dionysus

Alexander was not only investigating mountain peaks; he was also deep into the Hindu Kush, the western flank of that greatest range of mountains on the Earth, known as the Himalayas. Was this just the nearest range of mountains to Egypt, or were the ancient myths correct (in some respects) in this assumption as well? The 'fact' that Dionysus, Hercules and even Thoth, had apparently spent so much time in the Hindu Kush must have played a great part in Alexander's decision-making. He was undoubtedly on the trail of Dionysus, and perhaps thought himself even an equal of that god.

Dionysus was the son of Zeus and Semele and his upbringing was unusually 'modern' in concept. Dionysus' mother was killed while he was still a foetus in her womb, but the premature Dionysus was extracted and 'sewn into the thigh of Zeus' to develop to full term. [17] The name of Dionysus was given to him by Hermes (Thoth) because the swelling foetus made Zeus limp and Nysos, so the texts assure us, means 'limping' in Syracusan. [18]

Dionysus may seem like a diversion into obscure Greek myths at this stage, but he is more central to mainstream history than one might at first think. He was the god of wine, more commonly known under his more familiar appellation of Bacchus, and he was closely associated with the vine and also his symbol of office, the fennel.

That Dionysus should be closely associated with the vine and all things verdant (green) is perhaps not so surprising when his mythical origins are understood. According to the Greek historian, Herodotus, Apollo was a Greek version of Horus; Typhon a manifestation of Seth, and Dionysus, was none other than the Egyptian god, Osiris. [19] Like his Greek incarnation, Osiris was also associated with all things green. He was the only god to be depicted as having green skin and this was reinforced the greenness of the Osiris bed. The Osiris bed is a wooden or brick base in the shape of Osiris, into which soil and seeds are sown. It is said that the germinating seeds symbolised the resurrection of Osiris, but more likely the association was, like Dionysus, with the lush new green vegetation. [20]

Dionysus was, therefore, an image of Osiris and also closely associated with the new growth of vegetation. Indeed, sometimes this vegetation forms an image of the god, as it grows from his very form. What I am saying, of course, is that Osiris/Dionysus was the original template for the image of the Green Man.

The Green Man burst upon the European consciousness during the medieval period, as the great cathedral-building programme across

5. Alexander

Europe gathered pace. He is the decorative motif that has a tangle of foliage either around his face or growing out of the various orifices on his face. Historians are rather baffled by the origins of the Green Man. The tentative suggestion sometimes put forward is that he was a remnant of the Roman Bacchic cult; in other words, a representation of Dionysus/ Osiris. It is odd to see an image of Osiris in so many of the European medieval cathedrals; a notion that is also discussed in the book *Jesus*, but there are reasons to believe that the Green Man is a Templar device.

The Rosslyn Chapel, near Edinburgh, was built by William Sinclair in the fifteenth century. Sinclair was undoubtedly a very important member of the Knights Templar and it is quite apparent that he not only closely directed the construction of the Rosslyn Chapel, but also that the designs and motifs used throughout the building were Masonic/ Templar. It is reputed that there are more than one hundred images of the Green Man in the chapel, but only one of Jesus. It seemed to be obvious that the Templars, who were influential in the construction of many of the great cathedrals, were the prime motivators behind the Green Man motif.

It was for this reason that the mountain I was now looking at had first caught my attention. It was the supposed site of Alexander's last battle on the Indus, before he turned south and westwards once more; forced to turn back by both the terrain and disaffection within his officer corps. It was supposedly the mountain citadel that the god, Hercules, had failed to take during his legendary Indian war, but Alexander had taken it with his usual cunning and military prowess. The name of that citadel – Pir Sar, the Green Man.

I asked Altef, my sirdar guide, whether the name was ancient. He just indicated that it had always been called Pir Sar, as that was the name of the settlement at its base. Indeed, this was a fitting name, as it was an unusually lush and verdant slope that rose up precipitously in front of me.

Indian war

The reason for the god, Dionysus's, fabled war with the Indians is not entirely clear, but he undertook the adventure with some gusto. His followers were a varied group that included the Bacchant women, and Amazons, who brandished ivy wands that were capable of cutting iron.

5. Alexander

Aided by their other-worldly powers, these gods and mythical soldiers tore into the terrain of the Hindu Kush, felling everything in their path:

> ...they tore up the foundations of the ravines and cast them, or some crag, from the tops of the hills. Showers of splintered rocks were hurled, rolling on the heads of the Indians. [21]

Deep into the Hindu Kush they forged the battle front. Ever eastwards they pushed, just like Alexander, seeking the rays of the dawning Sun. [22] These supernatural armies had great powers at their disposal, powers that are nowadays claimed for the ancient Egyptians by some recent devotees; the power of levitation by harmonics:

> Amphon played the harp and at the tune a whole hill moved along of itself as if bewitched ... (The music) was only a work of art, you might have said, the immovable rock went lightly skipping and tripping along! When you saw the man busy with his silent harp, striking up a quick tune on his make-believe strings, you would quickly come closer to ... hear the music of seven strings which could build a wall, to hear the music which could make the stones move. [23]

The gods also appear to have had the ancient knowledge of precession and how the stars moved in the heavens:

> Beside the socket of the axle were the poles of the two heavenly waggons, never touched by water ... Between the two waggons he made the serpent, which is close by and joins the two separated bodies. [24]

Quite plainly, the two axles are the Ecliptic Pole and the Celestial Pole, and between them winds the constellation of Draco, the serpent. The fact that these two points are described as axles with wheels is a rather delightful, and accurate, graphical description of precession that shows that both of the axles 'rotated'. We all know that the Celestial Pole rotates, as we see this each day in the movement of the Sun and stars across the sky, but for the Ecliptic Pole to be seen to rotate shows a clear knowledge of the very slow rotation of the stars, known as precession. The Greeks had obviously held onto, and understood, much of the teachings of the Egyptians.

5. Alexander

Eventually, during this titanic struggle of the Himalayas, it was Hermes/Thoth, brother of Dionysus, who came from Zeus to assure him of victory against the Indians. Indeed, the victory was total, and 'many a black-skinned bride was dragged out by the hair' to begin a new life in the west. Dionysus distributed the spoils of war and the victors 'made haste to go, laden with shining treasures'.

Was this all that Alexander was looking for in the Himalayas: the fabled spoils and treasures in India, as told in the tales of Dionysus and his Indian war? Frankly, I think not. Alexander had already captured the treasury of the Persians, an incalculable wealth that far outshone anything else available in the known world. In comparison with the wealth and splendour of Persia, the Hindu Kush and the Karakoram were very poor cousins that provided nothing but a wealth of grinding poverty and a few impoverished warlords, overseeing the occasional modest palace.

Anyone could see that these high, inaccessible peaks were not going to produce any great wealth and if the final goal for Alexander was the Ganges and eastern India, as has been proposed by some, what was he doing in the Hindu Kush? His scouts and guides would have known that the Indus river was totally inaccessible and that the only route to the Ganges was to the south, via the lowlands around modern Lahore and Delhi. At any point in time, Alexander could have turned south but he remained resolutely in the Hindu Kush, until his officers finally rebelled at their hardships and privations.

So what are we to make of all this? Why were both Dionysus and Alexander high up in the foothills of the Himalayan ranges? What were they doing? Undoubtedly, in my mind, Alexander was searching for something. Indeed, the tales of Dionysus indicate something similar. There was not only a battle in the Himalayas, but also much moving of mountains – was Dionysus burying something in the Karakoram? This is a very tentative hypothesis at this stage, but it would certainly go some way towards clarifying some of Alexander's more bizarre actions.

Hindu Kush

The myths of Dionysus may have been well-known to Alexander, but what other new information had the priests of Siwa imparted on the new, impressionable pharaoh of Egypt. Certainly, it would appear that

5. *Alexander*

Alexander had endorsed the 'new' cult of the constellation of Aries with some gusto, as is explained in the book *Jesus*. Henceforth, he now wore the two horns of the ram, the cult of Aries. What he could not have known, despite his later furtive rummaging around the Himalayas, was that the, as yet undiscovered, Queen's Chamber deep inside the Great Pyramid, would be the first key to the true location of the Hall of Records. The key to this explanation lies in the shape and layout of the chambers and galleries that reside inside the Great Pyramid.

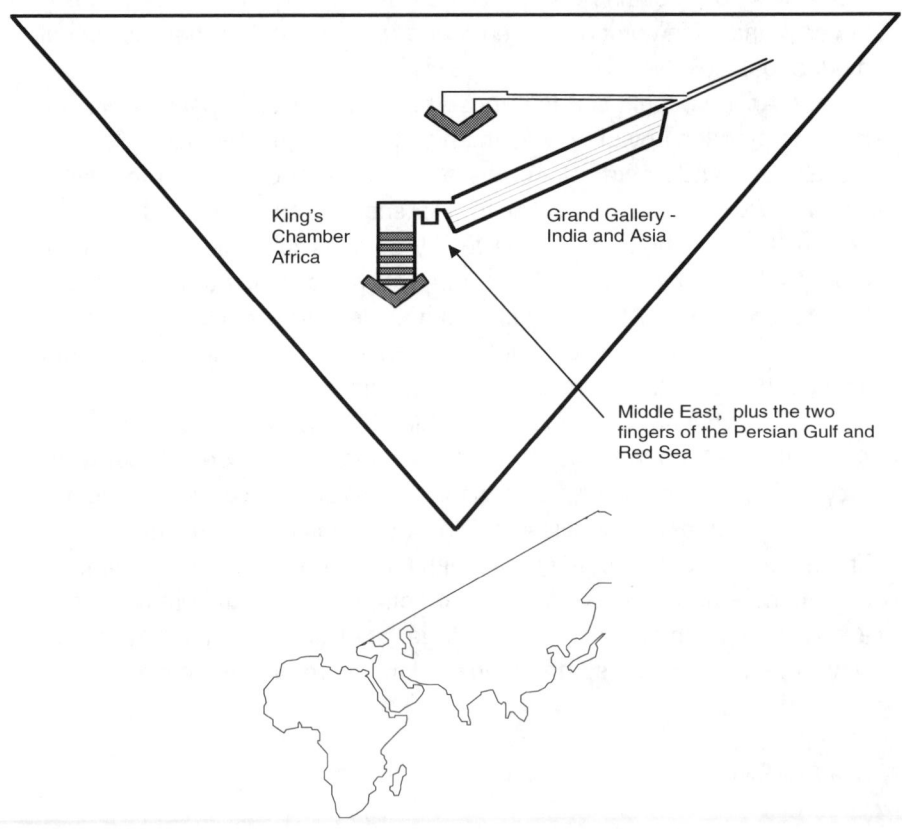

Fig 17.   The Great Pyramid's continents.

5. Alexander

In the book *Thoth*, I explained in some detail that I thought the plan-view layout of both the Avebury and Stonehenge sites in Britain strongly resembled the form of our Earth; they even came complete with lines of latitude marked on them. This was highly speculative, but the clinching factor that forced me to go into print with this discovery was the fact that the Great Pyramid's upper chambers did much the same. The layout of the upper chambers strongly resembled the continents of the Earth and, once more, some lines of latitude were also displayed on this megalithic map, as is shown on the previous diagrams.

It may take a while to see the image, so a few hints may be necessary. The sloping Grand Gallery represents India and Asia, and the small anti-chamber represents the Middle East, complete with the two fingers of the Red Sea and Persian Gulf protruding inwards on either side. Finally, the King's Chamber and its enigmatic upper chambers represent the continent of Africa. Was this a true image or was it a figment of my fevered imagination?

The deciding factor had to be the presence of lines of latitude on this image. The role of the enigmatic 'attic' chambers that lie above the King's Chamber have been a complete mystery, both to the classical and to the esoteric communities of Egyptian history. There seemed to be no logical rationale for making such a construction. They were not required for 'stress-relief' to the King's Chamber, which is the usual explanation, as the form of the Queen's Chamber clearly shows. If the Queen's Chamber did not require 'relieving chambers', despite having even more pressure on its roof beams, then why did the King's Chamber need them?

Indeed, the whole concept of these beams across the top of the King's Chamber being structural in any fashion is ludicrous. It has even been said in one serious work that these beams were 'overstressed' and hence one or two have broken but, in truth, they carry no more mass above them than a few grams of stale air (which is balanced by the air pressure below in any case). These beams provide no stress-relief whatsoever for the mass of masonry above the topmost gable-stones; all they do is provide a little stability to the chamber in keeping the walls beside them apart. In reality, the beams allow the King's Chamber to be much taller than is otherwise possible, and the reason for the cracks in some of the beams is that the northwestern floor of the King's Chamber has subsided by a couple of centimeters.

5. *Alexander*

So what was the design of this very tall chamber, with several crossbeams inside it, really for? The Africa theory at last gave a full explanation. These extra chambers above the King's Chamber not only greatly increased the height of the chamber, so as to resemble the outline of Africa more strongly, they also drew straight lines across this continent – lines of latitude.

One small additional factor that convinced me this was a true image intended by the designer, was that the final image had to be hung upside down to see it. This was perfectly in line with the lateral thinking that has to be applied to all of these hints and clues, for the image is impossible to see when in the normal orientation.

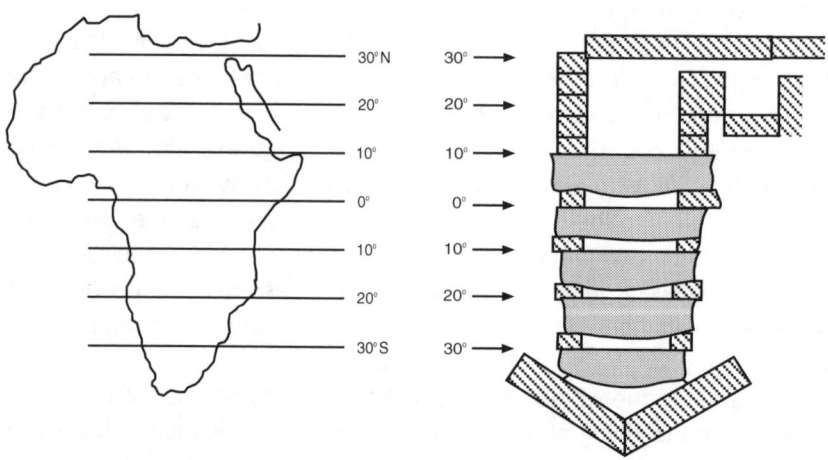

Fig 18.   Africa's lines of latitude.

Queen's Chamber

Here was a concise and simple theory that seemed to explain all of the upper chambers in the pyramid. Indeed, it explained all of the most puzzling aspects of the construction, down to the finest detail. It may have been highly speculative, but it was both simple and comprehensive.

5. Alexander

However, there were two troubling problems with the theory. Firstly, the theory was too far outside the mainstream explanations for the role of the pyramids; indeed, it was too much, even, for many of the alternative researchers to grasp. Secondly, as was said to me on many occasions, it did not explain the function of the Queen's Chamber. Which continent on the Earth was represented by the Queen's Chamber, I was invariably asked, with a wry smile and a tongue held in the cheek?

Which continent indeed! The answer to this had been formulating itself in my mind even at the time of writing *Thoth*, but the lure of the map of the Avebury henge indicated that the Atlantic was the correct location and so this continuously drew me off in the wrong direction. Time and time again I dismissed the Queen's Chamber as an aberration, yet in truth I understood the basic maxim of this whole enterprise – that nothing in this great construction was done without a purpose. In fact, I clearly stated this axiom in the book *Thoth*. The rules of the game were clear, but I was not prepared to play by them at the time because of a simple lack of understanding. The mountain theory for the pyramids at Giza gave the final clue that would jolt me out of this wayward thinking and back onto the right tracks.

The task was to look for snowcapped mountains, and there was a desperate lack of them out in the Atlantic. Yet, the biggest range in the world was just to the north-east of Egypt, the Himalayas. Looking at the Great Pyramid 'map of the world', it suddenly became apparent that the Queen's Chamber marked exactly the right point on this map to be the Himalayan range. More than that, Sir Flinders Petrie, *et al*, had long ago deduced that the center-line of the pyramid ran right through the exact center of the Queen's Chamber. This center-line then continued up to the upper end of the Grand Gallery, exactly up through the 'Great Step' that lies at the top end of this enormous gallery.

Clearly, this had been done for a reason, as was everything within this structure. This center-line of the pyramid has to be an important marker of some nature, as it is the very center of the whole construction. Surely, if anything of importance is to be built within the pyramid, it ought to lie on the center-line, as the chambers in many of the other pyramids do. A center-line has to be a prime location for any budding 'X marks the spot'.

This fact has taxed the minds of many would-be historians, Egyptologists or pyramidiots, for why should the King's Chamber – the most prestigious of the chambers in the Great Pyramid – be so off-center. This was not imperfect surveying, as the Great Step and the Queen's Chamber itself mark that center-line to the nearest couple of centimeters. Clearly, the original layout and position of the pyramid's internal chambers were known to the architect in the minutest of detail. So why was the King's Chamber not on the center-line?

Now, however, with the 'map' theory for the pyramid, the answer to this question can be clearly seen. The most important part of the map is no longer Egypt and Africa (the King's Chamber), but the location on that map that the architect wishes to describe to us. It was the 'X marks the spot' position that was the prime motivation behind building the entire structure and surely it is *this* point that must therefore lie on the center-line. It was the Queen's Chamber that held the *hidden* 'air' shafts, and it was the Queen's Chamber that was placed on the center-line of the pyramid, so this chamber *is*, therefore, of great importance. The Queens' Chamber is not to be dismissed so lightly as an 'afterthought'; perhaps it is the Queen's Chamber that marks the 'X marks the spot' position on this pyramidal map of the Earth.

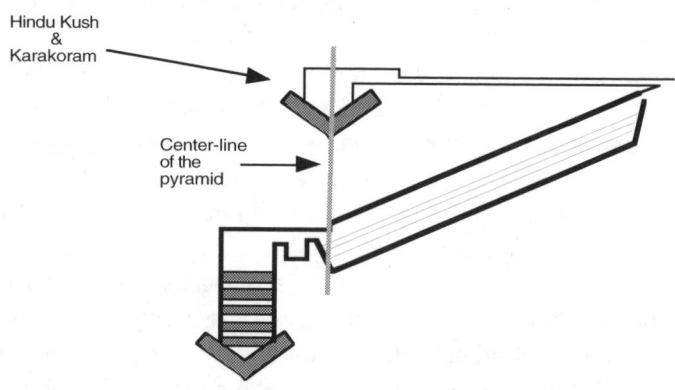

Fig 19. India and the Hindu Kush.

Looking at the center-line position in the pyramid, and comparing it to the real world, some interesting conclusions can be drawn. Due to the slight camber on the upper wall of the Grand Gallery, the center-line can be

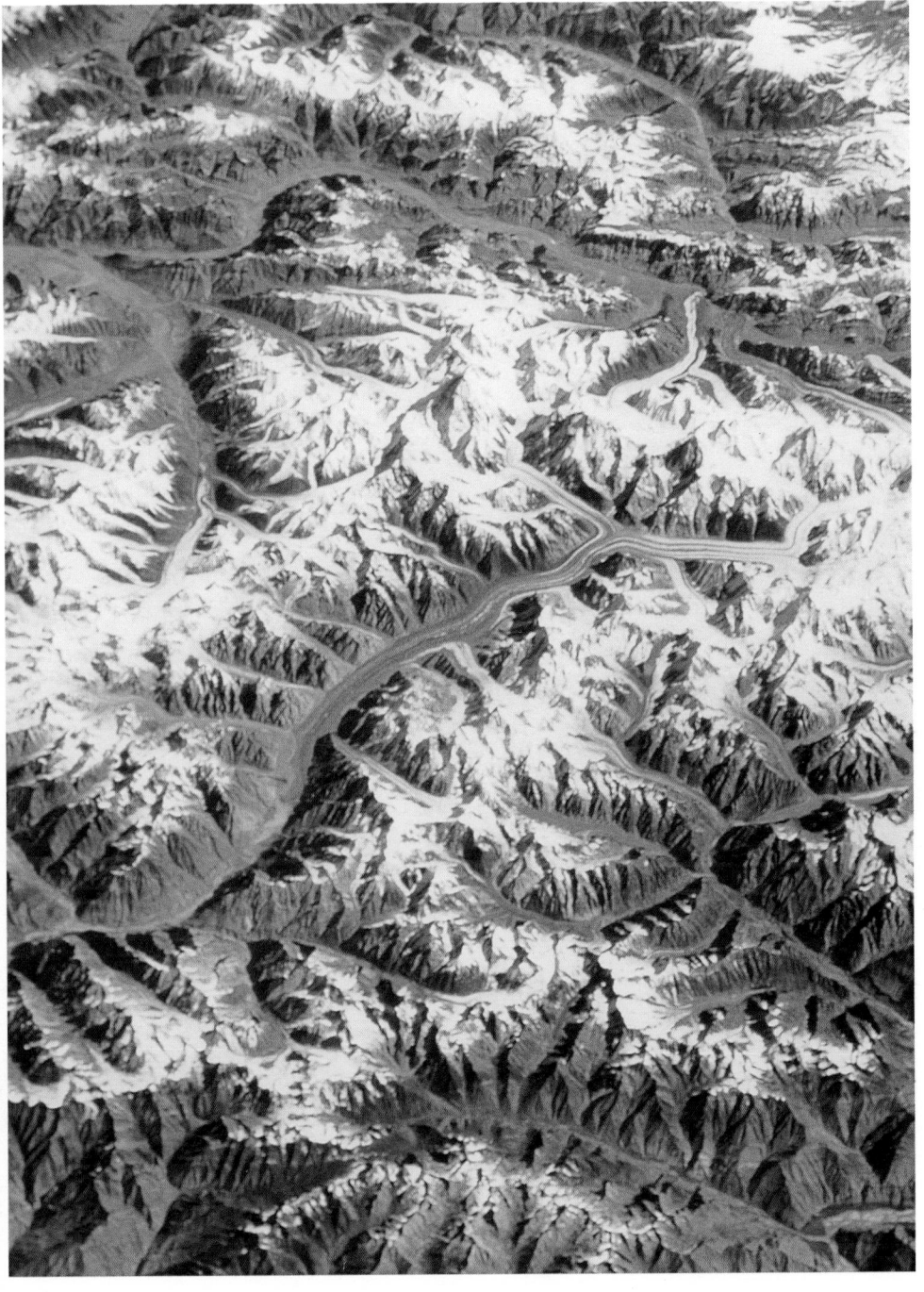

Plate 1. The Karakoram and K2. The Godwin Austen glacier winds its way up from the bottom-left to the middle of the picture. Turn left at the 'T' junction and K2 lies straight ahead.

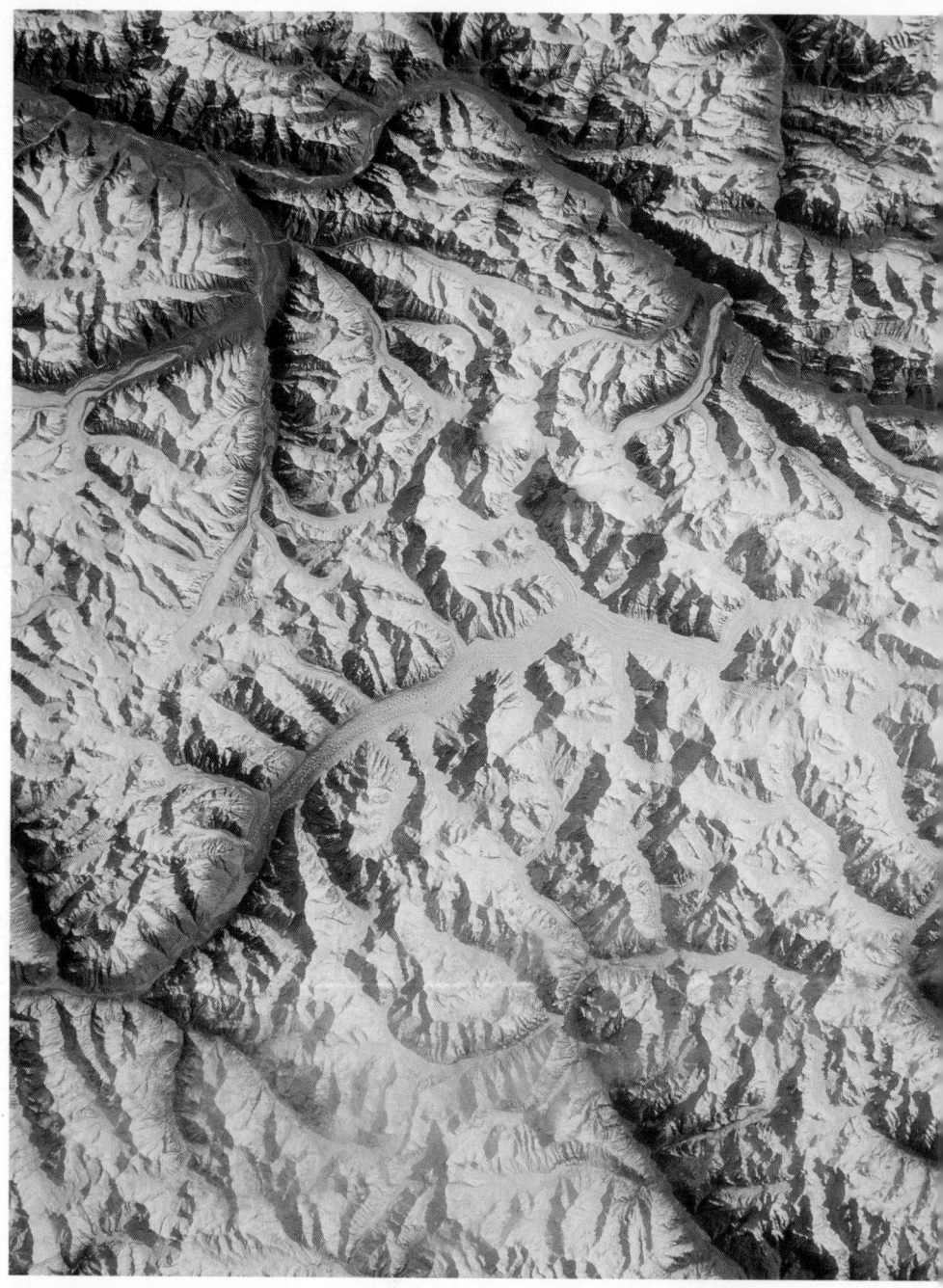

Plate 2. K2 in winter. The 'T' junction is less visible now, but at the end of the left-hand arm lies K2 with a puff of cloud on the top. With this shot from high above, the pyramidal form of K2 is readily apparent; it is separate from all the other peaks, has a marked square base and it clearly has a pyramidal shape. A small ridge protrudes from the southern face adjacent to the glacier.

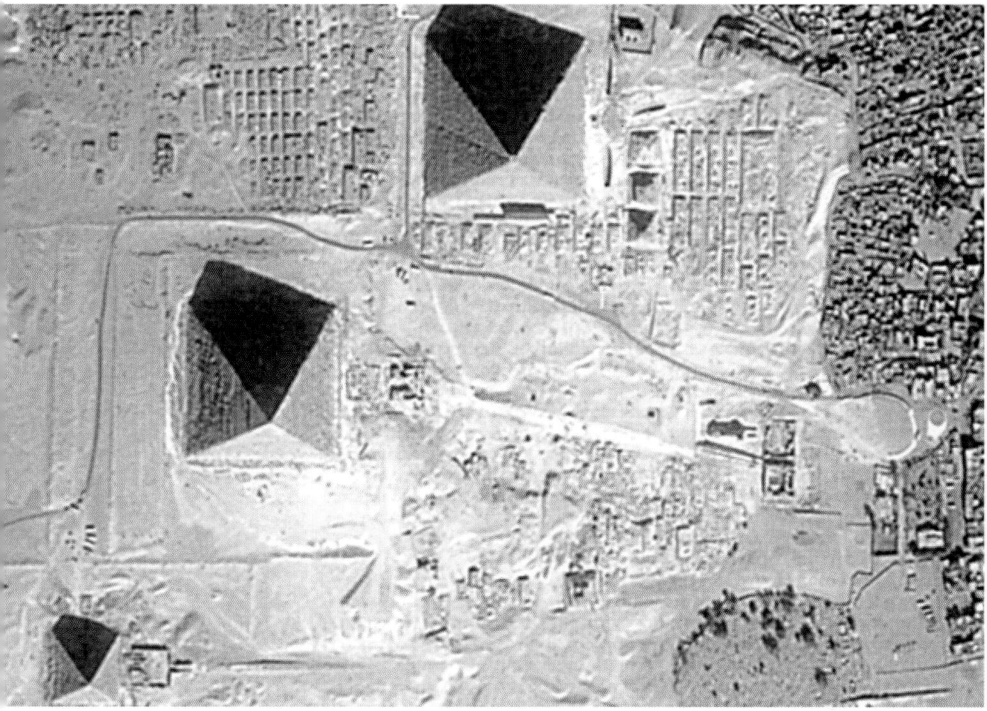

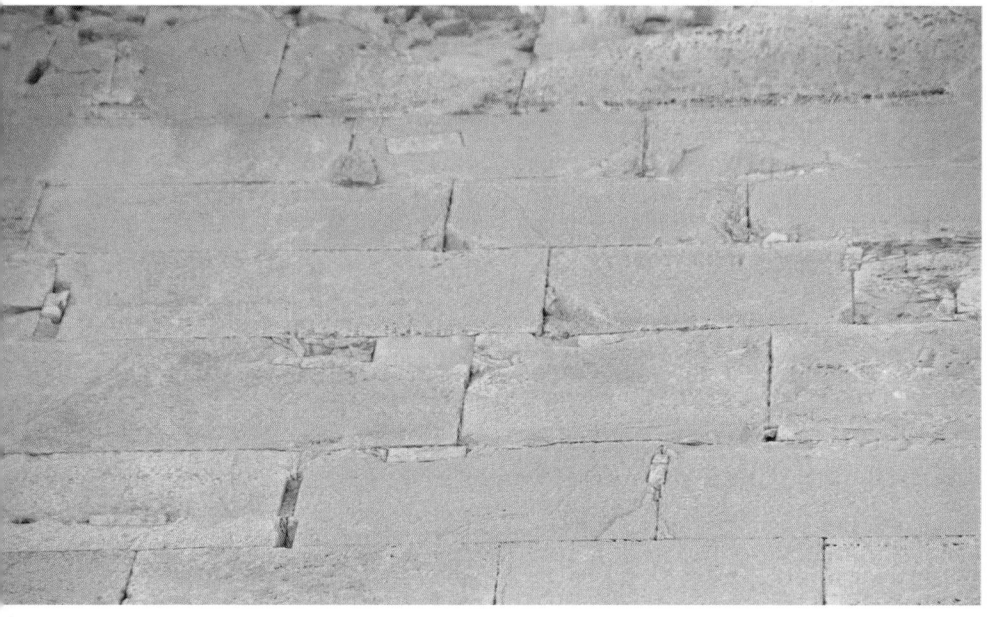

Plate 3. Giza, taken from Russia's Ikonos satellite.

Plate 4. A few of the thousands of repairs made to the Vega Pyramid at Dahshur.

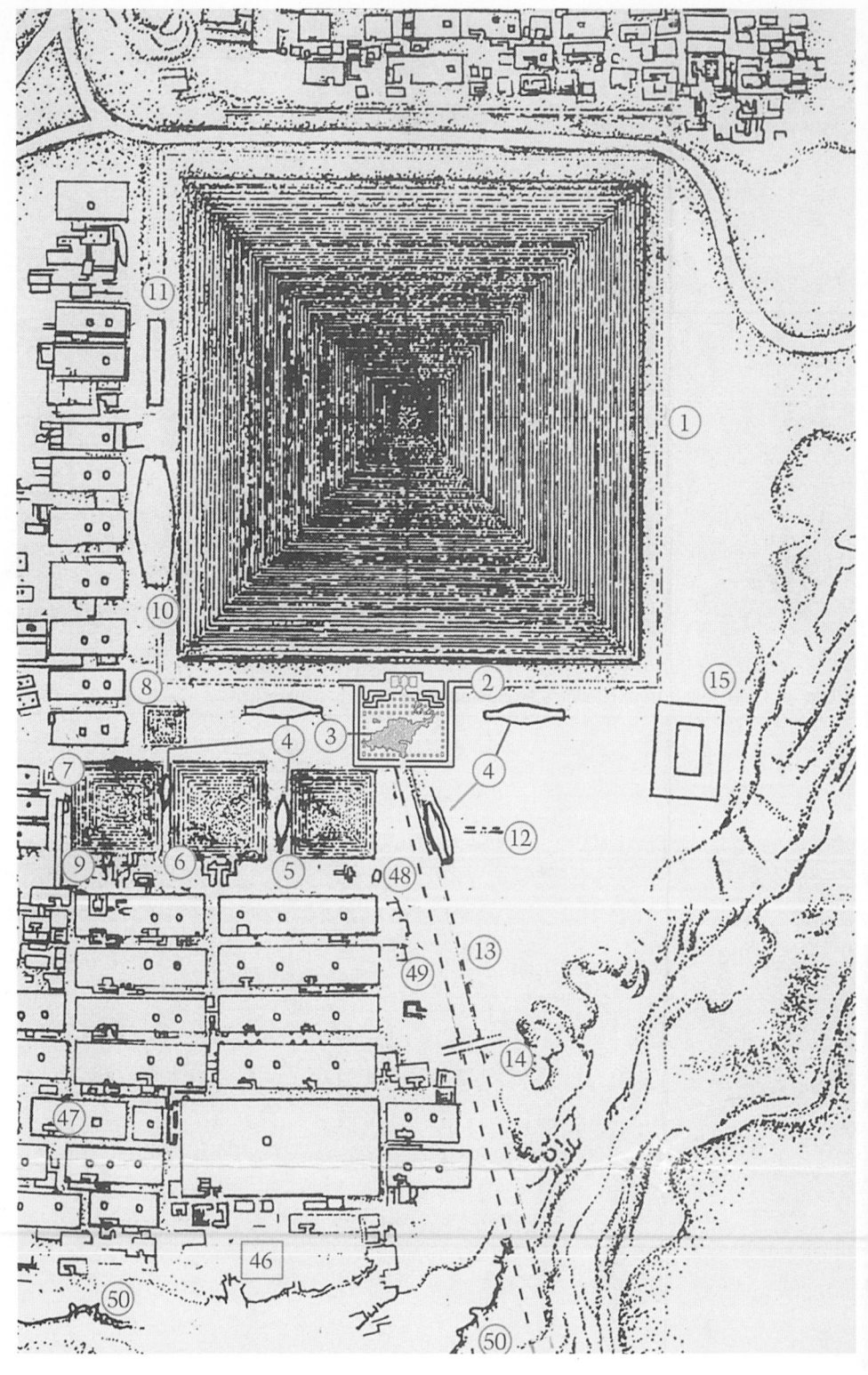

Plate 5. The Great Pyramid and its causeway.

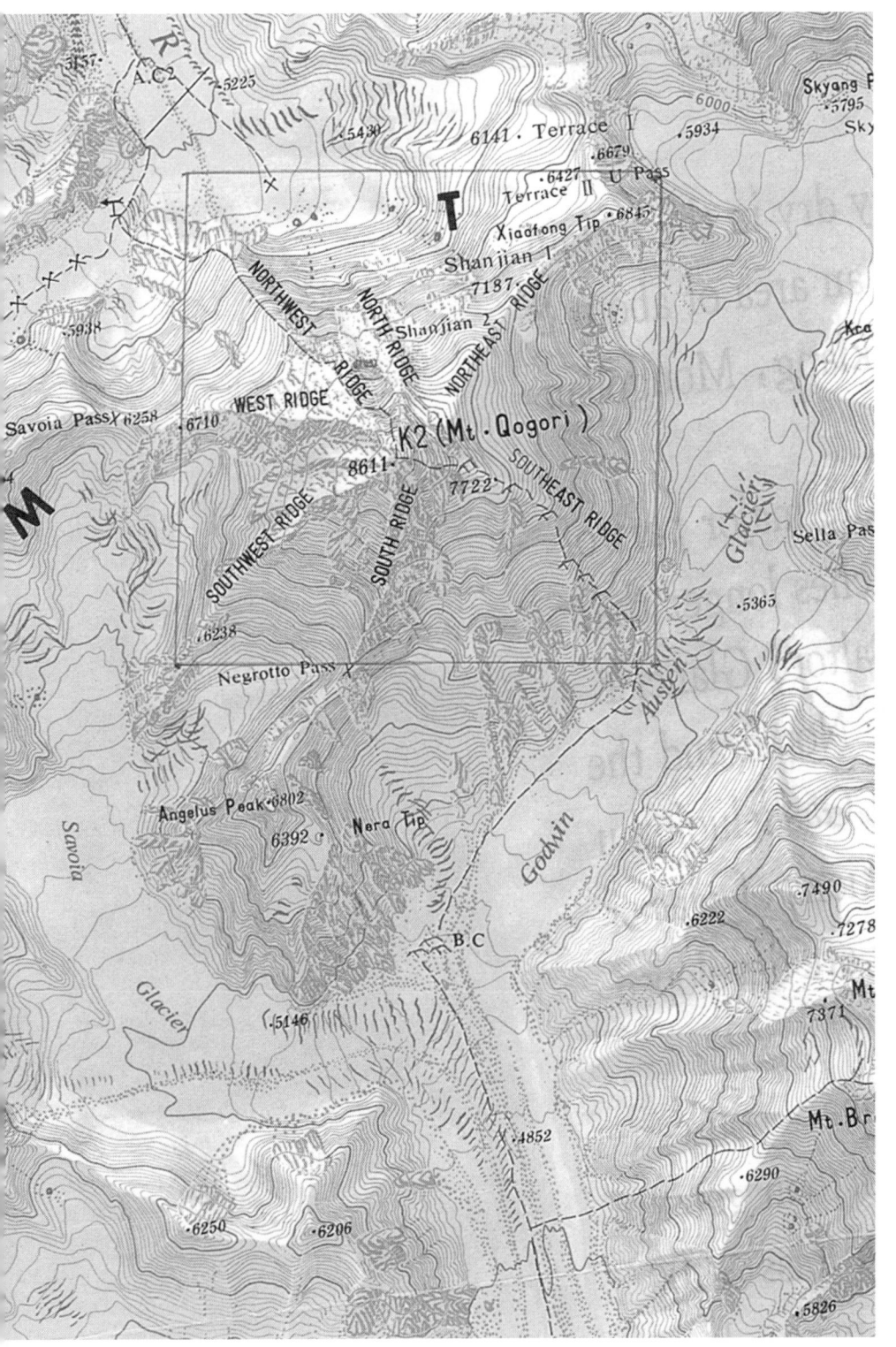

Plate 6. K2 and its causeway.

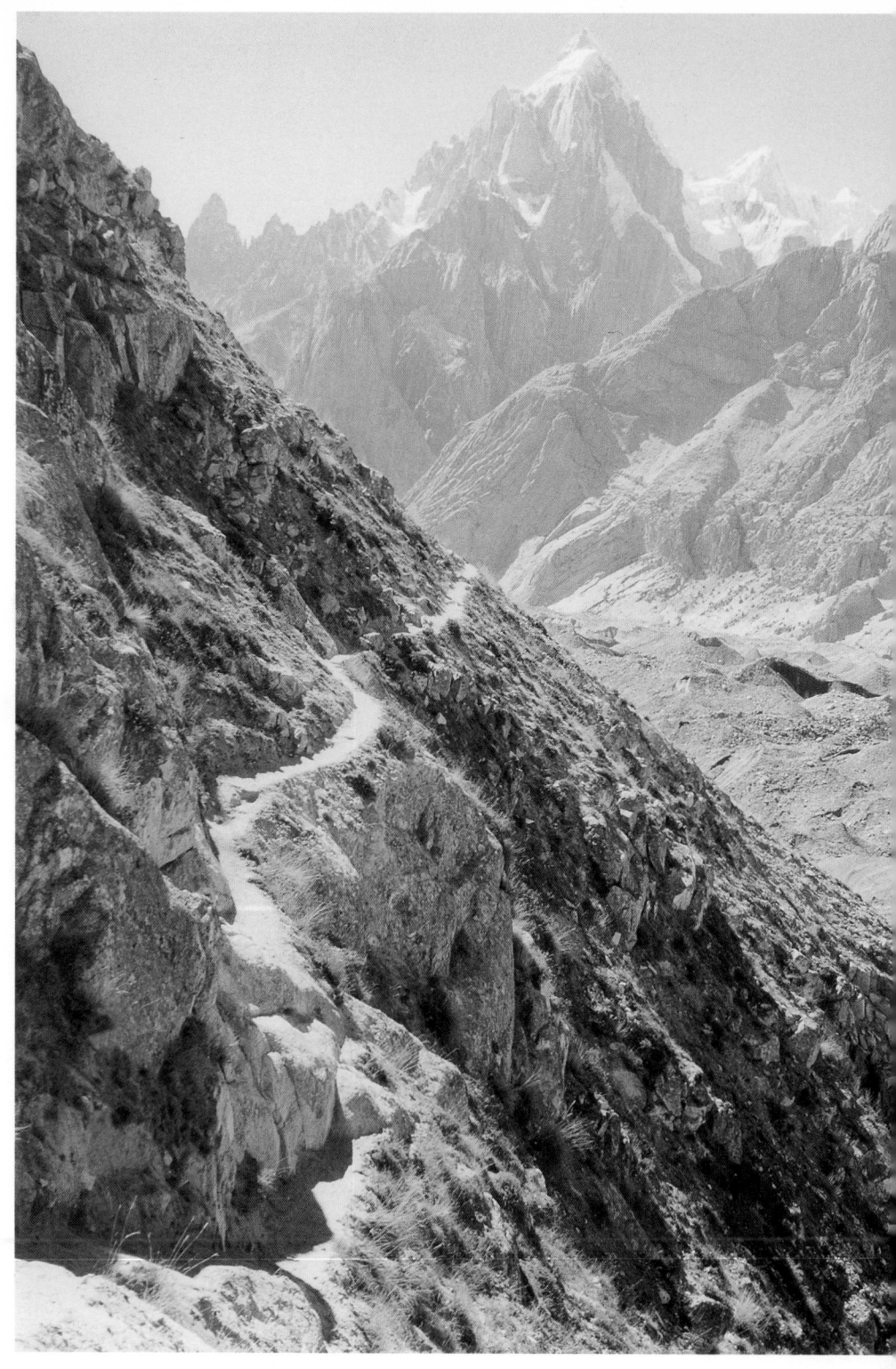

Plate 7. The high trail.

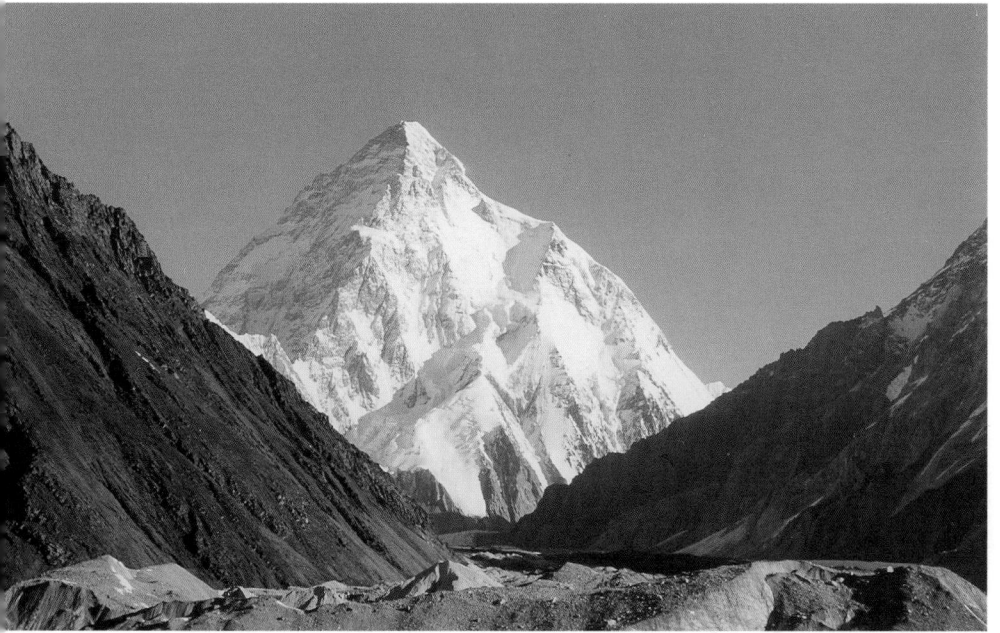

Plate 8. Standing at the junction of the Baltoro and the Godwin Austen glaciers, a point known as Concordia, and looking north towards the pure white peak of K2.

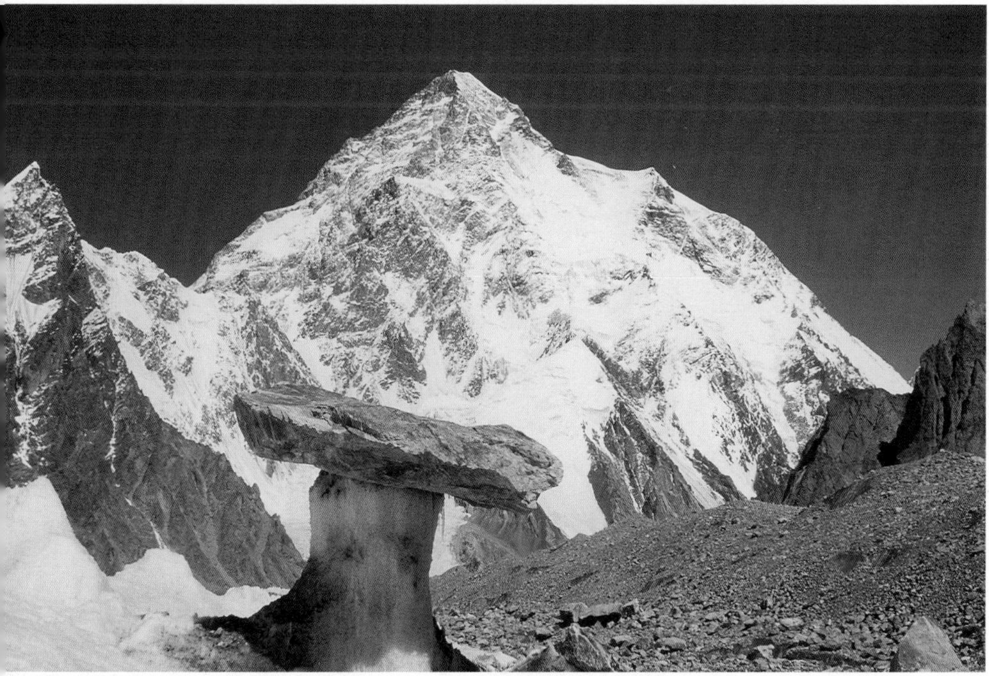

Plate 9. K2 and one of the many Himalayan Taule. See *Jesus, Last of the Pharaohs* for ancient Minorcan replicas of this phenomena.

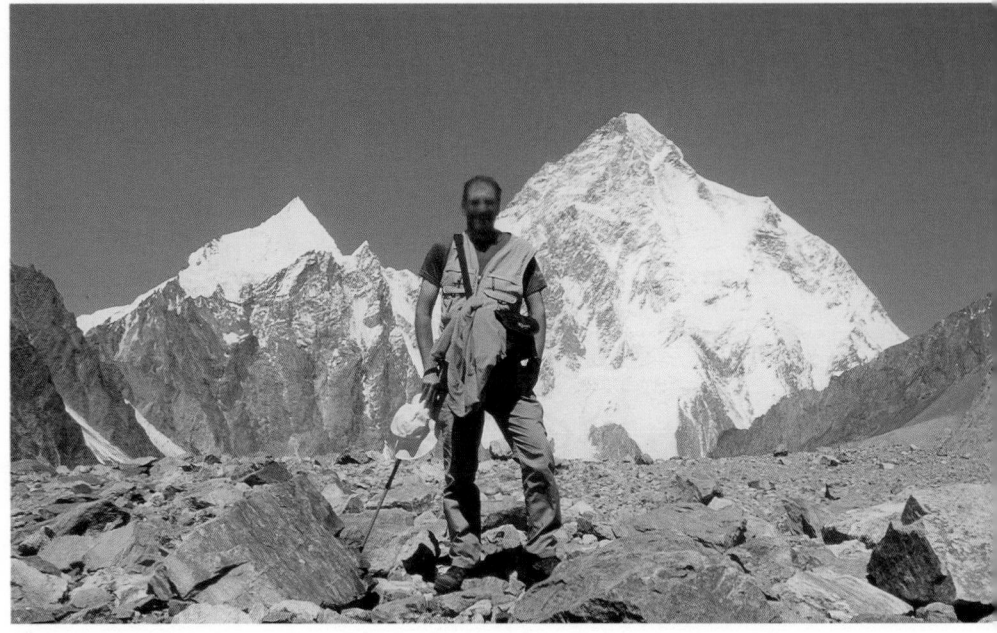

Plate 10. The author approaching K2 base camp.

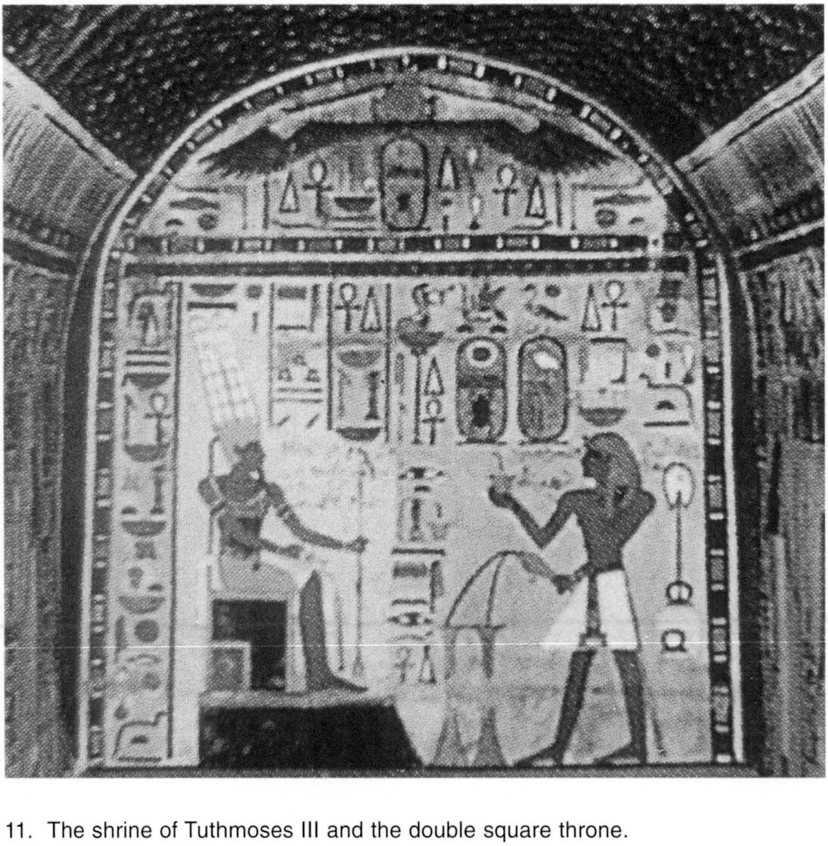

Plate 11. The shrine of Tuthmoses III and the double square throne.

5. Alexander

seen to be passing through a position at the 'tip of India', which is represented by the tip of the Grand Gallery. Follow this line 'up' (on the inverted diagram) towards the Queen's Chamber, which also lies on the center-line. On a real map of the area, this takes us up past Lahore and Rawalpindi, and into either the Karakoram or the Hindu Kush ranges. Clearly, if the Grand Gallery marks the line of India and Asia, the Queen's Chamber marks the next major topographical feature to the north of India – the Western Himalayas.

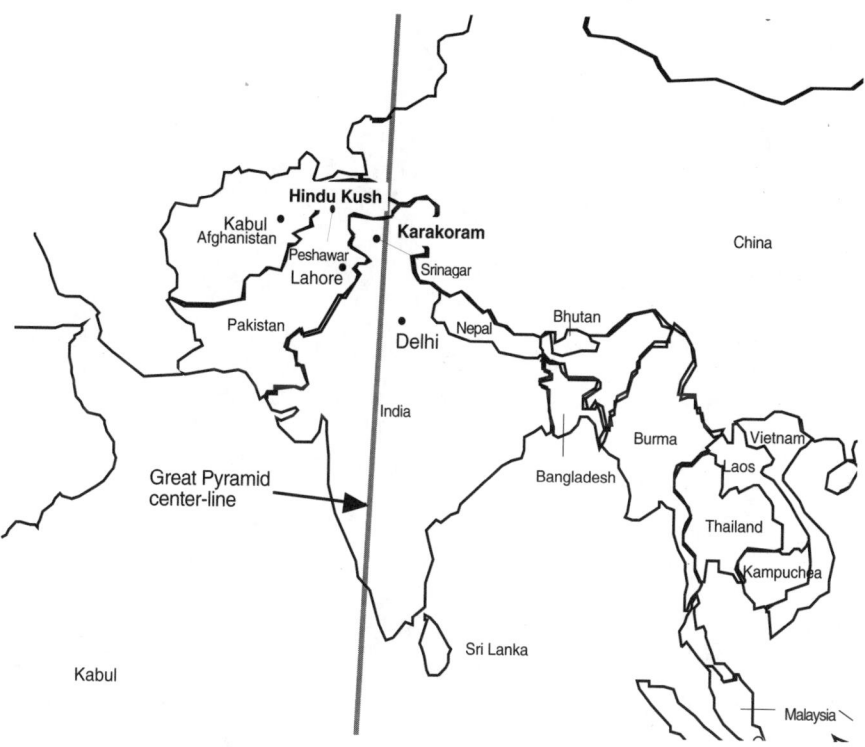

Fig 20. India and the center-line.

As Alexander knew in his heart, *this* is the most suitable area for the location of the legendary Hall of Records, in so many respects. Surely, for security's sake, the location of such a treasure would not be in the populated lower reaches of the Hindu Kush, but instead high up in the inaccessible highlands of the Karakoram. This is one of the few areas on the planet where man cannot live, however hard-pressed he has been for land space over the last few millennia. It is too cold, too dry, too lacking in oxygen, and too inhospitable to support much in the way of life. Here is a place where a treasure-trove of immense importance could lie undisturbed for thousands of years. This is the area I must travel to but, unlike Alexander, I shall be taking more than a few myths on these travels; there will be a complete and detailed map as well, with the final location marked to the nearest tens of meters.

Chapter VI

Karakoram Triangle

North of Pir Sar, the winding Karakoram Highway now took us up the original precipitous route of the Silk Road. Perhaps that is a little misleading for, especially at this point on the route, there was no one clearly defined trail. The route was originally, in effect, a series of trails that led to and from each of the principalities that lay on the route. Those trails did not necessarily converge either, for there was more than one pass into China and not all the trade consisted of a crossing over the Khunjerab pass.

The modern road was a tortuous ribbon of tarmac, blasted out of the rocks, high above the Indus. It was barely two lanes and as it wound its way through hairpin bend after hairpin bend, so the unfortunate vehicle on the outside lane had to teeter on the lip of the abyss to pass oncoming vehicles. As the road swung back and forth across the Indus – over suspension bridges erected by the Chinese – it meant that both sides of the traffic had equal turns in putting a wheel over the edge. My driver seemed fairly capable and experienced, so I put my faith in his abilities and tried to enjoy the view.

The journey was long and arduous, taking two days to cover a straight-line distance of just 250 km. We overnighted in Chillas, one of the slightly larger truck stops *en route*. The place was bustling with activity and some of the ornately decorated lorries were being prepared for a night's work. Presumably, some of the drivers prefer to drive at night, when the traffic is lighter and opposing vehicles can be more easily detected around the blind corners. Still, the huffing and puffing of

6. *Karakoram Triangle*

the antiquated Bedford trucks was a barrier to sleep, so I switched off the rattling air-conditioning and resorted to the stand-by earplugs for some peace and quiet.

The morning brought some cooler mountain air down from the northwest, a refreshing change from the stifling heat of Rawalpindi. We set off on the second leg of the journey up to Skardu, the starting point for all the Karakoram treks. The terrain was as rugged and inhospitable as before; a jumble of crushed boulders heaped upon each other to form mountains. I had hoped for something more spectacular, but geology and plate-tectonics had not been kind to the region. When India had crashed into Asia, it did so with so much force that the rock strata were not just uplifted into mountains – as is the case in the Alps – they were, instead, crushed beyond recognition.

During the entire journey to Skardu, I did not see one intact piece of strata; instead, the rocks were a jumbled mass of all types, crushed into small boulders and loosely held together with a sand/shale mortar. It is no wonder that there are no waterfalls on this route. Waterfalls need a solid strata of hard rocks to drop off the edge of; here there was not a single platform larger than a few meters across from which a river could launch itself. It was not so surprising that the Indus could cut its way so easily through these rocks to form such deep valleys. It was not a matter of cutting a valley, so much as rolling the loose stones downstream.

The precipitous gorge of the Indus begged the question as to whether Alexander had ever made his way north and east of Pir Sar, the Green Man. Skardu was, for instance, named after Skander, the common name for Alexander in the region. Had he managed to forge his way this far north? I asked Altef, my Sirdar, who shook his head rather gravely. He was a very pragmatic and imposing bull of a man, born in the valleys north of Gilgit and with a refreshingly detached view of Pakistan – its politics, religion and history. 'Everyone likes Alexander to have been in their town', was his jaundiced view. Initially, I was skeptical but, having looked at the terrain north of Pir Sar, I would have to agree that it would have been totally impassable for an army and all its baggage.

Nevertheless, an advance guard may have set off in this direction because Arrian, the original historian of Alexander, says that:

Alexander detached Nearchus with the light-armed units ... with his own regiments of Guards and two others and sent them out to reconnoitre. Their orders were to capture and question any natives they could lay hands on, and in particular to get what information they could about elephants, as this interested him more that anything. [1]

Are we really to believe that Alexander was this deep into the Himalayas and sending off armed parties of scouts to ask the natives about elephants? The story is just not credible; each and every local who was 'captured and interrogated' by Nearchus would have asked why on earth the supposedly sensible and intelligent Greeks were looking for elephants up in the high Himalayas, rather than down on the lush plains of India? The whole of this report by Arrian reeks of misinformation: Alexander was most probably interrogating the locals, but it was certainly not to get information from them about elephants.

Instead, Alexander was interested in sacred hilltops and, no doubt, Nearchus and his scouts were searching deeper into the Indus valley for any signs of a sacred summit. Altef, my sirdar guide, may be right in his assessment that Alexander never reached Skardu, but Nearchus and his light infantry certainly could have paid a visit.

Altef then put me straight on a few other points regarding this region and his hometown, near Gilgit, before the new road came to his town. Their previous contacts with the outside world had been a few traders on mule-back from China, following one treacherous branch of the well-worn Silk Road. Then, when he was nine or ten, a Jeep arrived in town, and contacts with the outside world became the norm. Suddenly, his town had electricity and schools, teaching unheard of subjects. It was a dramatic revolution for such a small village that mirrored the greater revolution of the whole area.

Most of the area had already been opened up to the wider world by the British in the nineteenth and early twentieth centuries, when many major roads and their associated bridges were put in place. The local history guide, however, summed up the influence of the British and their sudden departure in the typical propaganda tones of a new governmental system:

The clear background of the Gilgit revolution was a reaction to the century-long tyranny of British India and Maharaja of Kashmir. [2]

Once more, Altef had a much more pragmatic approach to history. He said that British rule was the best thing that ever happened to Gilgit and the Hunza. Before the coming of the Empire, the journey to Rawalpindi had taken up to six months, on a perilous journey by mule. With the building of the first roads, that time had been slashed to a few days. The roads had mainly been designed, it is true, to defend the northern borders of British India during the 'Great Game' with Russia. But, nevertheless, the flood of technology and ideas into the Hunza valley propelled the area through a thousand years of development in just a generation. The principality had joined the modern world.

The history of the region confirmed the severity of the terrain. Sadly, then, it would appear that Alexander did not reach Skardu, or at least not with an entire army. Perhaps a small expedition made their own way, backed by some of the unlimited funds from the Persian treasury, but the rest of the army headed down the Indus and into the fertile plains of modern Pakistan. What, then, was the furthest extent of Alexander's travels? How close to his objective in the Karakoram did he get?

Shaft location

We shall come back to Alexander in a minute, but the other question which will not go away is just what was I doing here, high up in the Karakoram foothills of the Himalayas? Was I so certain about Alexander's motives to have organised such an expedition? Was the position of the Queen's Chamber in the Great Pyramid, and the pyramid's similarity to mountains, sufficient reason to undertake such an expensive and arduous trek? No, there had to be more to the story that has been told so far, and there is, indeed, a lot more to it than this.

The Great Pyramid is full of devious little snippets of information, if one looks hard enough, and essentially, what has not been done so far in this investigation is to really look deeply at those enigmatic shafts that lead off from the internal chambers. They are not only, perhaps, the most difficult artifacts within the whole pyramid to build, but two of them were also deliberately hidden from view. This is just so typical of the architect's little games that these items *must* be central to deciphering the pyramid's function. If the pyramid is to be understood to the full, then these four small, but nevertheless very complicated, features must be completely explained.

As with everything the great architect did on the site, the answer is extremely simple, but nevertheless very clever. Rudolf Gantenbrink

6. Karakoram Triangle

nearly solved the riddle when he commented in his web-site that the King's northern shaft embodied the ratio of 7 : 11, as did the pyramid itself. In the recent updates to Rudolf's *Cheops* web-site, this snippet of information appears to have been deleted, which is a shame because it is probably the closet I have seen anyone getting to solving the riddle of the shafts.

What Rudolf was implying was that the shaft angle of 32.5° in the King's north shaft, gave this shaft a specific set of dimensions and so the <u>linear</u> dimensions of the shaft revolve around the ratio of 7 : 11. If the King's north shaft were to be resolved down into its simplest possible figures, the vertical rise of a triangle formed by this shaft would be 7 units, and the distance along the base would be 11 units – hence the 7 : 11 ratio mentioned by Rudolf. This was highlighted as being somehow special, because the pyramid itself also has a 7 : 11 ratio in its dimensions. If the pyramid's height were reduced down to 7 units, then the base length would be 11 units – the ratio of 7 : 11 once more. So, it seemed that the architect was using this ratio as a guide in many of his calculations.

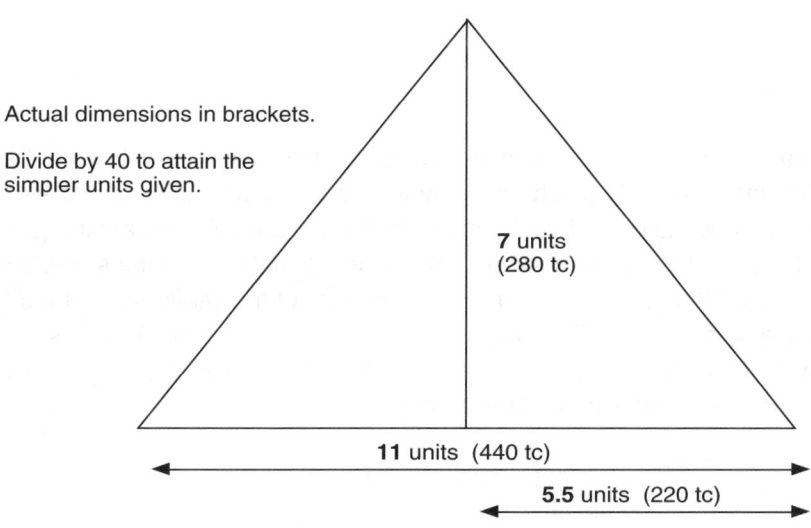

Actual dimensions in brackets.

Divide by 40 to attain the simpler units given.

7 units
(280 tc)

11 units (440 tc)

5.5 units (220 tc)

Fig 22.   Fundamental numbers.

6. Karakoram Triangle

Various writers have previously mentioned this 7 : 11 ratio for the exterior of the pyramid. It is in Petrie's *Pyramids and Temples of Gizeh* amongst many others. The 7 : 11 ratio of the Great Pyramid's external casing stones has occurred because the pyramid is constructed using the mathematical constant, Pi. The simplest Pi ratio that maintains whole-number values on both sides of this Pi ratio is 7 : 22, and it was from this ratio that the 7 : 11 ratio for the pyramid's external dimensions was drawn.

This evidence was taken a stage further in the book *Thoth*, as it was noticed that Pi was not simply represented in the exterior slope angle of the Great Pyramid; it was represented numerically, too. The pyramid's dimensions in cubits were exactly 40 times the values in the 7 : 11 ratio. The vertical height of the pyramid is 280 cubits (40 x 7) and the base length is 440 cubits (40 x 11).

This concept was taken to its final extreme by the extrapolation of the 7 : 11 (or 7 : 22) ratio to the various internal components of the pyramid, and even to the Stonehenge site and the Imperial Measurement System; these additions to the theory were all *very* new. All of these ancient monuments and measurements were based, in part or in full, upon the Pi ratio of 7 : 22. It very much began to look like understanding the pyramids' dimensions involved understanding where the Pi ratios fitted into each component.

Shafts

In a way, this is a bit of a sideshow to the main issue here, but what all this *does* do is to highlight, once more, the importance of the numbers 7, 22, 11, and 5.5 in the Great Pyramid's construction. The breakthrough in this quest only occurred when it was noticed that the numbers involved in the shaft <u>angles</u> (not the linear dimensions of the shafts) also embody these same ratios. The angles involved in the four small shafts that branch off from this pyramid's main chambers are 45°, 39.5°, 39.5° and 32.5°. The numerical difference between these angles are as follows:

$$45° \quad \text{minus} \quad 39.5° = \mathbf{5.5°}$$
$$39.5° \quad \text{minus} \quad 32.5° = \mathbf{7°}$$

The value of 5.5 is obviously half of 11. So, here are those same Pi ratio

6. Karakoram Triangle

numbers yet again (7 : 11), but involving *angles* this time, not *lengths*. Again, the complex nature of these shaft angles can be seen. They not only produce triangle lengths that are related to the dimensions of the pyramid, (as we saw in chapter 5), but the numerical differences between the same angles are also related to the dimensions of the pyramid.

This is a surprisingly complex thing to achieve, especially as the starting point for all these numbers is fixed by the constant, Pi! But these numbers of 5.5 and 7, formed from the differences in the shaft angles, were the prime clue to solving the location of the hidden chamber in the Himalayas, for there was a little mathematical problem with these numbers.

The Pi ratio of 7 : 11 is exclusively referenced to lengths, not angles. Those differences in angles of 7° and 5.5° are angular measurements, and therefore have nothing to do with the linear measurements that are fundamental to the Pi ratio. So here was a typical case of this architect's sense of humour, because it would appear that a question is being posed once more – 'When is an angle not an angle but a length?'

This may sound like an impossible question to resolve, but it happens that the answer to this conundrum lies on the chart table of any ship. A ship's navigation is governed by the shape of the Earth. Since there are no roads and signposts out at sea, a navigator, up until the middle of the twentieth century, looked to the stars and to a chronometer for the steady reference points required, and plotted a position using the latitude and longitude of the ship. The technique is much the same even today, but the 'steady' reference points used are now more likely to be man made stars instead – satellites.

When using this technique, it is convenient to have a distance-measurement system that is related to the latitude and longitudes on the chart; linear measurements that are related to the size of the Earth itself. The unit used in nautical navigation (and aviation navigation too) in most countries is the Nautical mile. This measurement is defined as being $1/_{21,600}$th of the circumference of the Earth, or $1/_{60}$th of a degree of latitude. As an aside, the length of the Nautical mile is thus double the Great Pyramid's circumference.

The answer to our architect's crafty conundrum lies in the definition of the Nautical mile, for this unit is not usually measured by a ruler but by a compass or a pair of dividers. Because the Nautical mile is

6. Karakoram Triangle

related to the size of the Earth, it can be measured as an angular measurement, focused on the center of the Earth. One degree of arc at the center of the Earth equals 60 Nautical miles on the surface of the Earth. Thus, we have found a very neat and logical occasion when a linear length is defined in terms of angular measurement. It happens every time a navigator plots a position on his or her map.

Plotting

Understanding this conundrum allows the Great Pyramid map to be plotted at last. We have four shaft angles that can be used for this exercise, and therefore four coordinates that can be plotted on a map. These angles are:

King's Chamber	45°	&	32.5°
Queen's Chamber	39.5°	&	39.5°

But how are they supposed to be used? When using coordinates, we need to know if these angles refer to latitudes or longitudes; that is, measurements that lie north-south or those that go east-west. There are a few variations in how these numbers can be placed on a map, but there is perhaps one clue that simplifies this task a little.

Both of the northern shafts in the Great Pyramid are curved in their plan-view. They snake around the Grand Gallery, as was discussed earlier. The reason for this curvature is not readily obvious, but it was suggested in the book *The Orion Mystery* that this shape may have been designed to represent the northern constellation of Ursa Major, or the Plough. This sounds like a reasonable argument and, if this is so, the values represented by these northern shafts can be considered to be northings; values of latitude to be plotted to the north. This considerably simplifies matters and now, all of the shaft angles can be plotted on a map in the normal fashion, as shown in figure 23.

Because the differences between these shaft angles were exactly 7 and 5.5 degrees, as explained previously, the two points on the map are in very specific locations relative to one another. If the points are joined up, as has been done in the diagram, the triangle (on the left-hand side) so formed measures precisely 7 x 5.5 degrees of latitude and longitude respectively. If the triangle is doubled up with its obvious

6. Karakoram Triangle

symmetric partner, then the resulting triangle drawn on the surface of the Earth becomes 7 x 11 degrees in size – which is exactly the same ratio dimensions as the Great Pyramid itself.

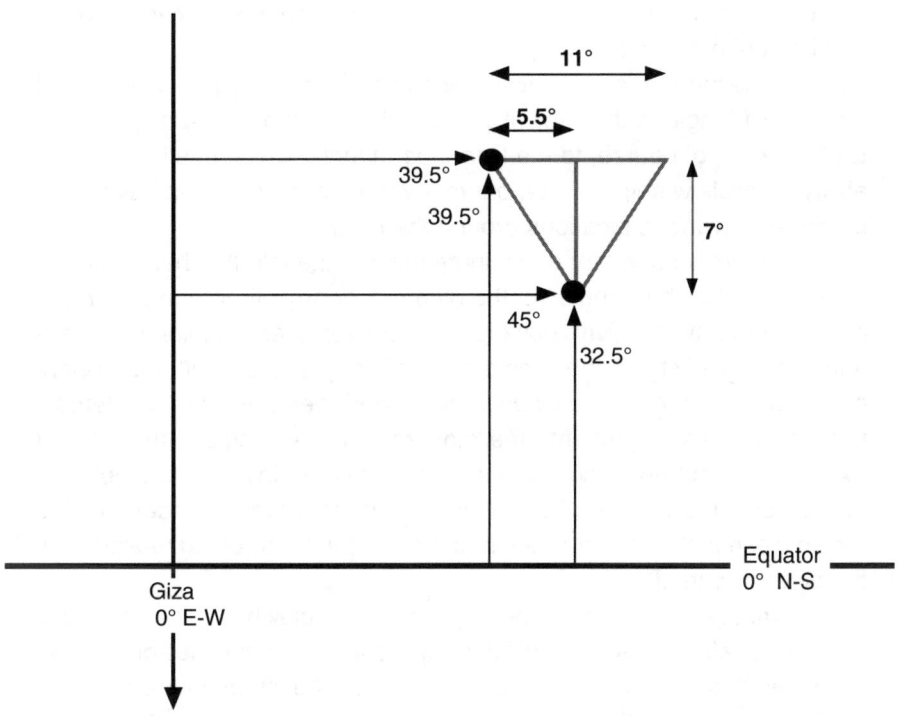

Fig 23.   Plotting the Great Pyramid's shaft angles on a map.

Here, drawn on the surface of the Earth, is an immense triangle that has exactly the same ratio of dimensions as the Great Pyramid, and this has been drawn using the angles given by the shafts inside the Great Pyramid itself. Is this a coincidence? I think not!

Bermuda

As an aside, it has been mentioned previously that the priesthood of Egypt knew of various rumours about the possible location of the Hall of

6. Karakoram Triangle

Records and, that these myths have been transmitted through the generations into our era. It was also noted in the book *Jesus,* that there are many other instances of these kind of rumours resurfacing in the more modern era. Among many others there is the Green Man of medieval architecture; the OK sign made with two curved fingers; and the all-seeing eye on the back of the US one dollar note. All of these traditions are firmly based both upon the myths of ancient Egypt, and the traditions of modern Masonry.

In the modern era, however, another fashion has grown up; that of the large triangle with magical powers drawn onto the surface of the Earth. I refer, of course, to the Bermuda triangle, which has the reputed ability to swallow ships whole; but many other such triangles have been proposed in various locations around the Earth.

I do not propose for one minute that the triangle that has just been drawn from the shaft angles of the pyramid, or any other triangle for that matter, has any 'magical' powers. These events and explanations are much more likely to be the simple result of people toying with the ancient myths they have at their disposal, or, indeed, perhaps clumsy attempts to promote these myths into the modern world. A magical triangle that swallows aircraft and ships is much more newsworthy than a simple trio of lines drawn on a map. But it is interesting that these 'modern' myths are so close in their interpretation to the facts that are being teased from the Great Pyramid.

Whatever the case, perhaps the complexity of these Great Pyramid shaft angles is now fully apparent; they have not only given linear lengths that mimic the dimensions of the pyramid's exterior in whole numbers, but they can also plot a triangle on a map that is exactly the same ratio dimensions as the pyramid itself! I do not believe for one minute that this was the result of the deliberations of a Bronze Age architect sitting in his mud-brick hut, for we have left that simplistic option behind many chapters and books ago. This designer was every bit as technically minded as any modern architect and perhaps much, much more so.

Karakoram triangle

The next question we have to ask is where, on the surface of the Earth, does such a large pyramidal triangle lie? To this end, the first thing we need to do is set the starting points for this exercise.

6. Karakoram Triangle

When plotting angles that refer to the north or south on a map, one has an obvious starting point – the equator, which is normally referred to as being the zero degree line. But when heading off to the east or west on a map, any starting position on the surface of the Earth could, in theory, be chosen. Witness the wrangling that has bedevilled our present east-west zero position.

In the modern world the zero meridian, as the reference point is now called, is the line that runs through Greenwich in east London. This odd little hamlet was chosen because the Royal Navy college was sited there and it was the Royal Navy that needed and used the meridian in their navigation. To pursue this goal of perfect navigation, the Royal Observatory was sited at Greenwich in 1675, and thus all British star charts and maps were referenced, from this time onwards, to the north-south meridian line running though Greenwich.

This rather infuriated the French, who had their own zero meridian running through Paris. Much to the dismay of the French, most of the world's shipping was using British charts for navigation, and thus the Greenwich meridian became the *de facto* standard. But it was not just navigation that was affected by the adoption of the Greenwich meridian.

As international communications became instantaneous with the invention of the telephone and radio, it became obvious that our time zones needed to be standardised too. Local time in the UK used to vary, depending on the longitude of the town; each location using the Sun as their guide to when midday occurred. Time was only standardised in the UK in the 1830s, to simplify the train timetables. It was not until the early 20th century that time between France and Britain was standardised, and the concept of a standard time, based on the Greenwich meridian, was accepted. The Greenwich meridian is now used worldwide, in both our navigation charts and our timing systems (Greenwich Mean Time).

The importance of being able to standardise a zero meridian is obvious, but the question still remains – what was the zero meridian that was in use in ancient Egypt? The obvious place to use as a reference point at this time would have been in Egypt itself. In fact, since the Great Pyramid seems to be so intimately associated with cartography, the exact location to use for reference just has to be a north-south line, or meridian, that runs through the Great Pyramid itself.

This does mean, however, that the values we use to measure coordinates on a modern map will be slightly different to the ancient Egyptian variety. But the calculation between the two systems is simple

6. Karakoram Triangle

enough; we just add 31° (31.1° to be exact) to the ancient Egyptian longitude (east-west) values we are given. For example:

Great Pyramid coordinate	Modern coordinate
45 E	76.1 E
32.5 N	32.5 N
39.5 E	70.6 E
39.5 N	39.5 N

It is these modern values that are then plotted on any standard world map and the locations that result are, perhaps, predictable enough.

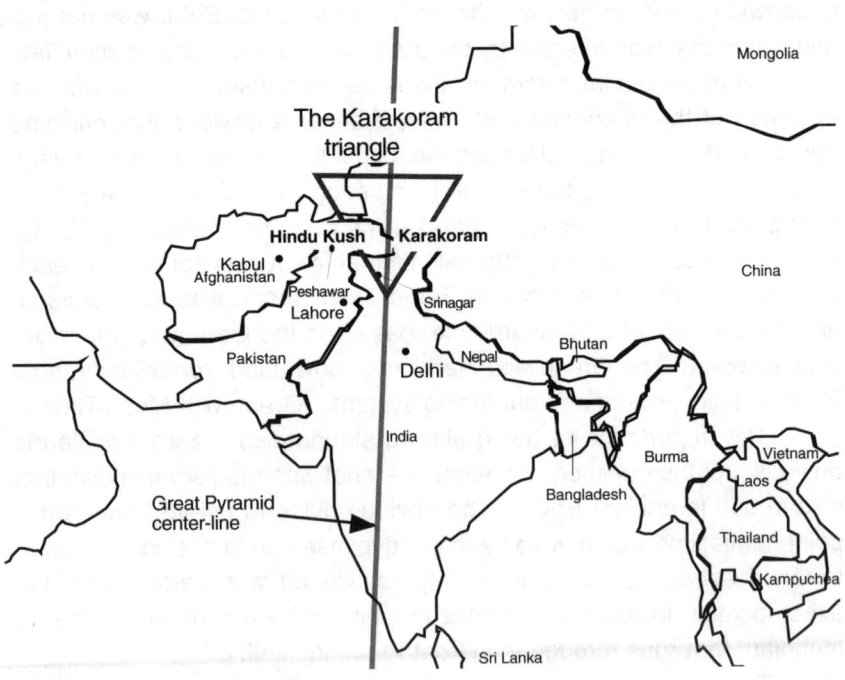

Fig 24.   The Karakoram triangle.

6. Karakoram Triangle

The first pair of coordinates mark a point on a map that is right at the base of the Karakoram range, just south of Srinagar. The second pair of coordinates gives another location which is in Tajikistan, just north of the Hindu Kush. If ever proof were needed of the type of quest that Alexander was really on, this is it. The two locations marked by the coordinates from the Great Pyramid straddle the Karakoram and the Hindu Kush, and this is the reason I am following in the footsteps of Alexander the Great.

Perhaps not only the general area to be searched, to locate the site of the Hall of Records, was known in ancient times. Perhaps these very coordinates themselves *were* also known. It may or may not be a coincidence, but the farthest reaches of the northeastern campaigns of Alexander, into Tajikistan, were surprisingly on the right track. Two campaigns went out from Samarkand in the summer of 329 BC; one to the east and one to the west. The eastern arm of the army established an outpost called Alexander the Furthermost – modern-day Khudzhand. This was the farthest to the northeast that the Macedonian army would travel, and the location is but a short distance from the northwestern apex of the Karakoram triangle that we have drawn – the 39.5 x 39.5 degree coordinate.

Whatever the truth in this matter, it is apparent that Alexander did not know, or realise, that these coordinates do not in themselves mark the site of the Hall of Records. All these locations do for us, is to mark out a vast pyramid on the face of the Earth, one with exactly the same measurement ratios as the Great Pyramid itself – 7 x 11. Note here that the large pyramid on the map that has just been drawn, the Karakoram triangle, is 'upside down'. Just as the Great Pyramid and its internal chambers had to be turned 'upside down' in order to see the layout of Great Pyramid's continents, so this larger cousin also appears to be upside-down. Once more, these uncanny symmetries are forcing the conclusion that this is the correct solution to the problems posed by our canny architect.

In fact, the new Karakoram triangle is a massive 660 Nautical miles (nm), or 1,320 Thoth miles (tm), across its inverted base, and 420 nm, or 840 tm, high. These figures are themselves interesting, because what we need now is some other form of supporting evidence that this image is the one intended by the designer. The architect is asking the potential researcher, in this case myself, to undertake an arduous and lengthy trek into the unknown, based purely on a few shaft angles and

6. Karakoram Triangle

similarities. Is this really enough to persuade someone to undertake such a perilous journey? Perhaps not, but the designer really does want us to go, for that was the sole reason for building the massive edifice called the Great Pyramid in the first place. What is needed is a little more evidence; something that will prove beyond doubt that this is the correct location.

Miles and miles

Perhaps a short diversion is due here, on the validity of the Thoth mile as a unit. In the book *Thoth*, it was pointed out that the circumference of the Great Pyramid is 1,760 Thoth cubits and the Imperial mile is 1,760 yards. It appeared that there was a correlation between the two, and a great deal of effort was placed into proving that the link I had found was both genuine and intended. It was also noticed that twice the circumference of the Great Pyramid equalled one Nautical mile. This had great relevance because it seemed to explain another long-standing conundrum.

It had long been thought, by new-age Egyptologists, that the perimeter of the Great Pyramid was linked to the circumference of the Earth by the factor of 43,200. The rationale behind this odd-looking ratio, however, was never fully explained to any great satisfaction. But the ratio of the Nautical mile to the Earth's circumference is 21,600, and it so happens that twice this figure is the magical new-age 43,200 ratio (21,600 x 2 = 43,200). It would appear that the perimeter length of the pyramid is an Earth-related dimension, just as many people had suspected. Thus, by extension, the perimeter length of the Great Pyramid can be thought of as an Earth-based unit of measure; the Egyptian or Thoth mile. For ease of calculation, it so happens that one Nautical mile equals two Thoth (tm) miles. This concept of the Thoth mile is fundamental for proving that the Karakoram triangle is a real artifact.

Trouble at the top

Using the Thoth mile as a unit of measure, I was doing some quick calculations on the dimensions of the Karakoram triangle. Since there are 120 Thoth miles (60 Nautical miles) per degree on the surface of the

6. Karakoram Triangle

Earth, my initial calculation suggested that the height and width were as follows:

height 7 x 120 = 840 tm
width 11 x 120 = 1,320 tm

Whoa there! There is a deliberate error here. Eleven degrees of latitude may well equal 660 nm, or 1,320 tm, at the equator, but is certainly does not at the latitude where the Karakoram triangle lies.

Because the Earth is a sphere, the lines of longitude get closer and closer, towards the poles, thus the distance between them gets smaller and smaller. So when measuring along a line of latitude (measuring the longitude), the distance between each degree being measured becomes smaller and smaller the further north or south one travels from the equator. In this case, the figure of 1,320 tm is completely incorrect. However, the figure of 840 tm for the height of the Karakoram triangle is unchanged, as measuring along the lines of longitude (measuring the latitude), is unaffected by one's position on the globe.

The previous results lie in tatters, for the figures simply do not add up. To calculate the width of the Karakoram triangle correctly, the 1,320 units that was found previously needs to multiplied by the sine of the latitude we are measuring along – ie: multiplied by the sine of 39.5°.

$$1,320 \times \sin 39.5° = 840 \text{ tm}.$$

That's more like it! In this case, although the Karakoram triangle measures 11 x 7 degrees – dimensions which are a copy of the ratios found in the Great Pyramid – the actual linear dimensions of the width and height of this triangle are both 840 x 840 Thoth miles (tm).

It would seem to be utterly amazing that one angle can do quite so much in its relationship to both Pi and the Great Pyramid. It can do all this simply because it is the sine of $^7/_{11}$, but nevertheless, let us remind ourselves of the abilities of this amazing angle of 39.5°.

* * *

6. Karakoram Triangle

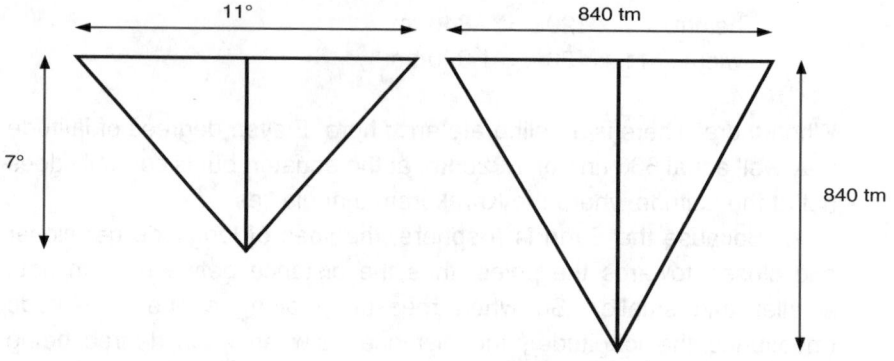

Fig 25.   Triangle by degrees.   Triangle by Thoth miles.

a.   It is (2 x Pi)²
b.   It is the sine of $^7/_{11}$.
c.   When 'beamed' towards the top of the Great Pyramid, it forms a ground length that is equal to the base length of this pyramid.
d.   As the 'midpoint' value between 45° and 32.5°, it forms the difference in angle of **5.5°** and **7°** – which is the ratio of the height of the Great Pyramid to half its base.
e.   When plotted as a coordinate on a map with the angles given in 'd' above, it forms a triangle measuring **11° x 7°** – which is the ratio of the height of the Great Pyramid to its base.
f.   It is the only latitude where **11°** of longitude measures the same <u>in linear measures</u> as **7°** of longitude at the equator.
g.   Remember that $^{11}/_7$ is $^1/_2$ of Pi.

Numbers like 39.5° do not drop out of a hat. They have to be cognitively conceived and designed into a project by a highly skilled architect; especially when they also have to relate to angles such as 32.5° (which is also Pi-related, being the tangent of $^7/_{11}$, as explained earlier in the book). These two numbers are not only both clearly related to Pi, but they also still manage to be 7° removed from each other; 7 being a Pi-related number once more.

Such matters are an unchangeable function of mathematics; it can happen no other way. But to have deliberately chosen these angles in a

102

6. Karakoram Triangle

related fashion, in the same construction project, is not a simple coincidence. Indeed, it is utterly impossible to derive such a string of coincidences by chance. Therefore, it is inconceivable that the design of the Great Pyramid has been achieved by a dumb artisan, squatting in a mud-hut. This has all the hallmarks of being conceived by a highly skilled technician; one whose skills are as far removed from the abilities of a Bronze Age mason as interstellar travel is from the Wright brothers.

Chapter VII

K2

It is at this point in the journey that we must leave the campaigns of Alexander behind us, for the route from here on is far too precipitous for an army and its baggage. Without the discovery of dynamite, the route to Skardu would be impassable to everything but a dozen donkeys in single file. However, had the lightly loaded advance guard of Nearchus, which was sent out by Alexander to interrogate the locals, reached Skardu, they would have been greatly amazed.

There is a confluence of valleys and rivers at Skardu, and the land opens up into a wide, flat and fertile basin, where the mighty Indus slows to a virtual standstill and gently meanders through the plain. For a small population, life in this valley could be quite agreeable. The altitude makes the climate cooler than the plains of India; there is plenty of water for irrigation and much fertile land to sprinkle it upon.

By all accounts, however, Alexander and his main army turned south at Pir Sar and headed for Taxila, near modern Islamabad. There, the victorious Macedonians scored yet another victory over Porus, king of the Pauravas. Following the battle, Alexander's ambition was to push on to the east once more, skirting the Himalayas just to the south and onwards to who knows where. Once more, it is difficult to see what the true ambitions of Alexander were. He had bettered the achievements of Hercules, defeated as many Indians as Dionysus – what more was there a great king could do with a roving army?

Behind him, all across the Middle East – the land he had already conquered needed consolidation – more immigrants from Greece were needed; more tutors of the Greek language and customs, more soldiers to police the indigenous populations; more defences to repel possible invaders; and perhaps more tax collectors to increase the already great wealth of Athens.

There was so much that Alexander should have been doing to ensure that his newly conquered lands remained under Greek control and influence, and the last thing he really needed was yet more conquered lands to protect and administer. So what was really on Alexander's mind: the location of the legendary Hall of Records perhaps? We may never find out exactly what Alexander's intentions really were, for as he tried to push his army towards the east once more, his generals at last tired of the campaign and rebelled. They had set off from Greece in early 334 BC, and it was now the spring of 326. The campaign had already lasted eight years and it had taken the resourceful Macedonians, on foot, over 10,000 kilometers of inhospitable, heavily defended terrain; across three continents and through innumerable battles. The men longed to see their homeland; their wives and children once more – enough was enough. Finally, a very brave general, Coenus, son of Polemocrates, spoke up for the common soldier:

> I do not propose to speak for the officers assembled, as we have already received the rewards of our services ... I speak therefore for the common soldiers ... Every man of them longs to see his parents again, if they yet survive, or his wife, or his children; all are yearning for the familiar earth of home, hoping, pardonably enough, to live to revisit it ... Do not try to lead men who are unwilling to follow you; if their hearts are not in it, you will never find the old spirit or old courage. [1]

It was a courageous statement to make to Alexander, in front of his assembled men. The men applauded Coenus and wept, but Alexander flew into a rage and called them deserters. Seeing that the men were unmoved by his rage, Alexander then went into a sulk hoping, says Arrian, that the men would take pity on him and decide to follow their great leader out of sheer respect. The stand off continued for three whole days until Alexander, ever the pragmatic leader of men, obviously decided that the men really *had* had enough.

But how was Alexander going to change his mind without loss of face in front of his men? The trick was simple, cunning and, more importantly, a tried and tested methodology in the ancient world. As was the tradition, the oracle would be consulted to see what omens the gods would give for the campaign to the east. A sacrifice was made and the pensive priest rummaged around in the innards of the slaughtered beast to divine the future for the Macedonians. The priest gave the prediction and, most unusually for Alexander's campaign omens, they were in this case predictably bad. It was the gods, therefore, that had decided the matter for Alexander; there was no choice but to turn back and head for home. The troops were, not surprisingly, elated and wept before Alexander, giving him every blessing. After eight long years, Alexander's quest into the Himalayas had finally ended, but ours has only just begun.

Askole

The two Landcruisers made laborious progress as they clawed their way up the gravel track. For seven hours, we had crashed and jerked our way across the landscape from Skardu to Askole, in the east, but unfortunately the road was now blocked by a landslide. Our party consisted of myself, Altef, a cook and fifteen porters. All the kit was unloaded, taken across the obstruction and we caught a 'bus' the other side. The 'bus' was simply another Landcruiser than runs a daily service up this road; the only problem being that we now had eighteen people and 500 kg of equipment on this one vehicle. Needless to say, it lurched and weaved its way down the unmade goat-track.

At last, the hamlet of Askole appeared on a hillside. Now we were deep into the Karakoram, the road finished and the trekking could finally begin. We climbed up a steep valley to the little village of Askole, which appeared to be unchanged from the time of its ancient Neolithic predecessors. There appeared to be nothing from the outside world that had penetrated this lonely outpost of subsistence farmers. Perhaps there was a portable generator here or there but, to be honest, the bother of carting fuel up that little valley made me doubt even this.

We purchased a small goat for the trip, at what seemed like an exorbitant rate, the village apparently doing a good trade with the passing trekkers and mountaineers. I named the hapless goat Lunch, and he was to be our lively companion for a week or so. The track took us along the Biaho Lungma river, which was itself a tributary of the Indus. The going was relatively easy and we made good progress up to the campsite at Korophon. The tents were erected and supper was on the

7. K2

brew in next to no time; something that would become a comforting routine as the going got rougher and tougher.

The next day's trek took us out of our way a little, to find the bridge to cross the Dumordo tributary. Unfortunately, the Dumordo river cut a little too deeply into its river banks at one point and we were forced to take to the hills to get around the fast-flowing and freezing waters. The track here was as narrow and as precipitous as any I have seen, just 30cm wide and with a 100 m drop, off to the right, in case you lost your footing. If I had stopped to think about my location it could have proved a little worrying, so I pressed on regardless of the possibilities. I soon learned that a good, solid walking stick is not a fashion accessory just because Prince Charles poses with one; it saved many a tumble ranging from the insignificant to the possibly fatal.

The night-time temperatures were cooler now as we pressed up towards Payu. From the stifling heat of the lowland plains, the overnight temperatures had now reduced to a more comfortable $5^{\circ C}$, but during the midday Sun that figure could easily rise to 20 or $25^{\circ C}$, making the walking unbearably hot. Still, as we were pressing on towards the Baltoro glacier, we might need all the heat we could get, so the hope was for more good weather.

It couldn't last and it didn't. It took us three days to get to Payu, at the foot of the Baltoro glacier, and at that point the wind and rain lashed the campsite and we had to sit tight for a day to let it blow through. It was at this point that Altef, the Sirdar guide, judged that we needed more protein and so Lunch, the goat, was about to have an unlucky day. Being a predominantly Muslim community, the resulting meat would have to be halal, which is a very similar concept to the Jewish kosher food preparation. As Islam is another offshoot of Judaism, perhaps this is not too surprising.

Halal meat involves a few simple prayers and the animal being bled to death, thus the method of dispatching the goat is to cut its throat. Unlike the Hollywood versions of these events, the real thing is a little more messy, with a great deal of sawing and hacking going on. Lunch, the goat, was not too impressed with this idea and struggled vainly, but eventually settled into a comatose position. After a few minutes, the procedure was over and everyone relaxed, except Lunch, who got up and tried to run away despite his head not being fully attached. The sudden panic eventually subsided, Lunch was caught and finally became dinner.

7. K2

Baltoro

Luckily, the next day brought fine, clear weather and we set off once more, climbing up onto the Baltoro glacier itself. I found the landscape rather peculiar. It was not quite as I had imagined it – there was no ice! What happens is that as the ice makes its sedate way down the valley, it gets contaminated with tonnes of falling rocks from the mountains above. The midday sun in the summer is powerful enough to melt the topmost layers of the glacier, and the resulting water finds little cracks and crevasses to run down to the bottom of the glacier. The result is that the surface of the glacier is covered in a thick layer of rocks, boulders, gravel and sand.

In fact, walking on the glacier is rather like one would imagine walking on the Moon to be. It is rough underfoot; it is often slippery because of the ice underneath; and it is full of rocky ridges and hills, some tens of meters high. Far from being an easy walk up a smooth ice-flow, it was a major scramble up and down great heaps of rock and rubble. The types of surface in one day of trekking was simply amazing. We might start on gravel; progress onto smooth granite boulders; hit a pocket of limestone nodules; trudge through some sand dunes; and slip on some shale scree, all in the space of a few hundred meters.

At one point, we had to come off the glacier due to a crevasse and climbed high up the mountain-side once more. We were on another of those goat-tracks suspended on a ledge the width of a sheet of paper, only this time the valley floor was some 300 m below us. I began to recall some climbing tips I had received when a student on a climbing expedition, and they began to revolve around my brain incessantly. Don't walk under unstable overhangs. Don't walk on top of unstable overhangs. Don't climb on scree slopes. Remove sand from your shoes before climbing.

Unfortunately, the majority of this trek broke every rule in the book along the whole of the route. Most of the trail was in, or around, alluvial deposits that were loosely bound with mud. The rivers and glacier were continually trying to reclaim these deposits, and this was the material we were walking over and underneath. Much of it was unstable in the extreme, presenting us with vast and fragile overhangs and undercuts, to be navigated as quickly as possible.

The trek along the Baltoro was, I have to admit, more soul-destroying than uplifting. The terrain was almost impassable and the scenery reminiscent of a coal-mining slag heap. In addition, we were now over 4,500 meters up (15,000 ft) and the atmosphere was decidedly thin. Every exertion sucked the breath from your body and I found myself hyperventilating after the smallest of climbs. Eventually, I had to give up my backpack to a porter, which made a great difference and I was able to stride on for another couple of hours with renewed vigour. The Baltoro trek took two whole days of hard slog, but eventually we came to a major confluence of glaciers – Concordia. At last, the beauty of the snowcapped mountain peaks could be viewed in all their glory. We were close to the ultimate goal, the whole reason for this arduous reconnaissance mission to the roof of the world.

But why did I have so much confidence that this was the precise location I should go to? The Karakoram triangle is a massive area to search, and it would have been foolhardy in the extreme to have gone scouting around without some more detailed information. Luckily, the area that needs to be searched can be whittled down considerably by just looking at a map and surveying the topography, because there is a specific location inside the Karakoram triangle that marks the true location of the Hall of Records, and that location lies in the very center of the triangle.

This is quite a dramatic development, because what we have here is another layer of deliberate obfuscation. The master architect has managed to provide precise coordinates within the Great Pyramid that *do not* point at the required location. This is an important point because it means that knowing just half or three-quarters of the answer is not good enough. The whole edifice of the Great Pyramid needs to be fully understood before the proper location can be found. If those deliberately hidden shafts in the Queen's Chamber, for instance, had not been found, then there would have been no possibility of finding the secret location in the Karakoram.

In addition, the Karakoram triangle concept prevents a cursory glance at a map – using the shaft angles as coordinates – from being successful. In fact I was trying out this technique years ago, looking at all the possible coordinates that the shafts could provide. Of course I found nothing, but now I find that the whole escapade was deliberately arranged specifically so that I would *not* find anything – for at that time, I had not made all the necessary deductions. This is fast becoming a battle of wills between myself and the Giza designer.

What, then, is so special about the middle of the Karakoram triangle?

7. K2

The center point of this triangle is marked by the coordinates of 45° east and 36° north, based on the Giza meridian. If those figures are plotted on a large-scale map of the area, the finger comes to rest on the site of the K2 mountain. Here is the final and fitting resting place of the legendary Hall of Records.

It is not just the fact that the mountain, K2, lies at the center of the Karakoram triangle that marks this particular peak out as being so particularly suitable as the desired location that the architect had in mind; K2 also happens to be the highest mountain in the whole area, and the second highest in the world. Mount Everest is a considerable distance away, on the northern borders of Nepal, and while it may be initially considered a more suitable location for that reason, I rapidly thought otherwise. Being the highest mountain in the world, Everest has become a magnet for adventurers and the whole area is now crisscrossed with tourists looking for the ultimate trek. K2, on the other hand, still lies in relatively lonely isolation. A great deal of thought appears to have gone into all of this.

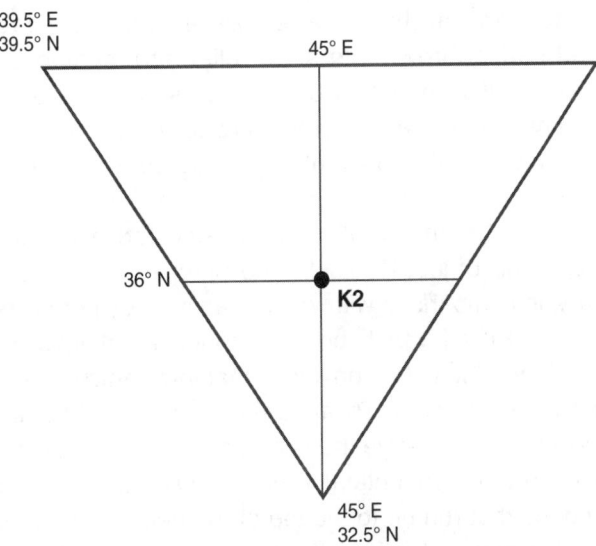

Fig 26.   The center of the Karakoram triangle.

7. K2

So, there does seem to be some merit in identifying K2 as the intended location that a researcher was supposed to come to, but what made me so sure about this? At first, and apart from K2's size, there seemed to be nothing particularly special about K2 and its environs. The small-scale map I had of the region just showed valley after valley, and peak after peak, running in every direction and off nearly every side of the map. It looked like an impenetrable and desolate region, dotted with small villages and snake-like tracks and roads. But every peak and every valley looked nearly identical, so what made K2 in any way special? Apart from the obvious fact that K2 was a mountain that would be perennially covered in snow, and the fact that I thought that the Great Pyramid represented a white mountain peak, there seemed to be nothing special about the whole region whatsoever.

But, when looking back over all the evidence I had unearthed so far, curiosity got the better of me. There had to be something that I had missed, perhaps something in the detail of the mountain itself. What I needed was a better scale map, and so I turned to all the specialist map retailers I could find. My first efforts were not very rewarding. All I managed to obtain were poor copies of maps based on Victorian and 1950s military surveys, and none of these showed any detailed features. Next, I turned to NASA and the photographic evidence taken from space. Some of the shuttle shots and satellite images were quite spectacular, with snowcapped peaks thrown into stark relief by a setting Sun, but the image of K2 itself remained frustratingly small. Nevertheless, the mountain seemed to be clearly pyramidal and white, even in the summer pictures; and it was sufficiently interesting to convince me to continue the search.

Eventually, I found what I was looking for: a detailed Chinese topographical map of just K2 itself. The precise detail of the map was extraordinary, in comparison with what I had already purchased, and the details of the peak itself were to be no disappointment either. Here was all the evidence I needed to be convinced that this particular mountain was the chosen site that the Great Pyramid was pointing to. Of all the mountain peaks in the Karakoram range, K2 is particularly pyramidal in shape. Not only is the base of the mountain surprisingly square, but there are also four main ridges that run up to the top of the peak, exactly as the Great Pyramid has. Furthermore, those four main ridges are clearly orientated with the cardinal points on a map – they are even labelled as being northwest, northeast, southeast and southwest. Thus, the peak of K2 is orientated with the compass points in exactly the same fashion as the Great Pyramid itself.

But that is not all. As was mentioned earlier in the book, the pure white Tura limestone on the pyramids was intended to be a representation of snow on a mountain peak. As the Great Pyramid has no granite at its base, the mountain peak that it mimics should also be pure white, with no trace of a seasonal snow-line around the base. The K2 peak lies so far up the Karakoram that it is permanently covered in snow. It is a pure white peak based on a square base that is orientated with the cardinal points. The similarity is so striking between these two peaks that the immediate thought that springs to mind is that the Great Pyramid may have been modelled on K2 itself.

Causeway

As I reached the confluence of the glaciers at Concordia and turned towards the north, there it was in all its splendour – K2. It was just as the maps portrayed it: a massive pyramidal edifice covered in a pure white cladding of snow and ice – a perfect model for the design of the Giza plateau. From Concordia, the view of K2 is seen through the valley of the Godwin Austen glacier and so in certain lights, at dawn or dusk, the brilliant white peak of K2 can be seen to sparkle through the dark and brooding valley sides.

Tired, hungry and gasping for breath, I sat down on a large boulder and surveyed the scene. By the time I had reached the camp, my tent was nearly up already and I could smell the first wisps of braised meat on the cooker: dinner wouldn't be long. It would be half an hour before the sun completely vanished behind the hills and plunged us into darkness, so I took the opportunity of studying the map in the fading half-light.

I had both maps with me, K2 and Giza, and it was quite evident that the list of similarities between K2 and the Great Pyramid carried on. The plan-view of the Giza plateau shows off not only the massive structures of the pyramids themselves, but also another key feature of the whole Giza site – the massive causeways that thrust out from each of the pyramids. In fact, looking at the Great Pyramid, it is evident that the causeway originally ran down the plateau; and thrust out over the edge of the plateau and it therefore had to be carried outwards on the top of a massive embankment. Herodotus, who was able to visit the site when the pyramids were still substantially complete, had this to say of the Great Pyramid's causeway:

> This causeway is five furlongs in length, ten fathoms wide, and in highest part, eight fathoms. It is built of polished stone, and is covered with carvings of animals ... It took ten years oppression of the people to make the causeway for the conveyance of the stones, a work not much inferior, in my judgement, to the pyramid itself. [2]

Clearly, the Great Pyramid causeway was a substantial feat of engineering in itself, as it seems to have contained a massive amount of masonry. For the designer to have gone to all this trouble – to extend the causeway out over the edge of the plateau in this fashion – indicates that the shape and length of the causeway must have been important. The causeways must, therefore, be somehow linked to the overall Giza plan; they must have an important meaning or symbolism.

Indeed, I believe that they are important, but this observation just serves to give us a further mystery to ponder on, for the causeways lead us straight back to the plans of K2. In my mind, the evidence is inescapable and the map of K2 explains exactly where the imagery for the pyramid causeways was derived from. Each and every mountain peak in the high Karakoram has its own causeway – a vast glacier moving slowly away from its base. K2, being the highest peak in the area, is no exception; in fact, it has a massive glacier that runs out to the south, slowly grinding the lower hillsides into submission. It was the very glacier that I was standing upon.

The pyramid causeways are nothing more than slightly stylistic, but nonetheless quite accurate, representations of those enormous ice-flows. Both the glaciers and causeways slope downwards as they track away from the mountain or pyramid. In addition, and quite incredibly, the Godwin Austen glacier, that flows from the base of K2, starts in the middle of the mountain's baseline, just as the Giza causeway does. It then flows southwards at an angle just about 14° to the right of the cardinal point, exactly as the Great Pyramid causeway runs 14° to the right of the cardinal point. Although the K2 glacier thrusts out to the south, whereas the Great Pyramid causeway runs out to the east, the angle at which they travel looks suspiciously familiar, and that 90° shift in orientation will be fully explained later.

Sitting in the doorway of my tent and looking up towards the peak of K2, I was now effectively standing on a copy of the Great Pyramid's causeway and looking at the pyramid itself. If one can imagine standing at the base of the causeway and looking up at the Great Pyramid, three subsidiary pyramids nestling at the left-hand base of the pyramid will be noticed. In a clear mimicry, as I looked from the vantage point of Concordia, there was a clear lump of rock with a pyramidal crest lying to the left-hand base of K2 – the Angelus peak.

That was not all. As I surveyed the scene in the dying rays and plummeting temperatures of late afternoon, I began to trace the line of the Godwin Austen glacier. Looking behind me, the glacier made a distinct left turn as it started rising upwards once more to the Baltoro Kangri. Maps of the original line of the Great Pyramid's causeway show the same kink; the line of the pyramid's causeway, which was built on top of a man-made embankment, shows a distinct and verifiable turn to the left. The symmetry is now complete; the two peaks are identical in everything except size.

Discovery

There was one important thing that cannot be over-emphasised in all of this. I started this quest as a paper exercise in my suburban office, looking at the dimensions and angles of the shafts contained inside the Great Pyramid. Without any preconceptions, those angles led me eastwards into the Himalayas – indeed my preconceptions, if I had any, were rather forcing me to look towards the Atlantic.

Having overcome my reticence to look at the Himalayas, it appeared that the location of K2 was being picked out as being somehow special. Having spent weeks tracking down a large-scale map of the site, I eventually discovered that this peak looked exactly like the Great Pyramid. In this case, the image of the continents and the angles of the shafts in the Great Pyramid, that consistently pointed towards the Himalayas, now seemed to point at an exact copy of the Great Pyramid itself! The edifice that started this whole madcap exercise points at a natural sister or mother monument! To be rewarded with such stunning symmetry was truly amazing and satisfying. There had to be some kind of deliberate causal element to all of this – a cognitive design.

In my mind, it is now perfectly clear where the concept of both the shape of the pyramids and the general layout of the Giza plateau came from in the first place. It was simply a copy of the K2 mountain and its immediate environs. The similarity between the two images is so close, it is almost as if the K2 peak had been uprooted and planted on the Giza plateau – they are identical concepts. This, then, is the Ma'at, the long-lost truth that the Egyptians and many others besides have been looking for over the past millennia.

To say that the Giza plateau was modelled on the K2 mountain may seem like a massive leap of faith, but this is only so if one is still thinking in classical terms. The whole point of this quest is to look beyond the possible and into the realms of the impossible. This is a quest of the 'gods' and, of course, the gods are capable of many things we might deem impossible. Thus, the bold assumption is that the Great Pyramid was modelled on the K2 peak and this was done for one specific purpose: to confirm that this is indeed the correct location to explore. This is it; the final resting place for the records of the gods lies somewhere in or around the K2 mountain.

Impossible

Having found the most likely location of the Hall of Records is not only a great achievement, it is also a little puzzling, perhaps even disturbing. The K2 peak was quite obviously the role-model for the design of the pyramids, while the Great Pyramid was itself designed with suitable internal structures that point back towards the location of the mountain that inspired its creation. And all this was done in order that the original mountain could be located.

So far, so good. The problems only begin to surface when one realises that finding the location of K2 was made possible by using the actual location of the Great Pyramid as a reference point. It is from this reference point that the cartographical journey begins and is sourced. But this appears to be a classic catch-22 situation. The shaft coordinates within the Great Pyramid, used to find the Karakoram triangle, are relatively fixed. Indeed, they are not only fixed by the dimensions of the Great Pyramid, but they are also fixed by their dependence on the mathematical constant, Pi. But the K2 peak is also, quite obviously, at a fixed location. It is a fixed topographical feature that cannot be shifted around to suit the coordinates, inside the Great Pyramid, that have been generated by Pi.

This leaves the Great Pyramid as being the only part of this whole grand design that appears to have any freedom of movement. Yet the pyramid also appears to be rather fixed in its location. The Great Pyramid lies almost exactly on the 30° north parallel and it also lies on the exact location where the Nile divides up into the cone-shaped marshes of the delta. Had K2 been located a little further westwards within the Karakoram range, the Great Pyramid would have had to have been built out in the Western Desert to get the coordinates to match. Would it really have been built in such a location?

The problems are not much easier to explain back at the Karakoram location either. The K2 peak lies almost exactly at the center of the Karakoram triangle, yet this triangle is clearly defined by its relationship to Pi. The longitude of the triangle (its east-west location) can be made to drift, depending on the position of the Great Pyramid, but the latitude (the north-south location) is fixed by Pi, especially that 39.5° latitude dependent on the sine of the Pi ratio, $^7/_{11}$. It is true that other mathematical functions could have been used as the coordinate system for finding K2, but it is still rather fortuitous to have found the second largest mountain in the world conforming so compliantly with the dictates of Pi.

Chapter VIII

Grand Plan

From our base at Concordia, we slowly and breathlessly made our way up the Godwin Austen glacier. Effectively, the journey was the equivalent of walking up the Great Pyramid causeway, from the edge of the Giza plateau towards the base of the pyramid. But the scale of K2 is rather larger than at Giza and the journey took another whole day. It certainly did not help matters that we were now at an altitude of 5,300 meters (17,400 ft) the going was getting rather tough.

I consider myself to be reasonably fit, but I soon found that I was stopping every 100 m or so to catch my breath. In the end, I had to relinquish my camera bag as well as my backpack. It was only another 2 or 3 kilos, but it felt like a millstone had been lifted from my neck. The pace slowed to a crawl as I huffed and puffed at every step; it was as if my boots were being pulled out of treacle. The going was slightly easier now, with the glacier's surface less contorted by the pressures that build up further down the valley; but still, every hillock seemed like a mountain, every pebble a boulder. Eventually, after a day spent sweltering in the glaring high-altitude sunshine, we approached the day's goal – K2 base camp.

What I was looking for was evidence of a Hall of Records, whatever that might be. But without any real data to go on as to the form that this mythical cavern would take, the best option seemed to be to look for more similarities between Great Pyramid and K2. The Great Pyramid contains many chambers, and if any of these chambers had once contained ancient papyri we would have had, in effect, an ancient 'Hall of Records'.

8. Grand Plan

If this great mountain in the Himalaya were indeed the model upon which the Great Pyramid was based, then perhaps we can take this similarity one stage further. The Great Pyramid has internal chambers; could there be a similar arrangement inside K2? The Great Pyramid has an entrance in the northern face of the pyramid; could there be a similar entrance, perhaps on the same face of K2?

The image of artisans, toiling away at these altitudes in the distant historical past, is all rather speculative, but this is what the myths of Dionysus were all about – the moving of large quantities of rock in the Karakoram. It was also the very reason that I was now standing at the base of K2 – to find any evidence of further similarities between these two structures. These myths had turned up so many interesting coincidences already, that perhaps just one more might reveal itself.

Big Brother

K2 is rather larger than the Great Pyramid, however, so to make any comparisons whatsoever between the two structures, what is needed is a scale to work to. How much bigger than the Great Pyramid is the peak of K2? This, I believe, is probably the true purpose of the morass of data that is explained within the appendix at the end of the book.

The easiest comparison one could make between the two structures would be simply to look at maps of them and make an inspired guess. It is only when we start this process that we begin to see even more remarkable similarities between the two structures. In order to make this comparison, however, the two maps need to be orientated properly. As in so many aspects of this story, there appears to be one more twist (literally) to the plot. It would seem that east is not east and north is not north.

Take a look at the following diagrams of K2 and the Great Pyramid. Yes, they do look incredibly similar, but in order to achieve this comparison one of the diagrams has been twisted by 90°. It is difficult to know why it has been done in this fashion. Perhaps it was an intended disguise, to confuse the uninitiated and casual observer. Perhaps the physical orientation of K2 did not fit the specifications for the Great Pyramid, where the causeways (glaciers) need to point towards the rising Sun in the east.

Whatever the reason for this layout, the justification for us being able to make the final twist in this story – and thus claim that it was an intended part of the original grand plan – is contained within the chambers of the Great Pyramid. Looking at the upper chambers of the pyramid, it will be noted that the Grand Gallery rises up to meet the King's Chamber from the north. It is only separated from the King's Chamber itself by the small anti-chamber, otherwise it could be thought of as abutting the north wall of the King's Chamber.

Looking instead at the Queen's Chamber, it can be seen that there is a very similar structure in this chamber. The 'niche' is a corbeled recess inside this chamber, which Egyptologists have claimed once contained a statue of the pharaoh, but it could just as easily be considered to be a smaller representation of the Grand Gallery. Indeed, many of its dimensions are exact $^3/_4$ scale duplications of the layout of the Grand Gallery. This niche, however, is not in the northern wall of the Queen's Chamber; it is in the east.

(Not to scale)

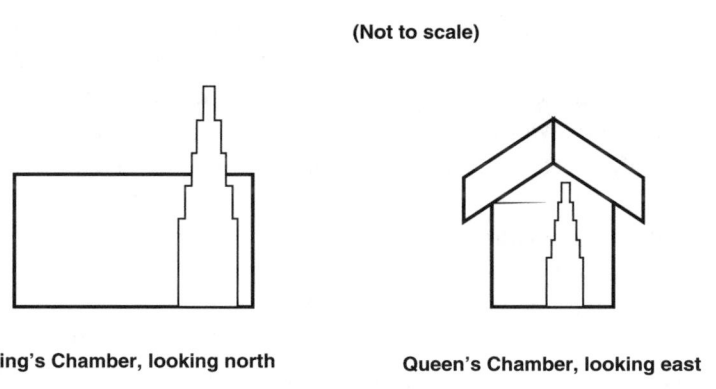

King's Chamber, looking north   **Queen's Chamber, looking east**

Fig 27. The two Grand Galleries.

In making the twist from the King's Chamber (where the Grand Gallery is in the north) to the Queen's Chamber (where the niche is in the east), a change of 90° has been made. The clear inference is that the Grand Gallery, and the entire pyramid structure, can be imagined as being twisted clockwise from north around to the east. If this change were also mimicked by the orientation of the causeway outside the pyramid, the real correlation with K2 itself can be clearly seen.

8. Grand Plan

The Great Pyramid's causeway, in reality, faces east. If it were turned in the same way as the Grand Gallery appears to have been, then it would end up running out to the south instead. On the plan of K2, it can be seen that the main glacier from the base of the mountain is heading off towards the south, just as the twisted plan of the Great Pyramid's causeway does. Not only this, but the angles of these structures are identical too. The angle of the Great Pyramid's causeway, relative to the base of the pyramid, measures 14° to the 'left'. The angle of the Godwin Austen glacier, relative to the base of K2, measures 14° to the 'left'. A remarkable coincidence if ever there were one.

In fact, the whole feel of the K2 peak is unerringly, and perhaps chillingly, familiar to any Egyptophile. Take a look, once more, at these similarities:

a.   The base of the mountain, just to the west of the Godwin glacier, has a series of small peaks. Likewise, the Great Pyramid has three smaller pyramids in a similar position beside the causeway.

b.   The Great Pyramid was originally cased in pure white Tura limestone, and it must have been an awesome sight when it was originally completed. Likewise, the K2 peak is above the winter snow-line; unlike the lower peaks, it is always covered in snow and shines as brilliantly in the sunlight as the Great Pyramid once did.

c.   The Great Pyramid is a four-sided pyramid, orientated to the four cardinal points. The K2 mountain is also a four-sided peak, aligned to the cardinal points.

d.   The Great Pyramid also has small indentations in the side of each face; each face being very slightly concave. These indentations are so small that they can only be seen in certain angles of sunlight, when only one half of a face of the pyramid is illuminated. The indentation is real, but it is only about a couple of cubits deep at its maximum. This may be considered an insignificant point, but in the book *Thoth*, I argued that this small indentation would considerably add to the structural stiffness of each face of the pyramid. When looking at the K2 peak, however, the original precedent for this design is to be seen.

The K2 peak is a precise, four-sided pyramid, orientated to the

8. *Grand Plan*

cardinal points, exactly like the Great Pyramid. Each face, however, is slightly convex. Instead of having slight indentations, each face of the K2 peak has a slight ridge protruding out of it. The design is exactly the same, with both pyramids being, in reality, slightly eight-sided instead of four-sided.

In this case, one might ask, why not make the Great Pyramid exactly like the K2 peak; with small ridges instead of indentations? The answer is that the small ridges are unstable elements in a design. This might be fine for a mountain, which (fault-lines apart) could be considered as being composed of one block of stone, but it might spell disaster for a pyramid. The Great Pyramid is composed of loosely-fitting blocks of stone, so it requires as many elements of stability as possible. For this reason, the ridges on the K2 peak have been mirrored on the Great Pyramid cousin as slight indentations; thus, the design remains essentially the same, but extra stability has been added to the pyramid version.

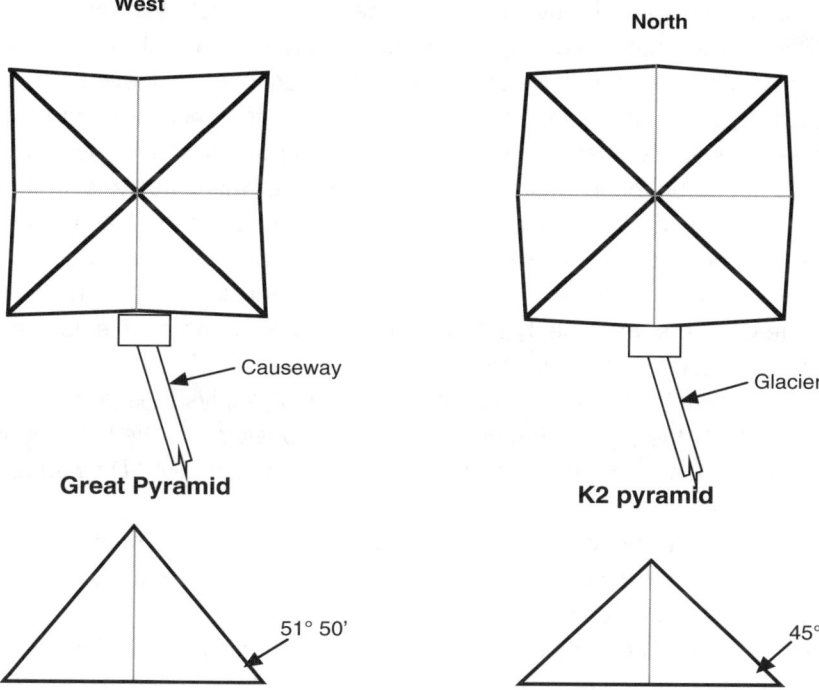

Fig 28.   K2 and Great Pyramid.

8. Grand Plan

The only way in which these two peaks differ is in their slope angles. The Great Pyramid is designed around the mathematical constant, Pi; it has a rise of 7 cubits for every 5.5 cubits along the base, which gives a slope angle of 51° 50′. The K2 peak is clearly at a different angle, and a quick look at the rough dimensions is quite illuminating. The base length of K2 seems to be about 5,200 meters at its widest point. The maximum height of the peak is 8,611 meters above mean sea level (amsl), and down at the base of the mountain it averages 6,000 meters amsl. Thus, the height of the peak above the surrounding terrain is about 2,600 meters. The K2 peak, where it thrusts its way out of the surrounding terrain, therefore forms a rather symmetrical, and unusually perfect, 45° slope angle.

Slope angle aside, the similarity of the K2 and the Great Pyramid is truly astounding. But this is not a simple similarity between a topographical feature and a pyramid. Remember that this discovery has only been made because the shaft angles in the Great Pyramid directed us towards this location in the first place. Having been mathematically 'instructed' to look further at the K2 peak, I duly purchased (with great difficulty) a large-scale map of the area, only to find that its layout is identical to the Great Pyramid. That this has been achieved in this fashion, and in this chronological order, seems to conclusively indicate that this was the intention of the designer and not a simple coincidence. *This* has to be the location in which the designer wishes us to search.

But where do we have to look? The area around K2 is a vast place. The base of K2 itself covers some 27 square kilometers, and if one includes the Great Pyramid causeways and the rest of the Giza plateau, there may be hundreds of square kilometers of equivalent terrain around K2 in which to search.

What we are looking for, in the final analysis, is a possible location for the Hall of Records, the fabled repository for the knowledge of the ancient gods. What form would this repository take? Do we have any clues?

It has been suggested in other works, based largely on the testimony of the 'sleeping prophet', Edgar Cayce, that the repository was an underground chamber, with twelve rooms arranged around the perimeter, and perhaps even a small golden pyramid in the middle. Such predictions, however, are likely to be complete fabrications to help entertain the faithful. The followers of these mysteries always want to know more, but there has always been very little information to give, so the next best alternative is to create some fanciful stories to satisfy their demands. Thus, the stories become ever more bizarre and the storytellers ever more wealthy.

But with all the information that has been gathered in this book so far, we are in a much better and realistic position to predict the likely form that a potential Hall of Records might take. It can now be clearly seen that, in the vast and majestic wastes of the Himalayas, there is a copy of the Great Pyramid (or visa versa). Thus, a sensible prediction might be that the actual chamber of records, which has been searched for for so long and by so many, would also be a copy of the original; a copy of the Great Pyramid chambers. These chambers would lie deep within the K2 mountain – a rather mind-boggling assumption perhaps, but that is to be the working hypothesis.

The chambers in the Great Pyramid, as we all know, were originally accessed through a small passageway that enters the pyramid through an entrance, a short way up the northern face of the pyramid. Originally, the totally smooth face of the pyramid made access to the entrance block rather awkward. In fact, the only practical method of reaching the entrance would have been to erect a suitably long set of ladders to reach the entrance stone.

Since the entrance is some 20 meters up the face of the pyramid, this is not something that could have been accomplished without drawing attention to one's actions. Anyone trying to gain access to the pyramid would immediately be spotted by the authorities, which is an obvious and sensible precaution, bearing in mind the urge that many might have to plunder the pyramid's potential contents.

The form that the original entrance itself took is also an interesting question. For the answer to this, as we briefly touched on previously, I am indebted to the works of Sir Flinders Petrie once more. He noted, among other things, that the layer of core and casing blocks, in which the entrance passageway met the casing stones, was arranged to be exactly as thick as the entrance was high. This is a sensible design arrangement, to prevent any small slivers of stone being required around the entrance itself.

Above this entrance layer were two smaller layers that, when combined together, made a very thick layer within which to place the massive blocks that normally sat on top of entrance-ways, and gave them both strength and stability. For the design of the door itself, Petrie noted the works of Strabo, who says:

8. Grand Plan

> The Great Pyramid, a little way up on one side, has a stone that may be taken out, which being raised up there is a sloping passage to the foundations. [1]

It sounds as if there is a door made of stone that is moveable in some way, such that it can be moved upwards and outwards at the same time. This sounds like a hinged arrangement with the hinge at the top of the stone. Is Strabo to be trusted with this report?

Well, certainly he is clearly aware that behind the entrance stone there was a sloping passageway to the 'foundations', and this is obviously not a hearsay report. If this were simply a guess based on the form of other plundered pyramids, he would have been more likely to have said the passageway terminated in a chamber. The comment that the passageway ends in the pyramid's 'foundations' is a reasonable assessment of the rough-hewn cavern that actually sits at the base of the Great Pyramid.

This allows us to assess Strabo's report with some confidence. Firstly, it means that the descending passage was well known in his day, Secondly, that the casing blocks and entrance were still *in situ*. And thirdly, that the entrance block seems to have been a moveable block, as has just been described.

Petrie also backed this up with a detailed study of the entrances to the Vega (Bent) Pyramid – the only pyramid that has the doorways to the entrance still intact. He found that, on either side of the entrance, there were round holes cut opposite each other, about 9 cm in diameter by 14 cm deep. These holes were just inside the entrance and only a short distance from the top of the passage. Petrie, not unreasonably, interpreted these as being the hinge sockets to swing the stone-block door from. Behind these sockets, the passageway extended horizontally for a small way, terminating in a vertical face with more door sockets. These were smaller vertical sockets for a very lightweight door.

The following diagrams were developed by Petrie, based on his analysis of the Vega Pyramid entrance. The hinged stone door is clearly marked as the large shaded stone. It needs to be this shape, with a long top extending backwards, in order to counterbalance the weight of the stone. The amount of counterbalance at the top would be judiciously arranged by the architect, so that the force required to open the stone was within normal human limitations; say about 25 kg of force.

Behind the hinged stone is the vertically hinged wooden door, which opens up backwards, in towards the body of the pyramid. A cutout in the descending passage has been arranged to accept the top of the door. The function of this lightweight door is most likely to be for weather protection, to stop sand from accumulating and eventually blocking the descending passage.

This is the recorded history of the original entrance to the Great Pyramid; a stone 'trap door' waiting to surprise the potential explorer. The original entrance to the Great

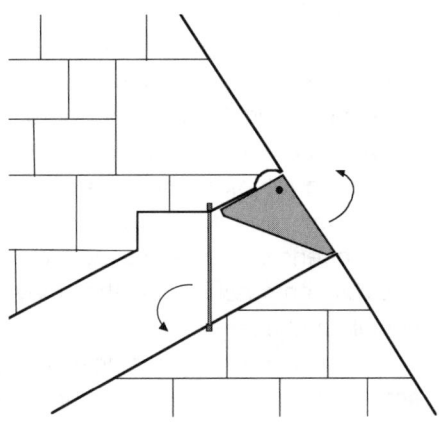

Fig 29. Great Pyramid entrance - closed.

Pyramid was probably left 'unlocked' in order to deter would-be tomb robbers; for there would be no point plundering a 'tomb' that was already open and manifestly empty. The K2 equivalent, were it ever to be found, would also most likely be left open, for who in the world would stumble across it in such a remote location?

Here, then, is the most likely scenario for the entrance to any potential Hall of Records. If K2 is itself an imitation of the Great Pyramid (or visa versa), then it is a reasonable assumption that the entrance would follow a similar arrangement – a simple hinged stone in the same position on the face of the K2 peak, just as is to be found on the Great Pyramid itself.

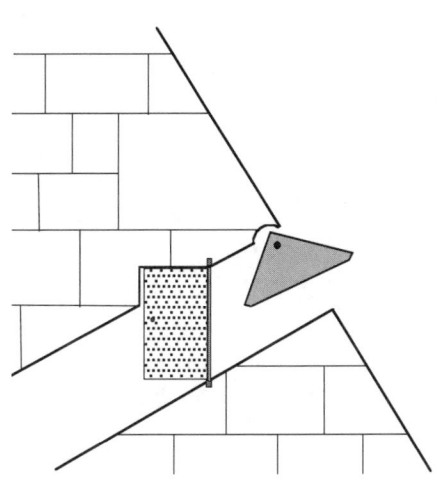

Fig 30. Great Pyramid entrance - open.

8. Grand Plan

Crevasse

Unfortunately, as our small exploration party trekked towards the south-eastern corner of the K2 pyramid, we stumbled upon a series of large crevasses in the ice. We were totally stuck; without proper climbing equipment and techniques, there was no way across. After travelling across much of the globe to reach this precise location, I was unable to even take a look around the corner at the eastern face of K2. It was a bitter blow and the return journey was made in an atmosphere of despondency. Thus, the exact nature of the eastern face of K2, and any possible entrance stone that may or may not exist there, remains a complete mystery.

But the story has now been told and the stage has equally been set. I am sure that there will be a return journey to K2 in the very near future; if not by me, then perhaps by another interested party. Perhaps that expedition may even include yourself...

Appendix 1

Squaring the Circle

The external dimensions of the Second and Third Pyramids have always posed a problem for adepts of sacred geometry, for when they are measured using the Thoth (Royal) cubit, these pyramids appear to have been constructed using dimensions that are composed of decidedly odd numbers of cubits. The base lengths of the Second and Third Pyramids appear to measure 411 and 201.5 Thoth cubits (tc) respectively. This has caused a great deal of head-scratching and a great deal of my time to be wasted in going through every permutation of new possible units of measure that may, or may not, have been used in the construction of these two pyramids.

Several possible measurement units (cubit lengths) were found that simplified the dimensions of these pyramids, including the very plausible 0.1915 meter and 0.544 meter cubits, which initially proved very versatile in fitting the dimensions of these two pyramids and producing whole numbers for the internal chambers. Unfortunately each and every new unit of measure that I created developed one or more flaws along the way, and these new cubit lengths were no exception. Either this dimension or that dimension within the pyramid would suddenly not fit into a neat set of whole or meaningful numbers and the plausibility of that new cubit would rapidly diminish.

I became convinced that the text books were wrong and the measurements that they gave were not as accurate as they claimed. So further time and expense was wasted in going to Egypt and re-measuring the pertinent chambers using a laser measuring device. Unfortunately, this caused great deal of consternation with one of the guides in the chambers and I was summarily ejected from the chamber. I am still unsure as to what he thought I was doing, with this little spot of light dancing off the walls. Anyway, the measurements of the chambers were eventually made on another day and the established texts were apparently as accurate as they could be, given the nature of the rooms they were measuring.

Looking more deeply into the subject once more, I then re-convinced myself that the Thoth cubit was indeed at the heart of these chamber dimensions. Many of the passageway lengths did appear to be made in Thoth cubits and some of the chamber dimensions were suspiciously close to these cubit lengths too. Perhaps the odd discrepancy that appears in these chambers, like the width of the Second Pyramid's chamber, was a simple lack of care in the design and construction of the chamber by the original artisans.

Yet the main problem for the Thoth cubit hypothesis did not simply concern the internal chambers; it was the troublesome external dimensions of these pyramids that remained stubbornly odd. It was most unusual for a pyramid in Egypt to have a base layout that did not include a mathematical function, and it was more worrying still to find a pyramid that was not designed using whole-number cubit lengths for the external dimensions. Something was desperately wrong here; but perhaps the fault lay not in the design of these pyramids, but with my train of thought. It was time for some more lateral thinking – there had to be a solution to all this.

Granite

At last, there was a glimmer of light at the end of the tunnel, kindly provided by Sir Flinders Petrie once more: how much poorer we would have been without his dedication to the survey of Giza. The problem I had been wrestling with was the external dimensions of the pyramids, but, as Petrie noted, there were actually two dimensions for each of the smaller pyramids on the plateau. These pyramids not only look different to the great Pyramid, with their contrasting granite bases and limestone tops, but these granite sections may also be another small part of the mathematical conundrum.

Certainly, as we have already seen, the granite bases were a part of the pictorial conundrum – with the dull, red granite symbolising the tree-line of a mountain-side, below the gleaming white of the Tura limestone snow above. So, if the granite layers have a pictorial role, why not a mathematical one too? As I flicked through Petrie's survey results, I saw that he had noted that the granite base on the Third Pyramid appeared to be exactly $\frac{1}{4}$ of the total height of this pyramid. The architect had been reasonably consistent in other parts of these designs in using simple fractions and whole numbers, thus a granite layer of exactly $\frac{1}{4}$ the height of the pyramid did not seem unreasonable. Should the measurements that are mathematically significant, therefore, just be the limestone portions on the top of the pyramid? Should the granite portions below be ignored? It was an intriguing thought.

As the slope angle of the Third Pyramid seemed to be variable to some degree, it was very difficult to establish the true height of this pyramid to check out this hypothesis. Petrie guessed at a slope angle of 51° 20′, which gave a height for the pyramid of 125.3 tc. Happily for the theory at this stage, the limestone height of the pyramid seemed to be almost exactly 94 tc. While this figure was not a nice, exact multiple of ten, at least the dimensions of the pyramid no longer seemed to be quite so stubbornly fractional. It seemed likely, therefore, that a distinction could be drawn between the lower granite dimensions of these pyramids and the upper limestone dimensions – each had its own tale to tell.

Likewise, when looking at the corner of the granite sections of the Third Pyramid, some more round numbers seemed to pop out of the calculations. The granite corner of the Third Pyramid appeared to measure 40 x 25 x 31.25 tc. These numbers were also more pleasing than the previous fractions, with tens and fives dropping out of the calculation.

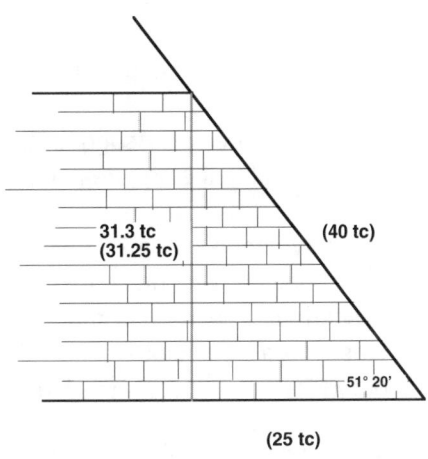

Fig 34. Third Pyramid corner.

Appendix 1. *Squaring the Circle*

The obvious way forward seemed to be to delete the dimensions of the granite base from the Second and Third Pyramids and to start the calculations once more with a slightly truncated pyramid, to see what difference this would make to the results. Unfortunately, the base of the (very) slightly smaller limestone section of the Second Pyramid would not yield a simple whole number answer and I began to suspect that the data I had for the Second Pyramid was wrong – and wrong in one simple respect.

Petrie had noted that the layer of granite at the bottom of this pyramid was constructed with large blocks measuring exactly 2 cubits high. This 2-cubit measurement did not in itself seem to be very enlightening and – no matter if the calculations were made with or without this layer – the external dimensions of the Second Pyramid remained obstinately fractional in both cubit and rod lengths. It was frustrating to say the least.

But the Second Pyramid was definitely designed around the concept of the 3 - 4 - 5 triangle; a Pythagorean triangle that has side lengths of exactly 3, 4, and 5 units. This is a fundamental piece of maths, as fundamental to squares and triangles as Pi is to a circle. It is odd that the classical texts do not acknowledge this fact about the Second Pyramid; they are happy enough to agree that the Great Pyramid is designed around the Pi formula for a circle, yet the dimensions of the Second Pyramid are equally mathematical and equally as advanced as the Great Pyramid's, but this fact is rarely mentioned.

The only reference I have found to this fact is a two line acknowledgement by Flinders Petrie. Yet I was surprised that Petrie let this snippet of information go past so easily. In regard to the dimensions of the Second Pyramid he merely states that:

> This seems to suggest that the square of the hypotenuse being equal to the squares of the two sides may have been known. [1]

May have been known? Petrie's pandering to his scientific patrons at the Royal Society, who had bankrolled his expedition, was obviously his chief concern. It is not hard to imagine that he was unable to speak his mind on these more contentious issues. Even if contemporary Egyptology still does not wish to do so, let us now face the facts. Just as has been demonstrated with the dimensions of the Great Pyramid, this is not a matter of the Second Pyramid being *possibly* or *nearly* equal to a 3 - 4 - 5 triangle; it is <u>exact</u>.

Appendix 1. Squaring the Circle

As I mentioned in the book *Thoth*, the classical texts about the pyramids, like *The Complete Pyramids* by Mark Lehner, give a slope angle for the Second Pyramid of 53° 10′. Petrie himself also gives a slope angle of 53° 10′. Mathematically, the calculated and precise angle for the 3 - 4 - 5 triangle is 53° 08′ – and I don't think that the 2′ of arc difference is worth quibbling about. It is quite plain that the Second Pyramid was designed to reflect this fundamental piece of maths. The ancient Egyptians were *fully* aware of the mathematical concepts of both Pi and Pythagoras.

However, the difficult question still remains to be answered. If the designer really intended this 3 - 4 - 5 geometry to be fundamental to the Second Pyramid's design, then why is this not replicated in the external linear measurements of the pyramid? The width, height and slope length of the pyramid are <u>not</u> divisible by 3, 4 and 5 in the way one would expect, so there is something very wrong with this design. Defeatists may take this inconsistency as a sign that there is no mathematical plan to the Giza plateau; sacred geometry adepts, however, will simply see this as a challenge.

Theoretical design

The answer lies in the depth of the granite layer at the base of the Second Pyramid. Strangely enough, the calculations appeared to suggest that one possible method for simplifying the external measurements of the pyramid – and also for providing a link to the 3 - 4 - 5 triangle – would be to double the height of the granite base. The first indication that this may be the correct solution for the design of this pyramid is that if the depth of the granite base is doubled, the little corner of the granite layer becomes an exact 3 - 4 - 5 triangle in cubit lengths, as can be seen in figure 31. The vertical height of this layer of granite becomes 4 cubits and, as the geometry and elevation angles of this pyramid are rather exacting, the rest of this little corner of pyramid *has* to conform to this fundamental Pythagorean 3 - 4 - 5 triangle.

Unfortunately, all the classical text books said that the Second Pyramid has only one layer of granite at the base, so is it stretching things a little too far to suggest that there were originally two layers at the bottom? Unfortunately, not everything we read in the orthodox text books can be taken at face value. The classical writers are simply reporting what they see and what they have read about – a single layer of granite. Since they do not wish to believe that there is any particular significance in the geometry of these pyramids, they are not really worried if there were originally one, two or three courses of granite at the base. Indeed they are not particularly concerned if many such minor details are accurate or not.

To the classical Egyptologist, such things are irrelevant and so, not surprisingly, none of the text books seemed to be of any assistance in solving this problem. Eventually I started e-mailing friends about the problem, with the intention of keeping them updated with the problems I was working on. I was somewhat surprised and more than a little pleased when an e-mail came back the next week from Mark Foster, my web-site designer. It appeared that he had solved my little problem by diligently reading the texts of Flinders Petrie, instead of glossing over them, and concentrating on the data as I had done.

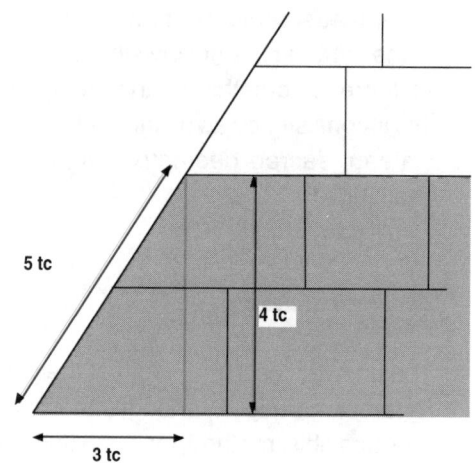

Fig 31. The Second Pyramid's granite base.

I had been buried in the measurements of Petrie's book and had neglected to read the introduction to the Second Pyramid at the beginning of chapter III. Although it was short, the introduction was nevertheless quite illuminating, as it described much of the data later in the chapter. Petrie later concentrated on the dimensions of the lowest layer of granite on the Second Pyramid, because it had an extra vertical strip at its base which was sunk into the pavement around the pyramid. But this close attention to the lowest layer did not preclude further layers above and so it would seem that the classical books are wrong and a lot of valuable research time had been wasted looking into this little piece of geometry. Turning to Flinders Petrie's 1883 work, at the beginning of chapter III he says:

> The lowest two courses of the Second Pyramid are of granite, very well preserved where it is not altogether removed. [2]

So the lowest <u>two</u> courses of the Second Pyramid were made of granite, just as I had suspected. Despite the wasted time, it was nice to have a theory proved correct by someone with the authority of Petrie. This confirmation also seemed to indicate that my idea was on the right track, for I had made this prediction based on the maths that the pyramid contained, and that prediction was later confirmed as being precisely correct by a historical text. This was nothing if not confidence-boosting.

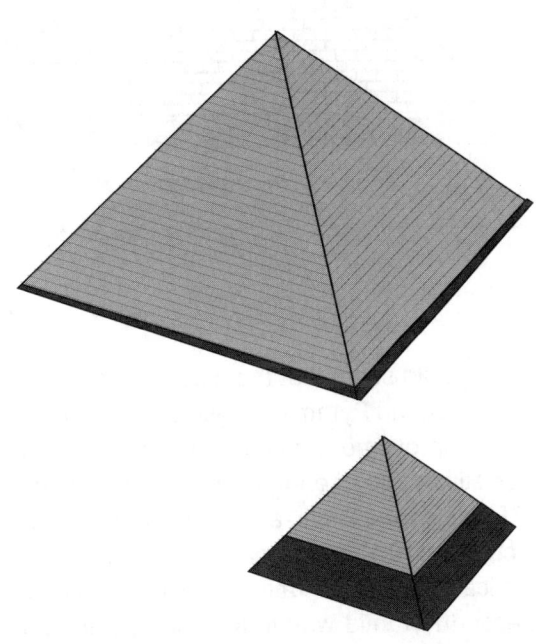

Fig 32. The granite bases.

As an aside, this also indicates that the destruction of the Second Pyramid has continued even within the last century, as there is now only the ragged remains of just one layer of granite blocks still *in situ*; a truly sad state of affairs. But the presence of an original double layer of granite, as reported by Petrie, was the key to the whole Second Pyramid geometry problem, for the external dimensions of the pyramid were now a little more even in their nature.

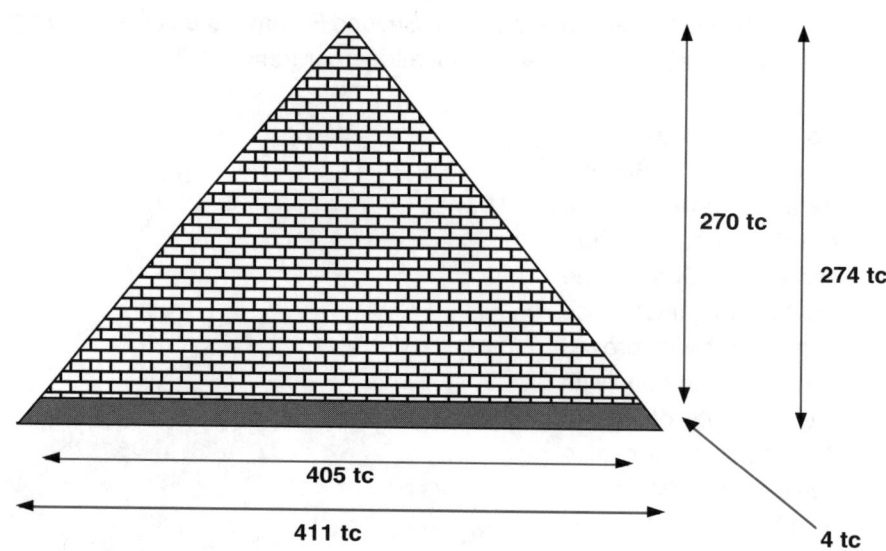

Fig 33. Second Pyramid dimensions, complete and limestone only.

So, it would seem that the external dimensions of the <u>limestone portions</u> of the Second Pyramid measured exactly 405 x 270 tc. Whilst this was a great improvement from the previous fractional dimensions, frankly, this was still not good enough. The Great Pyramid was designed around the Pi formula for a circle, and its external dimensions precisely mirrored that fact; the 440 x 280 tc base length and height were an exact 40-times replica of the 11 x 7 ratio of Pi when it is used in the circle formula. If the Second Pyramid was truly designed around the 3 - 4 - 5 Pythagorean triangle then surely its external dimensions should reflect this fact rather more precisely. The still infuriatingly odd dimensions of the limestone portions of the Second Pyramid were not in any way convincing enough to indicate that I had solved this whole issue.

Chamber

In fact, the dimensions of the Second Pyramid *were* based on the 3 - 4 - 5 triangle, but a little more lateral thinking is required before this can be seen. The evidence for this came to me from an unlikely source – the large and bare chamber that lies deep beneath the Second Pyramid.

Knowing the internal layout of the pyramids quite well, the first time I saw 'this' chamber I was a little confused. Having struggled down the narrow passageways I entered what seemed to be a small and roughly-hewn chamber; it was nothing like the diagrams, and so my disappointment was almost palpable. The reason for my disappointment was that the anti-chamber I was now in was not marked on my guide to the pyramids, and I had mistaken it for the main chamber. Shuffling a little further down the minute passageways, I eventually entered the main chamber and the contrast with the previous room could not have been greater.

Here was a chamber as impressive as anything to be found in the Great Pyramid, and although the chamber was not lined with granite, as is the King's Chamber, the walls were perfectly smooth and the dimensions perfectly accurate. If any of the subterranean chambers at Giza were to have some maths associated with them, this surely would be one of those.

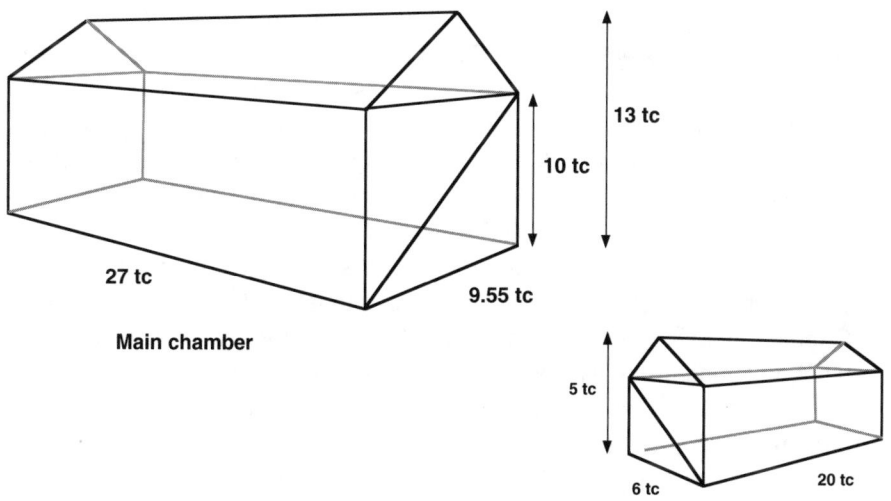

Fig 35. Second main chamber and anti-chamber.

Appendix 1. Squaring the Circle

But the solution to the Second Pyramid's chamber was not going to be as simple as I thought, and once more I spent some considerable time in a fruitless search for the intended geometry of this chamber. The problem was that, like the external dimensions of this pyramid, the dimensions of this chamber did not resolve into exact whole numbers when working in Thoth cubit lengths. Once again I tried other cubit lengths, until drifting back to the Thoth cubit once more.

The problem I still had to come to grips with, of course, is that not every mathematical function resolves itself into whole numbers; some will surely end up with odd fractions. The difficult part was going to be resolving an intended puzzle left for us by the architect, that ends with a fractional number. Indeed, is it possible for the designer to indicate that a particular fraction is in any way special?

Noticing that the King's Chamber measures 10 x 20 cubits is relatively easy and the problem can be quickly solved based on those secure and solid whole-number foundations. But how does one spot a 'significant' fractional number? Odd and fractional answers abound in this quest, so which of these are and which are not significant?

The answer was to lie in the symmetry of maths – in noticing that certain figures repeatedly fell out of the calculations, and that those particular figures corresponded to certain mathematical functions. The obvious example of this is the calculation of the true height of the King's Chamber in the Great Pyramid. The height of the King's Chamber is an odd fraction to fit a certain piece of maths (as explained in the book *Thoth*). The height should have been exactly 11.18 tc, but was this really the true height of this chamber? Because the height of the ceiling varies by a centimeter or two (up to 0.04 tc), it is difficult to tell exactly what this fractional measurement should be.

Luckily, the designer has resolved this issue quite conclusively for us, by a little fortuitous maths. It so happens that the diagonal of the King's Chamber is exactly double the required height of the chamber. Since this diagonal measurement is formed from the whole number chamber lengths of 10 and 20 tc, the result seems beyond doubt – the height of the chamber must be exactly 11.18 tc.

It would appear that there *is* a way of showing that a fractional figure is somehow to be regarded as being significant, and it is through such simple comparisons of lengths and angles that we can see what the designer was up to. The designer wanted us to be able to resolve these issues satisfactorily, so the gentle hints he made were both

Appendix 1. Squaring the Circle

obvious and numerous; the whole problem has been designed to keep us on the right track.

22.36 tc divided by 2 = 11.18 tc

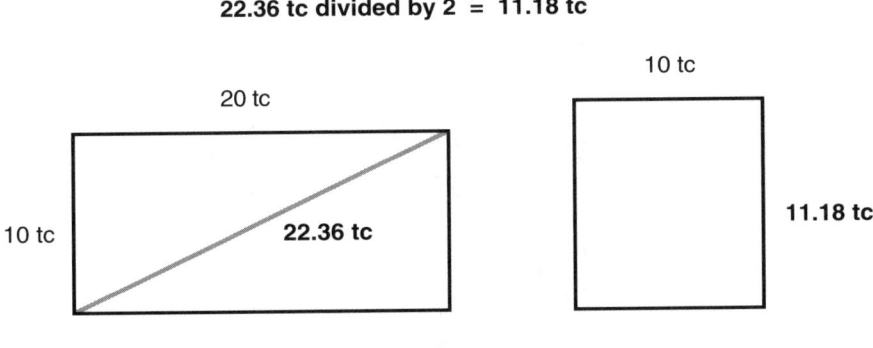

Fig 36. Floor of King's Chamber.   *End wall of chamber.*

The first glimmer of light in this unfathomable problem of the Second Pyramid's chamber dimensions, was that the linear dimensions of the chamber were in the same ratio that was required to 'square the circle'. Squaring the circle is a little mathematical trick that is explained later in this chapter.

The 'squaring the circle' formula is all about the sides and diagonals of a square and it did not dawn on me for quite some time that the Second Pyramid's main chamber was simply saying (mathematically) "I am a square". This statement may sound peculiar, but this is exactly what the designer was saying to us across the millennia; the dimensions are too exact for this to be anything else.

If the length of the Second Pyramid's chamber is divided by four; or rather, if it is folded up into the four sides of a square, the resulting square will have side lengths of exactly 6.75 tc (27 divided by 4 = 6.75). It cannot by any stretch of the imagination, be a coincidence that the length of the diagonal of this hypothetical square measures exactly 9.55 tc – the exact width of the Second Pyramid's chamber.

But is this what the designer intended us to see, or am I making a guess too far? Am I perhaps stretching the data too thinly and only guessing at the intended width of the chamber? Perhaps the chamber was intended to be 9.56 tc wide and therefore the little mathematical trick with the hypothetical square above would not work.

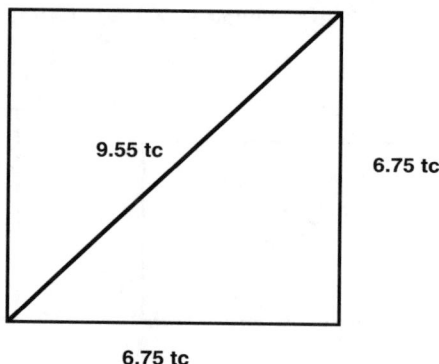

9.55 tc

6.75 tc

6.75 tc

Fig 37. The Second Pyramid's chamber's hypothetical square.

This was a genuine concern, but one that apparently is not justified. Although the resulting dimensions of this hypothetical square are in slightly fractional units (especially the diagonal), they *are* the intended units of length and we can be certain of this because this same length can also be verified from another starting point. The intended width of the Second Pyramid's chamber was actually 9.5459 tc, or a figure accurate to greater than 0.05 of a millimeter.

The reason that the theoretical width of the Second Pyramid's chamber can be calculated to such accuracy is due to a little mathematical symmetry, based upon precisely the same concepts as have been used to derive the exact height of the King's Chamber. Quite simply, the width of the Second Pyramid's chamber is exactly $1/3$ of the diagonal length of the chamber, and this in turn is dependent on the 27 tc length of the chamber. So in a stunning piece of metrological symmetry, it can now be seen that the height of the King's Chamber is <u>exactly</u> $1/2$ of the diagonal length of its floor, and the width of the Second Pyramid's chamber is <u>exactly</u> $1/3$ of the diagonal length of its floor.

It happens that there is only one width of chamber that will allow the floor diameter to equal three times the chamber width, and this is 9.5459 tc. How much more in the way of evidence do we need to start believing that these are the true dimensions for these chambers? How much more evidence do we need to believe that not only are these chambers fundamentally important in this quest, but that they were cognitively designed in <u>exactly</u> this fashion by the architect?

28.638 tc divided by 3 = 9.546 tc

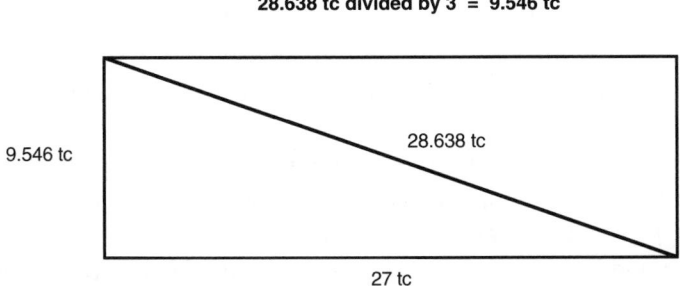

Fig 38.   Floor-plan of the Second Pyramid's chamber.

Square of the square

The exact width of the Second Pyramid's chamber has also just been calculated using the 'hypothetical square'; the square with side lengths of 6.75 tc, as already explained. But this gives us another little confirmation that this was the precise width for the chamber that the architect intended. The diagonal length of the Second Pyramid's chamber has now been defined as <u>exactly</u> three times the width – and that is so to at least nine decimal places! (9.545941546). This rather precise number is also the exact diagonal length of the 'hypothetical square'.

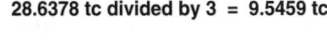

28.6378 tc divided by 3 = 9.5459 tc

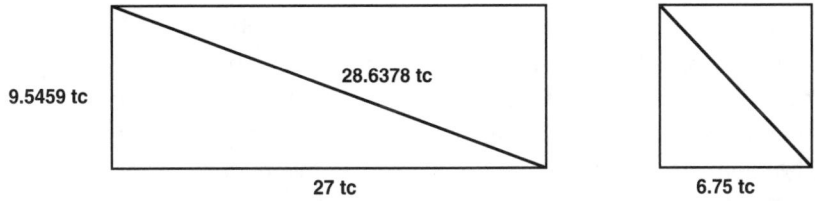

Second Pyramid's chamber's width.   *Hypothetical square's diagonal.*
Fig 39.

Appendix 1. Squaring the Circle

Of all the rectangles that could have been be chosen to form the floor-plan of a room, only a design with these proportions will perform this little trick. Thus, despite the fractional width of the chamber, the exact dimensions of the chamber are now quite obvious. The width that the designer intended for this room can now be calculated with great confidence and even greater accuracy, to no less than nine decimal places.

Just as a reminder, this is exactly the same process as we used to derive the height of the King's Chamber in the Great Pyramid. The height of the King's Chamber was half the diagonal length of the room; here, the width of the Second Pyramid's chamber is exactly one third the diagonal length of the room. This consistency in the function of these lengths and angles is crucial to understanding these problems and deriving answers to them. It gives a great deal of confidence in the results.

Thus, the 'hypothetical square', the one with side lengths of 6.75 tc, has to be a part of the designers intended answer to this problem; he is highlighting the 6.75 tc measurement as a fundamental unit of length. The diagonal measurement of 9.546 tc also looks to be 'special', but to what purpose? Why should these lengths be so special?

One possible solution for the 6.75 tc unit of length is that the designer seems to be indicating here that a different 'rod' length is being used within the Second Pyramid. The Great Pyramid used a rod length of 5.5 units, because that length is intimately involved and derived from the Pi ratio of a circle, and the design of the Great Pyramid itself rests upon the value of Pi. The Second Pyramid has nothing to do with circles but it has, instead, everything to do with squares, triangles and their diagonals. Thus, the 5.5 unit rod-length is largely irrelevant in a pyramid that has nothing to do with circles. The designer seems to be saying to us that the rod length being used in the Second Pyramid was 6.75 units in length – 6.75 Thoth cubits – and that this unit of length is somehow related to squares and their diagonals. Since this pyramid is often known as the Khafre Pyramid, I will call this unit of length the Ka rod.

Certainly, to be covered up in such a fashion, this unit 6.75 tc had to be of prime importance in this quest, but where and in what way was it used? For an answer to this question, the prime candidate had to lie in the dimensions of the so far unexplained, and particularly odd, units used in the base-layout of the Second Pyramid. Was this pyramid withholding some more fundamental maths in its fabric, but disguised within a new unit of length?

Some feverish fiddling with a calculator proved the point in less than 10 seconds. If the granite base of the Second Pyramid is removed from the calculation, and the dimensions of the limestone section are reduced into rod lengths using a 6.75 tc Ka rod length, then suddenly whole numbers start falling out of the calculator. The external dimensions of the Second Pyramid in these new 6.75 tc Ka rod lengths measure exactly 60 x 40 x 50 rods!

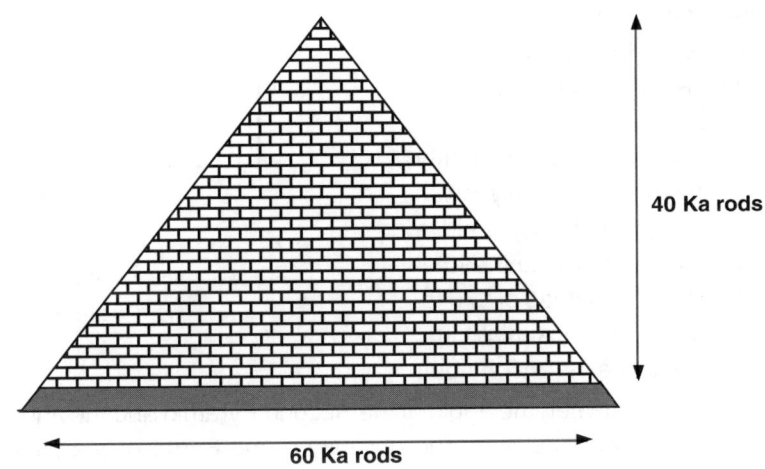

40 Ka rods

60 Ka rods

Fig 40. The Second Pyramid in rods.

Furthermore, the triangle formed by dividing the pyramid into two halves, measures exactly 30 x 40 x 50 rods. In other words, these measurements are exactly <u>ten times larger</u> than the 3 - 4 - 5 ratio that the pyramid was designed around. As I suspected from the start, the pyramid *should* have been designed in units that reflect the 3 - 4 - 5 triangle; now it does, and it does so very precisely indeed. Just as is to be found in the dimensions of the Great Pyramid, a fundamental piece of maths is firmly embodied within the external dimensions of the Second Pyramid.

This was all extremely satisfying. I was now in the privileged position of being able to predict what the design of the pyramids was going to tell us and the pyramids themselves were confirming these ideas in such a precise manner as to exclude wishful thinking. There was no forcing of the facts to fit the theory here; the theory only fitted so snugly simply because it *was* the correct answer.

Appendix 1. Squaring the Circle

Gnomon

One last question was left from all this geometry. Why did the limestone sections of the Second Pyramid, based precisely as they were on the 3 - 4 - 5 triangle, need that extra two layers of granite at the bottom? Was this just to put us off the scent? Or was there another rationale for the design?

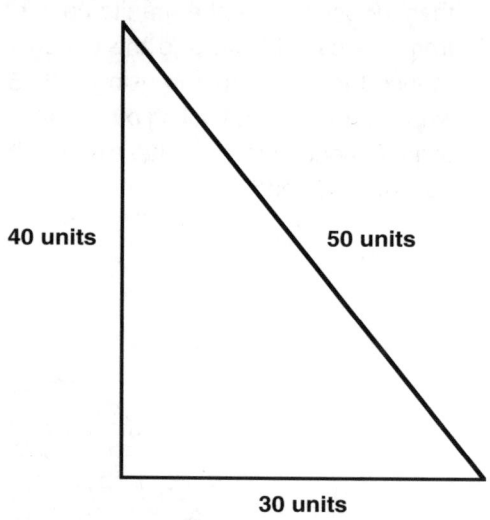

40 units   50 units

30 units

Fig 41. The Second Pyramid's 3-4-5 triangle.

There is a possibility that the extra granite layer was there to give the pyramid a slight lift up, to make the total height 274 tc instead of 270 tc. The reason for this might just be that there is an obvious symmetry between the angle of the Second Pyramid and the angle by the rays of the winter's Sun. The obliquity of the Earth, or the tilt angle, is 23° 26′. If we add this angle to the latitude of the Giza plateau, which is 29° 59′, the result is 53° 25′.

For comparison, the angle of the casing stones of the Second Pyramid is 53° 8′, a rather similar figure. Indeed, if the uppermost limb of the Sun were used, the former angle would be 53° 10′, in comparison with the Second Pyramid's 53° 8′ (see overleaf).

Therefore, the reason for the extra 'lift up' for the Second Pyramid upon its two extra layers of granite, is so that at midday on the midwinter solstice, the total shadow length of the pyramid is 365.3 tc. Such a shadow length is most likely to have been chosen because of its links with the annual cycle. Thus, at midday on the winter solstice:

a. The shadow length from the Second Pyramid is 365.3 cubits.
b. The angle of elevation of the Sun that forms this shadow is 36° 52′.
c. A 365.25-day year has just ended.

In fact, if a perfect midwinter Sun angle is assumed – ie, a theoretical angle that gives a shadow length of exactly 365.25 tc – the data just gets better and better.

a.   The shadow length from the Second Pyramid is now 365.25 cubits.
b.   The angle of elevation of the Sun that forms this shadow is now 36° 52.5´.
c.   A 365.25 day year has just ended.
d.   The declination of the Sun that produces this shadow (the opposite angle of the 36° 52.5´) is 53° 7.5'.
e.   The slope angle of the Second Pyramid is 53° 7.8´.

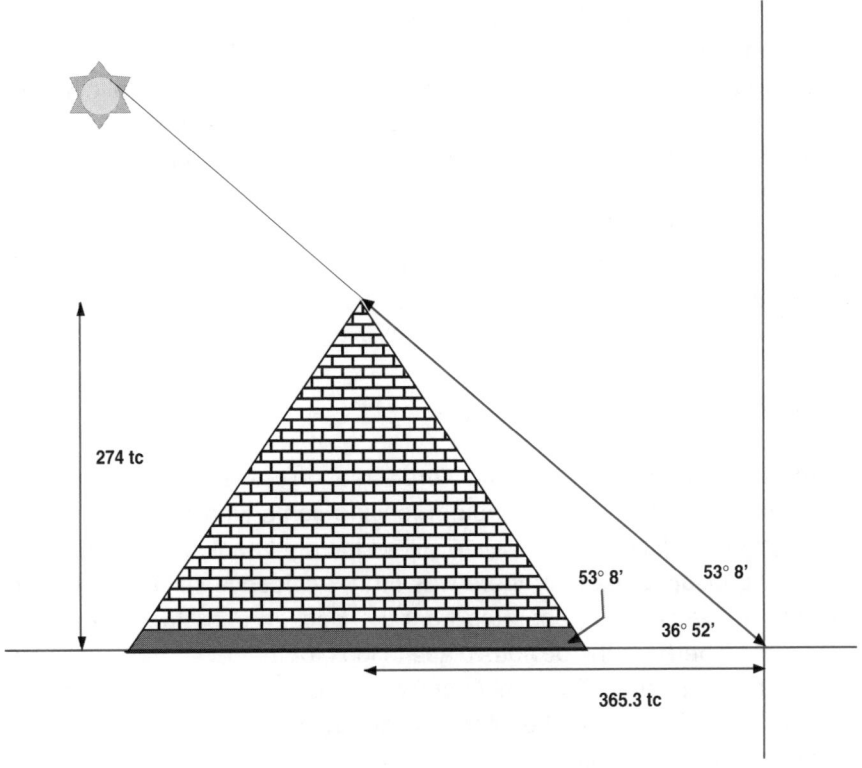

Fig 42.   Second Pyramid's midwinter Sun shadow.

This is a nice and unmistakable piece of symmetry that the designer just could not have missed – this has to have been deliberate. As confirmation of this whole concept of the pyramidal gnomon, there is also the linguistic paper-trail that was uncovered in the book *Tempest*. This shows that one of the prime rituals on the Giza plateau involved the observation of the shadows of the pyramids, either at the solstice or the half-solstice. This was further confirmed by a statement in the Koran that indicates that one of the 'signs of god' was the observation of the pyramids' shadows. It is my assertion that the prime reason for these observations in dynastic Egypt was to use the alignment of the pyramids' shadows with the pyramids causeways to define the seasons of the year, but quite obviously the designer has thrown in a mathematical trick on top of this basic secular function. Presumably, this was another one of those 'deeper layers' to these mysteries that was designed to entice people to look for more and more mathematical clues.

This may even be an indication of the precise angle of obliquity of the Earth when the pyramids were first constructed. It may have been that the position of the Giza pyramids, just below the 30° parallel north, was arranged so that the midwinter angle of the Sun matched the 3 - 4 - 5 triangle of the Second Pyramid. If this were so, then the perfect Sun angle that would have produced these exact figures would have had an associated angle of obliquity of the Earth of 23° 8.5'. This figure is still plus or minus 15 minutes of arc, depending on whether the upper limb, lower limb or the center of the Sun was the required visual picture.

Third Pyramid

If this new Ka rod unit of 6.75 tc were a real unit of length, however, the architect is normally in the habit of leaving some kind of mathematical confirmation – just to show we are still on the right tracks. As usual, I was not to be disappointed, for there was further evidence still to come. The theory above was all generated from the Second and Great Pyramids' main chambers, so the obvious place to look for further confirmation was in another chamber. The anti-chamber in the Second Pyramid proved fruitless, but then again, the interior of this chamber looks like it has been hacked out of the bedrock with nothing more sophisticated than an adze; it may well be a later addition to the structure.

The obvious alternative was to look at the chambers beneath the Third Pyramid, one of which was lined with granite, just like the King's Chamber. Once more, the dimensions of this chamber were fractional in the Thoth cubit. This had, once upon a time, indicated to me that the Thoth cubit was not in use here, but understanding that the answers required were sometimes fractional themselves made matters much easier, and the reason for constructing this chamber with these dimensions soon became apparent.

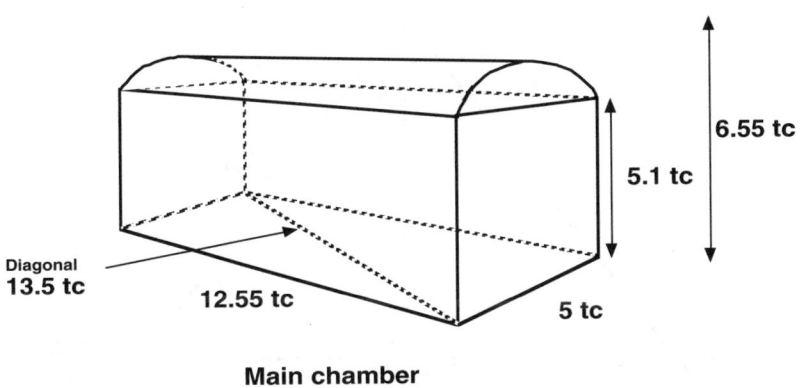

Main chamber

Fig 43.   The Third Pyramid's granite chamber.

The granite chamber deep inside the Third Pyramid measured a disappointingly fractional size of 12.6 x 5 Thoth cubits, which was neither a whole number nor divisible by either 5.5 tc or 6.75 tc. To make sense of the situation, a new rod length may be required once more, a rod length based upon the granite chamber's dimensions. The new rod length in the Second Pyramid had been derived by dividing the length of the internal chamber by four. Applying this logic to the Third Pyramid, the chamber length of 12.6 was also divided by four, which resulted in a rod length of 3.15 tc. A fractional value for this new rod length of 3.15 tc did not really look too promising: how many pyramidal dimensions were going to be simplified by using a unit of 3.15? The technique was getting off to a bad start in the smallest of these pyramids, but anything was worth trying.

So, was this new rod length going to resolve this pyramid's dimensions into more user-friendly units? Remarkably, the first calculation hinted at a positive result. Flinders Petrie gives the dimensions of the

Appendix 1. Squaring the Circle

Third Pyramid as being 105.51 m, with possibility of error of plus or minus 7 cm. This equates to a base length in the architect's units of 201.55 tc, which, when divided by the new rod length of 3.15, equals (as near as makes no difference) 64 rods. Against all the odds, a whole number had just dropped out of the equation. As this pyramid is often known as the Menkaure Pyramid, I will call this unit of length the Men rod.

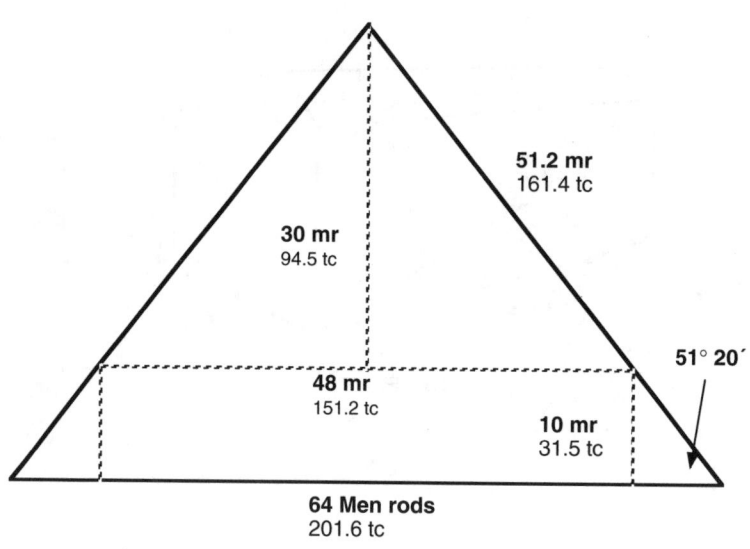

Fig 44. The Third Pyramid in rods of 3.15 cubits and (cubits).

This was worth pursuing further. For the angle of elevation of this pyramid, Petrie gives 51° 10′, whereas Mark Lehner, in *The Complete Pyramids* gives 51° 20′ 25″. Using Lehner's value gives a height for the pyramid of 126 tc. I was more than a little amazed to find that 126 divided by 3.15 equals exactly 40 rods. Was this the true height of the pyramid, or should I have used Petrie's angle of elevation, which gives 125.25 tc for the height of the pyramid?

I somehow think that Lehner's figure is the correct value, and simply because of another little piece of pyramidal symmetry:

a.   The height of the limestone sections of the Second Pyramid is exactly 10 times the length of the chamber underneath.

b.   The height of the Third Pyramid is now exactly 10 times the length of the chamber underneath.

c.   The height of the limestone sections of the Second Pyramid is 40 Ka rods.

d.   The height of the Third Pyramid is 40 Men rods.

It was apparent that this new rod length of 3.15 was a valuable tool in deciphering the dimensions of the Third Pyramid. But it was not only valuable in solving the Third Pyramid's design; it added greater weight to my solution for the Second Pyramid too. I had applied the same technique to two different pyramids, and despite the unpromising measurement units involved, the pyramid dimensions had both resolved into simpler forms. However, there was a problem with the Great Pyramid's rod length.

The geometry of both the Second and Third Pyramids indicated that the rod size to be used in making these calculations was always $\frac{1}{4}$ of the length of the chamber inside that pyramid. But the length of the King's Chamber inside the Great Pyramid is 20 tc, which would result in a cubit length of 5 tc and not 5.5 tc. This is not very helpful, as it has already been convincingly demonstrated that the cubit length that works throughout the Great Pyramid's dimensions is the Pi-based rod length of $5\frac{1}{2}$ tc.

But just a minute: there is another chamber in the Great Pyramid we could use in this calculation – the Queen's Chamber. It so happens that the Queen's Chamber measures exactly 11 tc in length and a quarter of this makes a rod length of 2.75 tc. Now, a rod length of 2.75 tc ($2\frac{3}{4}$ tc) would make much more sense, as it is exactly one half of $5\frac{1}{2}$ tc. It is now apparent that all the rod lengths that were used in all of these pyramids can be derived by simply dividing the internal chamber length by four.

But this new Great Pyramid rod length is half of the original value. Would such a rod length invalidate all the calculations that were made on the internal structure of the Great Pyramid earlier in the book? No, not at all. There are two possibilities here, neither of which alters the previous arguments in any respect.

a.   The designer has used the unit of a 'double cubit' throughout the pyramid. As mentioned in the book Thoth, this type of unit was often used at the Avebury site in Britain, and the unit of a double cubit would mean that all the measurements remain the same as before.

b.   The designer has always used the unit of the 2.75 tc rod, in which case all the results from the internal structure of the Great Pyramid have to be multiplied by 2. This does not alter any of the claims that have been made, as all the dimensions remain in the same relationships with one another. The fact that the true rod may have been 2.75 tc rather than 5.5 tc is mirrored, in a curious manner, by the Standard Gauge railways of the world. This subject forms the next chapter of the appendix and is an interesting read in its own right.

In fact, the accuracy of these pyramids in these new simpler rod units almost seems to be known about by the Egyptological establishment, but if this is so then they are not prepared to let us in on the secret. Look at the following table and see what I mean. On the left is the calculation using the simplified rod units derived from the pyramid geometry. On the right are the pyramid angles given in *The Complete Pyramids*, by the renowned Egyptologist, Mark Lehner.

Pyramid	Derived from	Equals	Angle	Mark Lehner
Great	Tan 7 / 5.5	Tan x 1.272	51° 50´ 34´´	51° 50´ 40´´
Second	Tan 4 / 3	Tan x 1.333	53° 07´ 48´´	53° 10´ 00´´
Third	Tan 40 / 32	Tan x 1.25	51° 20´ 25´´	51° 20´ 25´´

To put those similarities into perspective, the two slope angles of the Great Pyramid differ by just 6 seconds of arc. Thus, if the modern surveyor who was measuring this pyramid for the text books did not know the mathematical function that the pyramid was based on, the measurements in the height of the pyramid would have to have been made to the nearest 1.5 cm. Having been trained in surveying, I can assure the reader that this is a remarkable achievement, even with modern surveying equipment – especially as the building concerned is substantially ruined and is missing its top!

Likewise for the Third Pyramid, the measurements for the height of this pyramid seem to have been taken to within 2.5 mm of the mathematically derived value. This is an incomprehensibly minute error, especially bearing in mind that Petrie noted of this pyramid:

> For the angle of the pyramid, the data are rather divergent; the stones in situ are very irregular, and the courses not level. [3]

Because of this irregularity, Petrie took his value for the angle of elevation for the pyramid from his observation that the granite layer was $^1/_4$ of the height of the pyramid. Thus, he took linear measurements of the granite layers and back-calculated the angle of elevation. A survey cannot be taken to the level of accuracy indicated by Lehner's data, which leaves us with two possible options to explain this coincidence in angular measurements.

a.   Lehner's surveyor was remarkably lucky.
b.   The mathematical geometry of these pyramids is already known, but no mention is being made of this.

Conspiracies aside, it was also becoming clear that the granite bases to these pyramids had a dual function, as is so often the case with these structures. Yes, the contrast between the granite and the limestone *was* indicating that the pyramids were designed to mimic mountains, with snow on their peaks and rock at the bottom; but, at the same, time the two contrasting layers were also defining the exact dimensions that were supposed to be used in the calculations. This has been done for a good reason, because there is a similarity between the Second and Third Pyramids and it helps to know that the two structures are related before making the comparisons. It also gives the designer a chance to ensure that the researcher is on the right track once more; the two sizes of pyramid provide a little cross-check.

Circle and square

The way in which the two pyramids are related, however, is quite mathematical; it all seems to depend on the function of 'squaring the circle'. Now this phrase has been used often enough in everyday speech to allude to a very tricky problem that needs to be solved. But where did the phrase originate and what exactly does it mean? How exactly does one square a circle?

I would contend that the origins of the phrase are Masonic. As was strongly alluded to in my previous books, the origins of Masonry are deeply rooted in ancient Egypt and they are also strongly concerned with the nature and design of the pyramids. The Masonic deity is known as the Architect of the Universe, thus geometry and architecture are fundamental to the Masonic 'belief system'. The pinnacle of this belief system is, and always has been, the pyramids themselves and the measurements and geometry that they contain. In addition to this, the prime symbols of Masonry, their 'Coat of Arms', are the set-square and the pair of dividers. These are the precise tools that are required to draw a circle and a square. The Coat of Arms of the society is clearly stating that one of the most important aspects of their organisation is 'squaring the circle'.

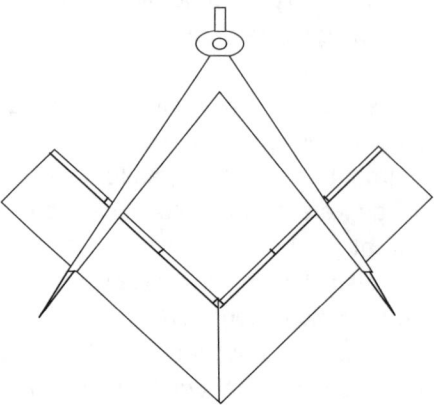

Fig 45. Square and compass

So what exactly is 'squaring the circle' and why is it supposed to be so difficult to achieve? I believe that it is not actually that difficult a concept to understand; it is simply the function of placing a circle around a square, and then a square around that circle. In doing so, a precise mathematical series can be built up, where the diagonals and sides of the successive squares relate to each other in a specific fashion.

Since, as I said before, the Second Pyramid's chamber is somehow related to the formula involved in this business of squaring the circle, this concept could also quite possibly explain why the unit of 6.75 was chosen for the 'hypothetical square' formed by the Second Pyramid's chamber. The rod unit of $5^1/_2$ tc, derived from the Great Pyramid, is fractional because it is derived from the Pi formula for a circle, and since Pi is not a whole number, anything related to it tends to become fractional itself. The new unit of $6^3/_4$ tc from the Second Pyramid may also be fractional because, although it primarily depends on squares and their diagonals, it also depends to some extent on perimeters of circles and Pi.

Appendix 1. Squaring the Circle

The first stage of 'squaring the circle' is to draw a circle around a square so that it just touches its corners. If the 6.75 tc 'hypothetical square', derived from the Second Pyramid's main chamber, is surrounded by just such a circle, the perimeter of this circle transforms itself from fractions to whole numbers. The 6.75 cubit square becomes exactly a 30 tc circle. (Using the standard fractional Pi value of 22:7, this result is exact to three decimal places.)

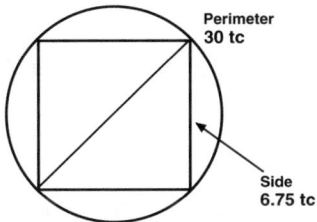

Fig 46. Circles around squares.

On the other hand, it can also be seen that if the diagonal of the circle is twice the width of the Second Pyramid's chamber, then this will also form a whole-number circumference (60 tc). The evidence that these numbers have been deliberately chosen in this fashion is simple to see, because the perimeter length of the King's Chamber in the Great Pyramid is also exactly 60 tc.

Thus, we now have the rather agreeable position of squaring the circle between the Second and Great Pyramids. A square with a diagonal of twice the width of the Second Pyramid's chamber (and a side length of half the length of this chamber), has a circumference that is exactly the same as the King's Chamber's perimeter length.

There is now a direct relationship between the Great and Second Pyramids. The exterior dimensions of the Great Pyramid are all about Pi and circles, so it is fitting that the King's Chamber's perimeter corresponds to the circle in figure 47. The exterior dimensions to the Second Pyramid are all about Pythagoras and squares, so in turn the dimensions of its chamber are related to the square in figure 47.

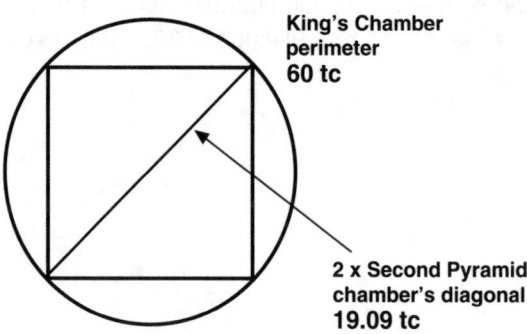

Diagonal = 2 x Second chamber's diagonal.
Perimeter = King's Chamber perimeter.

King's Chamber
perimeter
60 tc

2 x Second Pyramid
chamber's diagonal
19.09 tc

Fig 47. Great and Second Pyramids, circled and squared

The chambers of these two pyramids are 'squaring the circle', so a logical guess is that the exterior dimensions of these pyramids should do something similar. Indeed, this is so, but before embarking on that search, perhaps a deeper look into the function of 'squaring the circle' is required. As can be seen in figure 48, a series of squares and triangles have been drawn so that they just touch at their extremities, each nesting like a series of Russian Matrotshka dolls. In doing so, each square and circle is related to its neighbours by a specific ratio, irrespective of the actual size of that circle or square.

The sides and diagonals of each square mimic each other alternately, as do the circumferences of adjacent circles. Although the values for the squares can start with any number (n), they always follow the same ratio to each other, which is defined by the formula:

$$\sqrt{(n^2)} \times 2$$

This may sound complicated, but luckily this equation can be simplified to:

$$n \times \sqrt{2} \quad \text{or} \quad n \times 1.4142$$

Appendix 1. Squaring the Circle

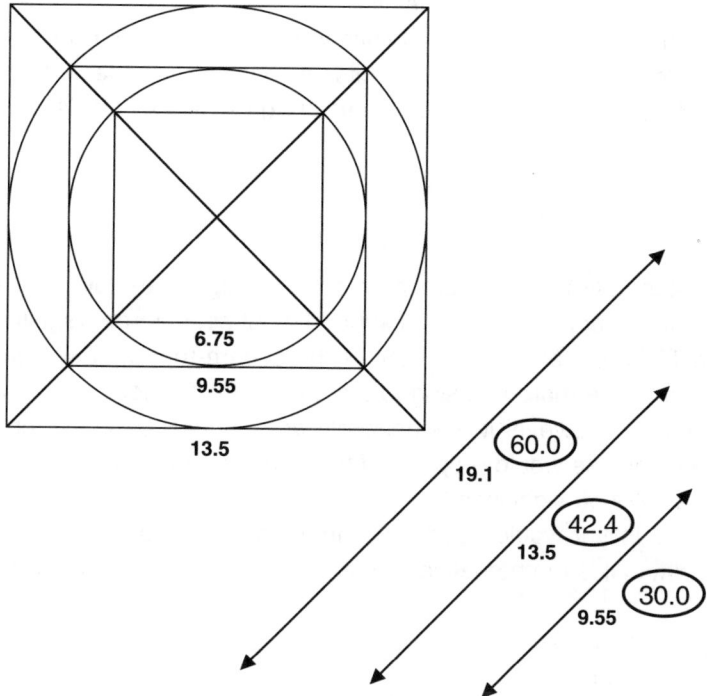

Figures beside lines are diagonal lengths of squares.
Figures in circles are circumferences of equivalent circles.

Fig 48. Squaring the circle.

This function of 1.4142 probably needs explaining in more detail. Perhaps the best way to visualise this number is to liken it to the Pi ratio of a circle.

a.   The diameter of a circle multiplied by Pi gives the circumference of that circle.

b.   The diameter of a square multiplied by 2.8284 gives the perimeter length of that square.

The figure of 2.8284 is obviously double 1.4142, and in turn 1.4142 is simply derived from √2. Since the figure of 2.8284 is such a fundamental

Appendix 1. Squaring the Circle

piece of maths, it deserves a Greek symbol and, for the sake of argument, I will label is as Ω. It so happens that this Ω function is not simply a function of squares, it is related to circles too.

The numerical value that links these two mathematical constants can be derived from some of the units that have already been used in the Second Pyramid's calculations. These are given in the calculation below.

$$\text{a.} \quad \frac{60}{6.75} = 8.888$$

So what is 8.888. Is this number in any way significant, or has it simply been drawn out of a hat? The number did not seem terribly significant at all, until it was realised that 8.888 is the square-root of 79. A figure like √79 was a little more pleasing to the eye, but it did not seem any more enlightening. However it was definitely worth pursuing the matter further to see what else would drop out of the equation – could such a peculiar figure as √79 be significant?

Actually it would seem that the figure 8.888, or √79, *is* relatively important in this mathematical quest, as it is derived from the formula:

Π x Ω
or
3.14286 x 2.8284

Where Π is the number that links the diameter of a circle to its perimeter.
Where Ω is the number that links the diameter of a square to its perimeter.

Thus √79, or 8.888 is a fusion of two very fundamental pieces of maths, which are in turn related to the diameters and perimeters of circles and squares.

So this unit of 8.888 is a figure that links the formula for a square with the formula for a circle, and so it is quite handy when 'squaring the circle', as we shall see. But it might be interesting to see once more how these numbers can be derived by using some of the pyramid measurements and ratios:

Π = 880 : 280 or 3.14286

Using the measurements for the height and double the base length of the

Appendix 1. *Squaring the Circle*

Great Pyramid gives the common Pi approximation that we have seen many times before. But what about the value of Ω?

$$\Omega \quad = \quad 27 : 9.546 \quad \text{or} \quad 2.8284$$

It would seem that Ω can be derived from the dimensions of the Second Pyramid's chamber itself, or 27 tc x 9.546 tc. Note also that Ω can be derived from the result of Π x 0.9. It would now appear that the very simple figure of 0.9 may link these two fundamental geometry units as well.

The maths here is relatively unimportant; what matters is that the ratio between the dimensions of the Second Pyramid and the dimensions of its chamber were apparently planned by someone with an intimate knowledge of maths. This must have been done for a specific reason and it only remains to find out exactly what that purpose was. The clue has to be the fact that the ratio of $\sqrt{79}$ is defined by the size of the squares and also by the dimensions of the circles. Thus, the figure of 8.888 or $\sqrt{79}$ can act as a link between the dimensions of the perimeter lengths of the squares and the circumferences of the circles.

As the Great and Second Pyramids themselves can be seen to be representations of squares and circles, it would also seem that we have a numerical ratio that can link these two structures together – $\sqrt{79}$ or 8.888.

Second design

This next section is a short description of one possible way in which the dimensions of the Second Pyramid were derived and how they relate to the other two pyramids on the plateau. As has often been suspected by many people, the pyramids were not simply piled up on the plateau until the masons ran out of stone. Firstly, the pyramids themselves were designed as statements of mathematical knowledge, and secondly, the precise dimensions chosen for each structure were designed to relate to each other in a specific way.

Each pyramid has a real size and then, as we have just seen, each pyramid has it own multiplier (rod length) in order to vary the physical size of the monument mathematically. The rod size for each pyramid was very simply defined as the length of the internal chamber, in cubits, divided by four. The system is very simple in concept, but it is flexible enough to hold a vast array of information.

Appendix 1. Squaring the Circle

So why was the Second Pyramid chosen to be the precise dimensions that we see today on the plateau? Well, the designer may have started with a circle. This circle was divided into the usual 360 degrees. Each degree was then subdivided into ten units, giving a circle with 3,600 units around its perimeter. What happened next, mathematically, is that the 3,600 units were divided by 8.888, the answer to which equals 405; and this is the base length of the Second Pyramid.

As has just been demonstrated, the figure of 8.8888 is defined as being Ω x Π. Thus, this piece of maths can be demonstrated pictorially as well as figuratively. Dividing the perimeter of a circle by Π gives the diameter; dividing a diameter of a square by Ω gives half the base length. In this case, the picture that is defined by this formula looks like this:

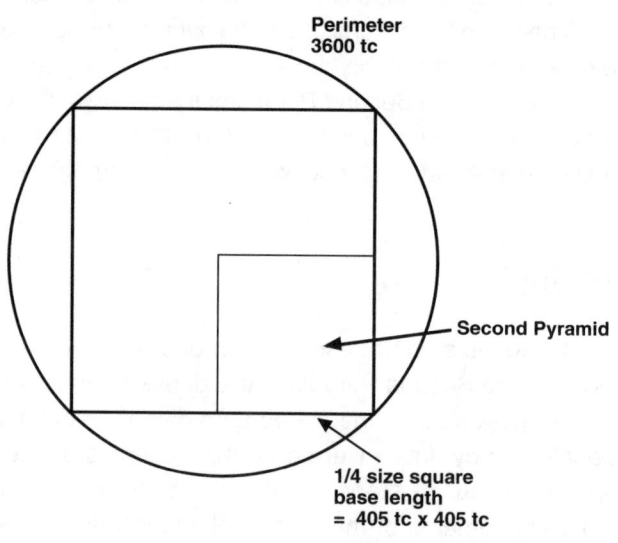

Fig 49. Defining the Second Pyramid's dimensions.

This may have been how the Second Pyramid's base dimensions were originally derived by the architect. If so, then this concept must have been transmitted down through the generations as a piece of sacred geometry, as the Egyptians have consistently used this design as the form of the throne for one of their chief deities, Amun. The photo of this throne, in the

Appendix 1. *Squaring the Circle*

colour-plate section of this book, is from a shrine of Tuthmoses III at Deir el-Bahari, dedicated to the god, Hathor. The main content of the frieze is the king making an offering to the god Amun, who sits upon the pictorial representation of the mathematical formula that has just been illustrated. It would seem that the symbolism of this mathematical function was known in the priestly and regal circles of dynastic Egypt, but we could speculate that the true meaning of this diagram was not necessarily known. Like the sacred measurement systems, this was probably just a piece of an arcane and unfathomable sacred design that was handed down by the gods long ago.

Second rods

The next step was for the architect to define the size of the chamber that lies at the heart of this pyramid. The requirements here were to create a rod length that would divide the Second Pyramid into 60 units – so that the 3-4-5 triangle would be displayed with whole-number unit lengths along the base of the pyramid.

This is simplicity itself; just divide up the base lengths of the Second Pyramid into 60 equal portions. (405 divided by 60 equals 6.75). This will not only instantly make each portion 6.75 tc in length – the rod size for the Second Pyramid – it will also make the half-base length of the pyramid 30 rods long, which is the length required for the 3-4-5 triangle. Adding to this compendium of symmetry, the 60 small squares on each side of the Second Pyramid now mean that there are a total of 60 x 60 squares throughout the base of the pyramid. 60 x 60 equals 3,600 squares, and remember that the perimeter length of the outer circle was 3,600 cubits.

This was a real part of this pyramid's design; the number of squares that could be fitted into the base area of the pyramid was made to be equal to the perimeter length of the circle that encompassed the pyramid. This was done in this fashion so that the design of the pyramid could encompass some very basic pieces of maths, both Ω and Π.

This may appear, at face value, to be a bit of mathematical trickery – simply find some formula that fits a particular pyramid and claim that was the design the architect intended. So, is this trickery or a real explanation? The balance of probability can be weighted in favour of reality by looking at the other structures on the plateau. If they, too, follow the same rules, then surely this has to be a real explanation.

Appendix 1. Squaring the Circle

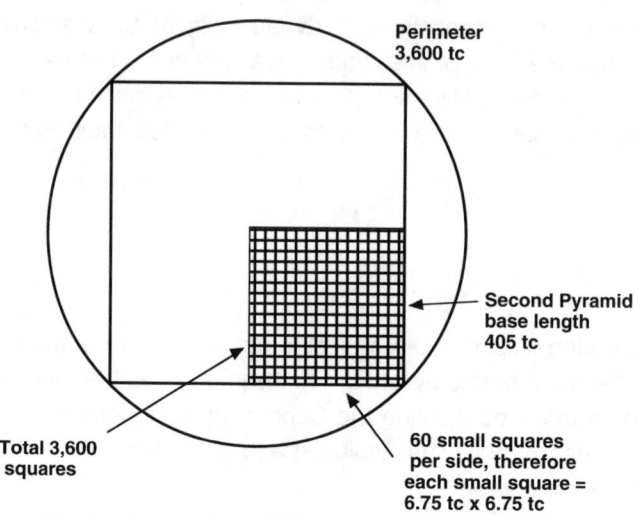

Fig 50.   3,600 squares in the Second Pyramid base.

The next pyramid we shall look at is the Great Pyramid, and exactly the same calculations will be performed here. What we find with the Great Pyramid, however, is that because the rod length used is so much smaller, the number of squares that can be fitted into the base area of the Great Pyramid is rather larger.

Just like the Second Pyramid's calculation, the base length of the pyramid has been divided by the rod length applicable to that pyramid. The rod length at the Great Pyramid is clearly 2.75 tc, and when dividing that figure into 440 the result is 160. Therefore, the number of squares measuring 1 x 1 rod that will fit into the base of the Great Pyramid is 25,600.

This is a number that could have slipped by unnoticed, and thus the meaning the designer intended would have remained hidden; so it is just as well that this particular figure has gained a particular prominence in recent years. 25,600 is the number of years in the precessionary cycle of the Earth.

Appendix 1. *Squaring the Circle*

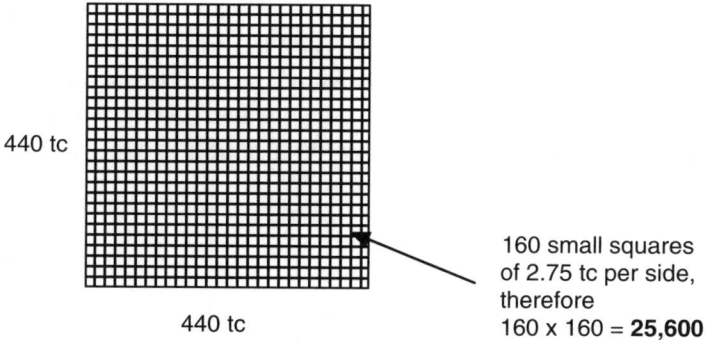

440 tc

440 tc

160 small squares
of 2.75 tc per side,
therefore
160 x 160 = **25,600**

Fig 51. Great Pyramid base area.

The questions remains as to whether this is coincidence. There is only one pyramid left on the plateau to prove or disprove this hypothesis; the Third Pyramid. The Third Pyramid, as has already been demonstrated, has upper limestone portions measuring 151.2 tc along the base length, and the rod length defined by the granite chamber inside this pyramid is 3.15 tc. Therefore, there are 40 rods to the side length of this pyramid, as in the diagram below.

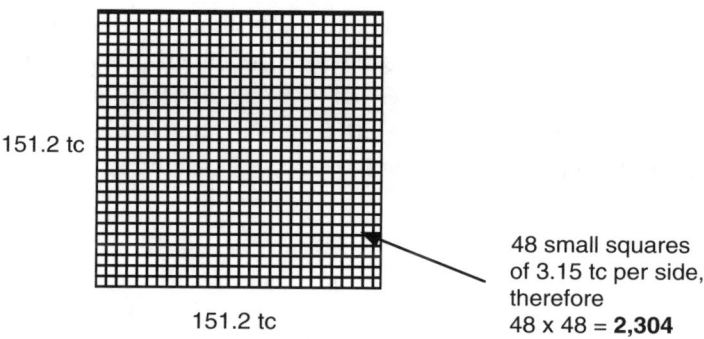

151.2 tc

151.2 tc

48 small squares
of 3.15 tc per side,
therefore
48 x 48 = **2,304**

Fig 52. Third Pyramid base area.

Appendix 1. Squaring the Circle

The number 2,304 does not initially look very inspiring, and it did not seem to fit any of the other numbers thus far derived from the base areas of the pyramids. But, knowing that 'squaring the circle' was an important function gave a further clue. The number 25,600 is related to a circle; it can be imagined as a circle that is described by the Earth's celestial pole as it wobbles around the northern and southern skies. If the number 25,600 is drawn as a circle and a square is drawn within it, things begin to make sense. The perimeter length of that internal square is exactly 23,040 units in length.

Great Pyramid's area as a circle
Third Pyramid's area as a square

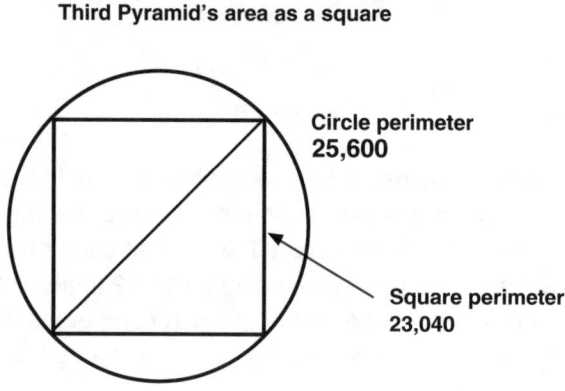

Circle perimeter
25,600

Square perimeter
23,040

Fig 53. Pyramid areas as squares and circles.

Strangely enough, the number of small squares that have been fitted inside the Third Pyramid base area is exactly ten times smaller than the perimeter of the square that lies inside the Great Pyramid precessionary circle. The perimeter length of the square is 23,040 and the number of squares inside the Third Pyramid's base is 2,304 (48^2).

Orbit

Thus far, we have three numbers. The Great Pyramid's 25,600; the Third Pyramid's 23,040; and the Second Pyramid's 3,600. Are these linked in any way? The number 3,600 seems like an unlikely number to be used in

Appendix 1. *Squaring the Circle*

any precessionary calculations as it does not appear to be linked in any way to the value of 25,600. Nevertheless, the Egyptians did appear to use 3,600 in precessionary cycles for some reason, as the historian Manetho relates.

If the value of 3,600 has been used in the ancient past, this probably infers that it is somehow useful in precessionary calculations; that perhaps the ancient priesthood was informed of its connections. After a great number of false leads over a number of days, it became apparent that actually, the number 3,600 is unexpectedly and intimately associated with the precessionary cycle. Looking at the precessionary cycle, if one divides 25,600 by 3,600, the answer is 7.1111. Such a number does not look very inspiring mathematically, as it hardly represents an easy multiplier of large whole numbers. But when working in powers, the results are remarkably different.

The very simple solution to this conundrum seems to betray an ancient understanding of powers. The square of a number has already been used extensively in these calculations – a square simply being a number multiplied by itself. But there is no limit to the number of these multiplications that can be made; one can multiply by the power two, three, four, five.... For example, 2^3 represents 2 x 2 x 2 = 8. Whereas, 2^4 represents 2 x 2 x 2 x 2 = 16. The power multiplies that can be found when using the rather odd looking number of 7.1111 are as follows:

$7.111^1 = 7.111$ x 10 = 71.111
The number of years in one degree of the precessionary cycle.
$7.111^2 = 50.6$ x 10 = 506
The number of years in 7.111 degrees of the precessionary cycle.
$7.111^3 = 360$ x 10 = 3,600
The number of small squares in the base area of the Second Pyramid, and the number of years in 50.6 degrees of the precessionary cycle.
$7.111^4 = 2,560$ x 10 = 25,600
The number of small squares in the base area of the Great Pyramid, and the number of years in 360 degrees of the precessionary cycle.

The answers are not exact to every numerical placing, of course, but the fact that this little mathematical symmetry occurs at all must have been spotted and incorporated into the design of these structures.

In fact, the symmetry that nature herself plays in this little game is also worth looking at in more detail. What we are saying here is that the precessional cycle of 25,600 years is related to the degree measurement system – one degree of precessionary movement takes 71.111 years to complete.

The degree system is obviously the simple division of a circle into 360°, but this is not a man-made system; it is plainly derived from the motions of our planet. The year comprises 365 days, or, to be a little more technical, during one orbit of the Earth around the Sun, the Earth revolves on its axis 365 times. Thus, during each day, the Earth moves (roughly) one degree around its orbit. The 360° to a circle is plainly derived from the orbit of the Earth.

Therefore, the 71.111 years per degree of precession is not a man-made convenience, it is a part of nature – rounded to the nearest whole number. In this case, it may sound a little strange to say that there is a mathematical solution for the number 71.111, that is derived from the squares and circles that we have already been looking at. Strange perhaps, but true.

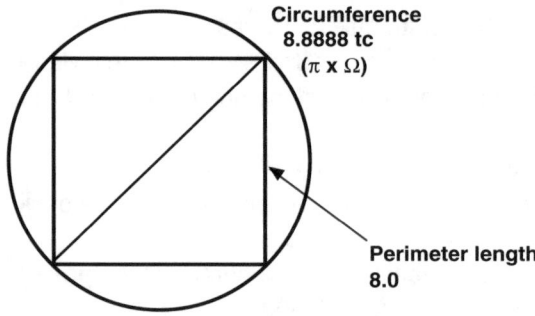

Circumference
8.8888 tc
(π x Ω)

Perimeter length
8.0

Fig 54.   8.888 square and circle.

As had already been shown, the function of 'squaring the circle' depends in part on the number 8.888. This number can be derived in a variety of ways; here are a few of them.

$$8.888 = \Omega \times \Pi.$$

$$8.888 = \frac{8}{0.9}$$

Appendix 1. Squaring the Circle

What this second equation infers is that the circumference of a circle is related to the perimeter length of the square inside it, by the simple ratio of 0.9. This can represented graphically as on the previous diagram.

As can be seen, the circumference of the circle multiplied by 0.9 gives the perimeter length of the square. It may sound surprising that the circle and square are related by such a simple ratio, but that is a fact of maths. A simpler square and circle diagram would be the relationship between a square with a perimeter length of 9 units and a circle with a perimeter of 10 units.

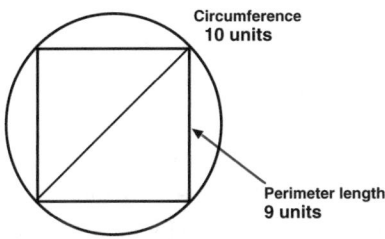

Fig 55.   10 x 9 square and circle.

A little mathematical spin-off from this observation is that Π is directly related to Ω in exactly the same fashion. Taking the diagram above, if we make the square equal to Ω x Π or 8.8888 units of length, then the circle that goes around that square measures exactly 9.877 units. This may not exactly stand out as a significant number, but it is, in fact Π².

This is why the 'squaring of the circle' function was deemed to be so important in sacred metrology. It is just a very simple piece of rough maths to calculate everyday engineering problems. It is not absolutely mathematically precise, but it is good enough for everyday usage. The quick and easy calculations are:

a.   The base of a square multiplied by 4.4444 equals the circumference of the circle around it.

b.   Therefore it follows that circumference of a circle multiplied by 0.9 equals the perimeter length of the square inside it.

c.   That Π² equals 7 x W.

Appendix 1. Squaring the Circle

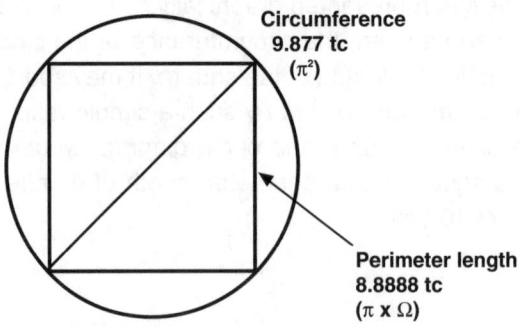

Fig 56. Pi square and circle.

These are simply quick and easy mathematical approximations that are fundamental to all of nature. They are not simply derived from the pyramids, or from the Earth and its various motions. Therefore, it is a little strange to find out that the motions of the Earth are related to this same calculation and the same underlying maths. The figure 8.888 is derived from the constants $\Omega \times \Pi$, and if those constants are squared, the result is 79 – as previously demonstrated. If the same diagram is drawn once more, using a circle circumference of 79 units, the result is that the square inside this circle has a perimeter length of 71.111 units. As a reminder, 71.111 is the number of years in one degree of precessional movement of the Earth's axis.

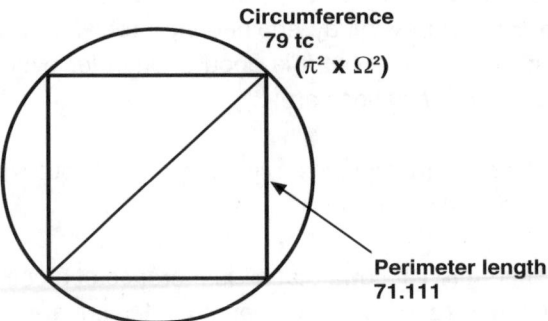

Fig 57. 71.111 circle and square.

Appendix 1. *Squaring the Circle*

Currently, the Earth's daily rate of rotation is slowing down, due to tidal forces derived from the Moon. When the length of the Earthly day reaches 24hrs 35 minutes, there will be exactly 360 days in the year and the above symmetry will be exact rather than approximate. There will be 25,600 days in a degree of precession, and 25,600 years in one precessionary cycle.

This does not necessarily infer divine intervention, of course. The precession rate of a spinning body depends on the rate at which that body is spinning on its axis. Thus, the spin rate of the Earth (the length of one day) will directly influence the precession rate of the axis (the number of years in a precessional year). In a spinning top, the slower the rate of spin around the axis, the slower the precessional rate becomes. But this is partly an influence of gravity on the spinning mass, which the Earth itself will not experience.

Obviously, the rounding in this calculation has all been advantageous. Many texts will give the rate of precession as 25,800 years rather than 25,600, although there is a great deal of uncertainty in this. The degree system was also rounded down to 360 degrees rather than rounded up to 370, as the unit of 360 is much easier to use in calculations. Nevertheless, the symmetry that nature has given the Earth's precession is relatively remarkable. The Earth's precession rate is defined by the natural geometrical constants, as in the following formula:

$$(\Omega \times \Pi)^2 \times 360 \times 0.9 \quad = 25,600$$
$$\text{or}$$
$$\Omega \times \Pi \times 360 \times 8 \quad = 25,600$$

Conclusion

Finding something useful from this great morass of data was tiresome, to say the least. What was the architect hinting at? Was this all simply a compendium of maths just for the sake of it – to prove that the designer was competent at his craft? Or was there something deeper, something more meaningful?

Unfortunately, this particular line of research has come to the end of the road and so far, it has turned out to be a disappointing cul-de-sac. Nevertheless, the research has highlighted certain identifiable numbers that are embedded in the structure of these pyramids, and that are bound

Appendix 1.   Squaring the Circle

to stand out and be noticed, numbers like 2.828, 3.142, 7:22, 3-4-5 and 360 stand out from the innumerable other combinations as being something special. Indeed, the number 25,600 is certain to stand out from the crowd to any astronomer, and so there is likely to be some kind of astronomical or calendrical significance in these calculations. What this is all supposed to mean, however, remains a mystery.

Appendix 2

Ancient Egyptian Railways

I discovered an interesting letter on an Internet chatroom, regarding the origins of the width of the track, or the gauge, of the British (worldwide) railway systems. Perhaps the author was being a little tongue-in-cheek, but he suggested that this gauge originated with the Romans, who made waggons of a particular dimension. Because deep ruts were made in roadways and tracks, as can be clearly seen at the famous Roman quarry trackways of Malta, all the succeeding wagon designs had to use the same width or gauge – or risk damaging their wheels on the ruts.

Much later, coalmining tracks used the same gauge, and it was from these early horse-drawn mining trucks at Tyneside in Britain that George Stephenson designed one of the first railway engines in the world, the Rocket. The author then went on to observe that Thiokol, the designers of the solid rocket boosters on the space shuttle, were constrained in their design by the need to transport the Shuttle's boosters by rail. Thus, in the words of this Internet wit, the dimensions of the shuttle were ultimately decreed by the width of the rear-ends of a couple of Roman horses.

But, as is often the case, there is nothing new under the Sun. Having researched the subject a little, I found an almost identical quotation (minus the space-shuttle quip) in a venerable old tome, which was penned by one Stuart H Holbrook. I never did find a precise date for Mr Holbrook's work but, unfortunately for the claims to originality by the Internet wit, this original posting was written in nineteenth century English.

Whatever the date for the origins of this quote, it was an interesting and humorous posting that had more than an element of truth as a backdrop. Just why have our standard measurements and designs come into current usage? Was this by design, accident or, as this author would have us believe, an historical comedy of coincidences? This was a question I had already tried to tackle in the book *Thoth,* and the surprising answer that I came up with, was that most of our measurement systems are based on the dimensions of the Great Pyramid (GP) and the Thoth or Royal cubit of ancient Egypt.

This claim may seem to be pure unjustifiable speculation at this stage, but let's run with this scenario for a while and see what it delivers. My Egyptian speculation was primarily driven by one glaring, and undeniable fact – that there are exactly 1,760 yards in the Imperial mile unit, and there are also exactly 1,760 cubits in the Great Pyramid's perimeter length. It seemed to be obvious to me that the British Measurement System was based either upon the dimensions of the Great Pyramid itself, or, perhaps, upon the same principles that the Great Pyramid's designer had used.

Thus, it was natural for me to investigate the railway gauge in terms of Egyptian units, as we shall see shortly. So, how was this worldwide railway gauge derived in the first place? The 'standard' railway gauge, as it became known, measures 4 ft 8.5 inches; so what was the reason for using this rather peculiar dimension? The history of the unit is that it was used at the coal mines in Tyneside, and then the horse tramways in Newcastle-upon-Tyne; both being east-coast towns in England. This gauge was subsequently copied by George Stephenson, presumably for economic reasons, for his Stockton to Darlington railway. His son, Robert, then used the same gauge once more for his Liverpool to Manchester line. As Britain made the majority of railway engines at this time, this gauge width was then subsequently adopted by the majority of countries across the whole world.

I have not seen a definitive rationale for the original Tyneside gauge width, but the influences on its choice would have included the size of the mine shaft tunnels, or drifts, and the amount of coal that a horse or two could pull. But, nevertheless, the actual gauge measurement they finally chose is rather perplexing; why would anyone choose a dimension of 4 ft 8.5 inches? Why not 4 ft, or 5 ft, or perhaps 4 ft 6 inches? The Russians chose 5 ft, and the Spanish, 5 ft 6 inches (these were not metric, but Imperial measurements, due to the British and American lead in locomotive design). Both of these alternative gauges comprised whole-number or simple fraction dimensions, and so the reason for their choice would seem to be more than obvious. The dimension of the standard gauge's 4ft 8.5 inches, however, is 4.7083 feet, and it does not resolve into a simple fraction at all. So why was it chosen?

Could it be, by some remote chance, that the reason for this strange measurement lies in the conversion of this Imperial dimension into Egyptian Thoth cubits – where it then produces 2.75 cubits? It has to be said, that this measurement is a much simpler fraction than the Imperial version, so did this fact somehow influence the strange choice of gauge width? A dank coal mine on the moors of northeast England may be a strange place to find an Egyptian cubit, but bear in mind that the coalmine barons of the eighteenth and nineteenth centuries were amongst the most wealthy and influential industrialists in the world. It is also true that the waggon gauge of ancient Greece was apparently 'between 4ft 6 inches and 5 ft',[1] which is undeniably close to the 'standard' gauge width. Did such an ancient custom, somehow or other, find its way into Britain?

The Rod

Even if the Thoth (Royal) cubit from Egypt did lie behind this strange choice of railway gauge, why on earth should anyone choose a unit of 2.75 cubits rather than a whole number like 3 cubits? The answer could well be, as I have said many times before, that just about all the dimensions of the Great Pyramid (GP) are based on the 5.5 cubit rod length; and the ease with which this measurement unit works throughout the Great Pyramid's dimensions has already been demonstrated. But remember, also, that the arguments in Appendix 1 further refined this unit, and suggested that the real rod unit in use should be half that size, or just 2.75 Thoth cubits (tc).

It just so happens, of course, that the 'standard' gauge of the railways also measures 2.75 tc. (To be accurate, 2.75 tc actually measures 4 ft 8.65 ins, if a cubit length of 52.33 cms were used). I am not sure, however, that this intriguing coincidence was derived via the size of a pair of horses' backsides or the width of the ruts in a Roman road, because in fact there is a much more logical way in which this adoption of a foreign unit may have come about.

The first iron rails for tramways were forged in Britain in 1789. The world's first real railway, Richard Trevithick's locomotive 'New Castle', on the Pen-y-darren Tramway near Merthyr Tydfil, South Wales, was built in 1804. George Stephenson copied this idea, but his Stockton to Darlington line, built in 1825, was not what one would really call a railway. The Stephensons' first real railway was the Liverpool to Manchester line of 1829, where Robert Stephenson's stage-managed event with the locomotive 'Rocket' eventually stole all the railway accolades from the true pioneer, Trevithick.

Isambard Kingdom Brunel's revolutionary Great Western Railway was not commenced until 1836, when his much wider seven-feet gauge railway was first proposed. It is clear that, although the 4 ft 8.5 inch gauge was widely adopted around the early nineteenth century by Stephenson and his followers, this was obviously not a universal British standard, enshrined in law, at this time. Each railway proposal came before Parliament with its own set of specifications and was approved on its merits. The original specification for the Great Western railway proposed the standard gauge, but Brunel then changed the bill to specify a seven-feet gauge track and Parliament accepted it. The real battle of the competing railway gauges did not start in earnest until 1845, in Bristol.

But if the Egyptian cubit was to be in any way influential in the design of the British railway system, they would have needed to have been rediscovered before 1800. That this is indeed so, can be conclusively proved because we know that Sir Isaac Newton had discovered the exact size of the King's Chamber in the Great Pyramid; and he wrote up the results of his investigations in his booklet called the *Dissertation upon the Sacred Cubit of the Jews*. Newton used John Greaves' measurements of the pyramids to try and discover the exact length of this 'sacred' cubit and he came up with a length of 52.33 cms, which is remarkably close to the figure that is currently accepted. Although I have a copy of Newton's original booklet, there is unfortunately no date upon this extract; but since we know that Newton died in 1727, it is certain that the exact dimensions of the Thoth cubit were known of, and in wide circulation, in Britain by the time that the railway gauges were created and standardised.

Egypt

It cannot be stressed enough that the designs of Egypt were quite influential in the late eighteenth and early nineteenth centuries in Britain. Napoleon had just won the Battle of the Pyramids in 1798, and then Admiral Nelson defeated the French fleet in the Battle of the Nile later that year; forcing Napoleon to surrender. Britain then claimed the spoils, both of Egypt herself and also from the 150 French archaeologists who had been working at all the great sites in Egypt. So, it was in this kind of climate that Brunel, ever the great engineer, proposed a design in 1830 for the longest suspension bridge in the world; the ambitious 630 ft span of the River Avon at Clifton, Bristol. The design he proposed included Egyptian towers, and this Egyptian theme to the project was warmly received. Brunel records that a major sponsor, William Beckford, said of this design:

> He admired the (plans to the bridge) and praised strongly the architecture I had adopted – approving the Egyptian but condemning in strong terms all the others. [2]

But the opinions of Beckford obviously did not win the day, and although the the Clifton Suspension Bridge was an engineering triumph, and is still taking vehicular traffic to this day, the towers were not built entirely in the Egyptian style.

As explained in the book *Thoth*, certain other influential characters like Mr Charles Piazzi Smyth, the Astronomer Royal for Scotland, had more than a passing interest in the Giza pyramids and their measurements. Smyth, like Newton, thought that the measurement systems used in the Great Pyramid had been preserved by the biblical patriarchs and had ultimately found their way into Britain. Sir John Herschel was another astronomer who was passionately in favour of the Imperial Measurement System. Sir John stood on the Standards Commission for measurements and he was central to the prevention of the metric system being adopted in 1855. Although this was a later chapter in the history of Britain's measurement systems than the railways dispute, it is not beyond the realms of possibility that other astronomers, with a similar interest to that of Sir Isaac Newton and Piazzi Smyth, were influential in measurement standardisation in the early nineteenth century.

Returning to the railway gauge dispute, there was still no particular standard gauge width in the eyes of the British law in 1835. Matters came to a head, however, when the different railway systems started to join up in 1845. A Royal Commission was duly appointed in July of that year to investigate the matter, and the legal battle for the standardisation of the British railway gauge was to be overseen by three commissioners: Sir Frederick Smith, Inspector of Railways; Peter Barlow, a Woolwich military mathematician; and (wait for it) George Biddel, the Astronomical Observer for the Greenwich Observatory. The reason for the appointment of the latter two individuals to the commission, neither of whom had any engineering experience, was rather baffling. But it has to be observed that Woolwich and Greenwich were both influenced by the Royal Navy and were within throwing distance of each other along the Thames.

The whole scenario seems uncannily like the problems that the horologer, John Harrison, had had with the same Greenwich Observatory nearly a century earlier. Harrison had invented a very accurate chronometer to measure the Earth's longitude, as an aid to maritime navigation. Meanwhile his rival, the Astronomer Royal at Greenwich, Nevil Maskelyne, was using a complicated system of Lunar observations to derive a ship's position. Quite sensibly, a competition was held to see which system was the superior, and ships sailed off, navigating with the rival systems. While competition is normally healthy, the fact was that the Astronomer Royal, Maskelyne, also sat on the commission that decided the result of the competition.

Harrison's far superior clock system was stifled and rejected by the commission at every turn, when it was obvious, even to the King, that the commission's decisions were biased and wrong. Harrison eventually got his prize, but the delay had cost decades – during which time British ships continued to flounder on unexpected shorelines and Harrison's clock design was progressively poached by others. [3] (By the way, if you find a Harrison clock in the attic, treat it with some respect as it is probably worth a few million GB pounds).

Competition

In an all too familiar fashion, the railway commission of 1845 quite sensibly devised a competition between the rival train systems to decide which of the designs was the superior. Each of the steam trains – the standard and the broad gauge – ran a route of about 50 miles carrying various loads, to see which was the faster and more reliable design. Because Brunel's broad gauge allowed a much bigger steam engine to pull the carriages; had a lower center of gravity for cornering; and larger wheels with less rolling friction; the seven-feet gauge railway produced the best results in every statistic being measured by the commission. This success was despite the fact that Brunel was using a much older engine design than

Appendix 2. Ancient Egyptian Railways

the standard gauge company, whose brand-new steam engine and carriages eventually came off the narrower tracks during the trials and crashed.

Following this pitiful exhibition by the standard gauge design, and in true British tradition, the commission therefore pronounced that the smaller 4ft 8.5 inch 'standard' gauge was the superior design and should be adopted as a legal standard throughout the country! Brunel was understandably furious and, like Harrison before him, told the commission exactly what he thought of them in the local vernacular.

Thus, the first British law to ban the construction of more broad gauge railways was passed in 1846. Despite this legal statute, however, Brunel was determined to build new broad gauge railways. Brunel's title of 'engineer' belies his true status; in reality, he was Commander in Chief and he managed every last detail of the entire project. Such a character was not going to be put off by mere trifles like an Act of Parliament, so he gathered together a 'private army' of 2000 navvies and defeated the opposition at the 'Battle of Mickleton', thereeby managing to complete the Bristol to Birmingham line in the broad gauge. But economics as well as the law were now opposed to Brunel; the vast majority of lines had been built in the standard gauge – it had become the *de facto* standard.

But, in the light of all the above, I would respectfully suggest that it is entirely possible that Egyptian influences were really behind the invention of this standard railway gauge of 4 ft 8.5 inches:

a. Many influential characters, like Sir Isaac Newton, really thought that the Thoth cubit from ancient Egypt was somehow a 'sacred' measurement system supplied by 'god'.

b. These individuals also thought that the Imperial Measurements were somehow descended from these 'sacred units' and they therefore sought to include this newly discovered 'sacred' measurement system, from the Great Pyramid, into the British statutes.

c. The newest development of the era and the next change to the statutes book was the inclusion of the new fangled 'iron road', as the Irish still call it.

d. There are two possibilities as to how the Egyptian system was subdivided into 2.75 units for use in the railway system.

    i.   The railway pioneers used the Egyptian cubit measurement system, but copied the standard Imperial Measurement's subdivision of the rod, which measures 5.5 units. A rod width of 5.5 cubits (9 ft 5 inches) would have been far too wide for a railway, whereas half a rod was just about right.

    ii. Alternatively, perhaps it was already known through myth and tradition that the Egyptians had an equivalent to our rod system, and also used the 5.5 or the 2.75 cubit subdivisions in their measurements. In this case, there would have been no argument as to what measurements should be used.

I would suggest that Sir Isambard Kingdom Brunel lost his fight for a 7 ft gauge railway on purely religious grounds. Brunel came up with a far superior specification based on sound technical and engineering principles that took into account the stability of the train, the size (power) of the engine and, equally, the practicality and comfort of the carriages that would be carried.

    Brunel then proved to the world in an open competition that his design was far superior to the 'standard' gauge – but his proposals were still rejected by the Royal Commission. Brunel rightly derided the authorities and politicians for their stupidity in not adopting his proposal. What Brunel probably did not understand, however, was the depth of feeling in political circles for the concept of sacred measurement systems. Had he opted for a 9 ft 5 inch gauge instead, he might have been taken more seriously. It is therefore quite probable that the dimensions of our railways were chosen purely because the width of the tracks are exactly $\frac{1}{4}$ of the length of the Queen's Chamber in the Great Pyramid.

Notes & References

Chapter 1

Chapter 2

Chapter 3

1. Rudolf Gantenbrink, http://www.cheops.org
2. Ibid.
3. Ibid.
4. Ibid.
5. Ibid.
6. Pyramids and Temples of Gizeh, Flinders Petrie.
7. Rudolf Gantenbrink, http://www.cheops.org
9. Redshift II, p.c. planisphere.
10. M Foster, http://www.rosetau.com
11. Strabo. Quoted from Pyramids and Temples of Gizeh, Flinders Petrie.
12. M Foster, http://www.rosetau.com
13. Pyramids and Temples of Gizeh, Petrie.

Chapter 4

Chapter 5

1. In the footsteps of Alexander the Great, Wood M.
2. The Age of Alexander, Plutarch.
3. Josephus Antiquities 11:334
4. In the footsteps of Alexander the Great, Wood M.
5. Campaigns of Alexander, Arrian.
6. In the footsteps of Alexander the Great, Wood M.
7. Thoth, Architect of the Universe, Ellis R.
8. Timaeus & Critas (Penguin), Plato, p98.
9. Ibid p41.
10. Ibid p51.
11. Ibid p54
12. Ibid p53.
13. Ibid p59.
14. Ibid p84.
15. Modern reference manuals indicate one layer, but Petrie says there were two. The appendix will confirm that the latter is correct.

16. The White Goddess, Graves R, p 195.
17. Dionysus, Nonnos IX:10.
18. Ibid IX:15.
19. Euterpe, Herodotus, 144.
20. British Museum of Ancient Egypt, p215.
21. Dionysus, Nonnos XVII:135.
22. Ibid XXI:315.
23. Ibid XXV:420.
24. Ibid XXV:395.

Chapter 6

1. The campaigns of Alexander, Arrian, bk 4.
2. Northern Pakistan, R A Quazi.

Chapter 7

1. The Campaigns of Alexander, Arrian, bk 5.
2.. Euterpe, Herodotus, 124.

Chapter 8

1. Strabo. Quoted from Pyramids and Temples of Gizeh, Flinders Petrie.

Appendix 1

1. Pyramids and Temples of Gizeh, Petrie.
2. Ibid.
3. Ibid.

Appendix 2

1. History of Rail, E Berghaus.
2. I K Brunel, L Rolt.
3. Longitude.

List Of Diagrams

Photo credits

All pictures taken from the authors own library, except where credits are given.

Plate 1.　The Karakoram and K2.
　　　　　Earth Data Analysis Center,
　　　　　University of New Mexico, Albuquerque, USA.

Plate 2.　K2 in winter.
　　　　　Earth Data Analysis Center,
　　　　　University of New Mexico, Albuquerque, USA.

Plate 3.　The Giza Plateau.
　　　　　Taken from Russia's ikonos satellite.
　　　　　Space Imaging 2000, www.spaceimaging.com

Plate 4.　Repairs made to the Vega Pyramid at Dahshur.

Plate 5.　The Great Pyramid layout, Sir Flinders Petrie.

Plate 6.　K2 and its causeway.
　　　　　Lanzhu Institute of Glaciology, Chinese Academy of Sciences,
　　　　　174 Donggang West Rd, Lanzhou, China.

Plate 7.　The high trail on the Baltoro Glacier.

Plate 8.　Concordia, looking north towards the pure white peak of K2.

Plate 9.　K2 and one of the many Himalayan Taule.

Plate 10.　Approaching K2 base camp.

Plate 11.　The shrine of Tuthmoses III.

Index

Symbols

√2 ~ 154.
√79 ~ 156, 157.
20 - 21 - 29 ~ 14.
22 : 7 ~ 10.
25,600 ~ 160, 162, 163, 167.
3-4-5 ~ 153.
7.1111 ~ 163.
7:11 ~ 102.
71.111 ~ 164.
8.888 ~ 156, 157, 158, 164, 166.
8.8888 ~ 156.

A

Afganistan ~ 66.
Africa ~ 81, 82.
Alexander the Great ~ 7, 8, 52, 59, 61,
    62, 65, 70, 90.
  aims ~ 62.
  Aries ~ 63.
  Asia Minor ~ 61.
  Dionysus ~ 66.
  Egypt ~ 61, 63.
  elephants ~ 88.
  extent of campaign ~ 88.
  Giza ~ 71.
  Hall of Records ~ 85.
  Himalaya ~ 66.
  Hindu Kush ~ 66, 79.
  Issus ~ 62.
  Jerusalem ~ 64.
  Jesus ~ 66.
  Nearchus ~ 88.
  Persia ~ 65.
  Persopolis ~ 65.
  Phoenicia ~ 62.
  Pir Sar ~ 75, 77.
  reason for following ~ 99.
  retreat ~ 106.
  Siwa ~ 65.
  Skardu ~ 105.
Alexandria ~ 67.
Alps ~ 88.

Altef ~ 77, 88, 107, 108.
America
  dollar bill ~ 39.
Amun ~ 40, 158.
  Siwa ~ 65.
Angelus peak ~ 115.
angle of obliquity ~ 146.
Aornos ~ 75.
Apis Bull ~ 63.
Apollo ~ 76.
Archimedes ~ 67.
Aries ~ 63, 65, 80.
Aristotle of Stagira ~ 61, 63.
Arrian ~ 88, 89, 106.
Asia ~ 7, 81, 85.
  geology ~ 88.
Asia Minor ~ 61, 62.
Askole ~ 107.
Assyria ~ 65.
Aten ~ 41.
Athens ~ 106.
Atlantic ~ 52, 68, 83.
Atlantis ~ 83.
atoms ~ 69.
Atum ~ 40.
Atum-Ra ~ 41.
Avebury ~ 4, 18, 24.
Avon ~ 173.

B

Babylon ~ 65, 67.
Baccus ~ 66, 74, 76.
Baltoro glacier ~ 108, 109.
Baltoro Kangri ~ 115.
Barlow, P ~ 173.
Battle of the Nile ~ 173.
Battle of the Pyramids ~ 172.
Bauval, Robert ~ 5.
Bazira ~ 75.
Beckford, W ~ 173.
Bent pyramid. *See* Vega pyramid.
Bermuda ~ 95, 96.
Biaho Lungma ~ 107.

Index

Index